"It'd be nice to make out under the stars," Kelly said as she swung the hammock a few times. She climbed up on it and grabbed Gina's hand as she lost her balance and fell into the hammock.

Kelly's startled gasp loosened Gina's tight lips. She laughed and climbed on the hammock, straddling Kelly. "You're not very graceful. I thought you were some wonder-karate-kid. Don't they teach you balance?"

"Yes. But apparently I lose my footing when you're near me," Kelly teased. She grabbed Gina and wrestled her way on top. The hammock swayed back and forth, threatening to tip them both out. As soon as she had Gina underneath her, Kelly paused to kiss her. "Okay, enough fighting."

"Oh, I see, as soon as you win one round you think the game is over? Oh no, chica, this fight's just—"

Kelly kissed her again, stopping Gina mid-sentence. She pressed her tongue lightly into Gina's mouth then moved lower to kiss her neck. Kelly unbuttoned Gina's shirt and ran her hands over the black silk bra. She felt Gina's nipples grow firm with her touch.

Gina rubbed Kelly's shoulders. "Your muscles are tight," she observed, pressing her fingers on the knots.

"Too many push-ups in karate, I guess," Kelly replied. She kissed Gina's belly as she unzipped her shorts.

Visit

Bella Books

at

BellaBooks.com

or call our toll-free number

1-800-729-4992

Call Shotgun

Jaime Clevenger

Bella
BOOKS

2005

Bella Books, Inc.
P.O. Box 10543
Tallahassee, FL 32302

Printed in the United States of America on acid-free paper
First Edition

Editor: Christi Cassidy
Cover designer: Sandy Knowles

ISBN 1-59493-016-3

*To everyone who smiles in spite of the rest of the world.
Special thanks to my mom (for trusting me), Norman (for being there
to pick me up), Jackie (for making me laugh) and Corina (for the sleepless nights and the dancing).*

About the Author

Jaime Clevenger lives in Northern California. She currently works as a veterinarian. Some of her other job titles have included karate instructor, chemistry tutor, baby-sitter, horse-ride trail guide and closet writer. It's good to be out.

Chapter One

Beads of sweat dripped down Kelly Haldon's neck, skirting under her collar and drenching her back. The wet cotton undershirt clung to her skin like cellophane and salt stung her eyes as she focused on Sam Lee. He lunged forward with a spear strike aimed at her chest, then turned his Bo staff at the last second to catch hold of Kelly's Bo staff. In one fluid movement, he yanked her Bo from her grasp and sent it flying across the room. The wood clattered on the mat several feet away and before she could reach it, Sam swung at her chest again. She dodged this blow and dove for the Bo just as a knock sounded on the back door. Kelly rolled onto her back and saw Sam's Bo poised over her. He had stopped his strike inches from her body.

"Expecting anyone?" Sam asked. The dojo was always closed on Sundays and a sign hung in the window as a reminder of the hours. No one ever knocked at the back door.

Kelly shook her head. Her heart was thumping loud in her ears and her attention was focused on Sam's Bo. The knock sounded again, impatient. Sam pulled his Bo away and backed off his guard. With an exaggerated sigh, she whispered, "Saved."

"Only temporarily," Sam replied. He bowed off the mat and headed to the back hallway. "You know, that's the third time this morning that I've showed you the same sweep technique. When are you going to show me the counterattack?"

"When I figure out how to hold my damn Bo," she muttered under her breath.

Sam reached the door and glanced back at her. "Be inventive."

She leaned down to retrieve her Bo staff and slid her hand over the length of the wood.

Sam unlocked the door and gave a stiff greeting. "Didn't expect you today. Something wrong?"

Kelly couldn't hear the reply. Knowing Sam wouldn't want her eavesdropping, she turned to face the mirror and practiced her counterattacks. The Bo whistled softly as it sliced the air and she repeated the same move just to hear the sound. At six feet the smooth-grain maple Bo was a hand's-length taller than her, its color only a shade lighter than her skin. She trusted the Bo like her own arm. The fact that it had slipped out of her grasp three times in the past hour was due to a late night at the dance club, not any fault of the Bo staff. Although she knew she had an early private lesson scheduled with her sensei, she had gone dancing with Gina last night anyway. Gina had wanted to stay at the club until the DJ announced closing time and Kelly hadn't argued.

She glanced again at the back door. Only Sam's back was visible in the doorway and she couldn't see who had interrupted the lesson. At this point, she didn't really care. All she wanted was a shower and an excuse to crawl back into bed. She tightened the knot of her black belt and tucked the loose strands of sweat-soaked hair behind her ears. Her hair was a shade too short to tie back and too long to keep out of her eyes. Stifling a yawn, she gave up on the Bo techniques and started her stretch routine.

Sam finally opened the door and ushered in Rick Lehrman.

Kelly hung her head as soon as she saw Rick. He followed Sam through the mat area and took a seat in the waiting room. Sam picked up his Bo and bowed toward Kelly. "Ready for another round?"

"Another round?" Say no, she coached herself silently. Saying no would be nearly as bad as cussing. "Sure, why not? Maybe one more round will improve my oh-for-five score."

Rick cleared his throat, as if to remind everyone of his presence. Without looking into the waiting room she knew his eyes were on her. She didn't want him to watch her lose, but he seemed intent on staying for the next match.

Sam tapped his Bo against hers, bringing her attention back to the mat. "You could win this match."

"Sure. Miracles happen every day."

Sam brought his Bo staff into position. "I never wait for miracles."

"Some of us don't need them, I guess," she replied with a hint of sarcasm.

Rick laughed.

Kelly tried to focus on Sam. She was exhausted and the simple act of holding Sam's gaze felt like too much of a challenge. Dancing with Gina until two in the morning had definitely been a bad idea. Now Rick and Sam would be her judges, and neither would miss any mistake. She stepped into the on-guard position and raised her Bo. "Ready."

"Ah-saahh!" Sam yelled, signaling his attack. He instantly swung his Bo at her head. The wood whistled through the air.

Shielding her face, she twisted to the side and spun her staff. There was no time to think. The wood moved like butter in her hands, slipping between her fingers until Sam's weapon clashed against it with a loud crack. Fading to the left, she narrowly missed his second attack, a quick strike that hissed by her ear. She tried to plan a strategy, but Sam stepped up the pace of the match and she fell into her usual tack of blocking his assault. She couldn't risk missing one of his strikes or letting him inside her guard. He could

3

slip inside her thoughts with one side glance and make her doubt her every move.

He jabbed suddenly and the butt of his Bo slammed into her ribs. As she recoiled, he caught hold of her Bo and tried to wrench it out of her handhold. She fought against his grip, tightening her fingers on the wood. He kicked at her knee and she shuffled to miss his foot as her hold on the Bo slipped. She threw a round-house kick at his head, tapping her foot lightly against his temple. The kick didn't stop him and she knew she should have struck harder. Before her foot landed from the roundhouse kick, he swung his stick at her supporting leg. Her shin swept over the stick just as she dove for the mat to roll past Sam's reach. He caught up to her before she could stand and swung his Bo toward her face. She blinked reflexively and felt her breath catch in her throat. The Bo hung over her, frozen in space and quiet.

When she opened her eyes again, Sam was staring down at her. His Bo staff was at his side, and he offered his hand to help her rise. "Not bad."

"Not bad?" Kelly shook her head.

"Well, you weren't expecting a miracle." He smiled. There was no consolation this time.

"I wouldn't mind a miracle."

"Maybe you should just practice more."

"Yes, sir." She couldn't argue with him. "But swinging a long stick at imaginary objects and making loud noises attracts too much attention at the park. Last week I scared some kids at the soccer field. They thought I was a witch training with a broom handle."

"Were you chanting curses on their soccer game?" he asked, grinning.

"No, I was just swinging my stick around, you know. Some six-year-old kid spotted me when he was chasing after a runaway ball. He asked me why I was playing with a broom handle." Kelly paused and smiled at Sam. "So, I told him I was a witch, in train-ing, and that all witches had to practice with broom handles." The boy had nodded, believing this explanation, and then trotted off after the soccer ball. As soon as he returned to the soccer field, he ran up to another boy who was fielding his kicks and whispered something in his ear before pointing at Kelly. She guessed he was sharing the secret. Although the boys in the park were entertained, she couldn't help feeling a little silly with the witch story. "Anyway, I decided to practice in the dojo from now on so I don't scare the entire Ashton Youth Soccer League with witch stories."

"Maybe we'd get more students if you kept up the act." He winked at her and then placed his Bo on the wall mount, just under the spear and above the Escrima sticks. Chinese stars and Nunchakus hung alongside them, and a broad sword was mounted near the doorway leading to the waiting room. He nodded at her. "Joking aside, your speed is improving. You blocked almost all of my attacks."

"I don't like coming home with so many bruises," she admitted. Rick was still in the waiting room, watching her. She had forgotten about him in the heat of the match and wished he hadn't stayed to watch her lose.

"Maybe you should try striking first, rather than trying to block every strike I throw. You won't survive most fights just by outlasting your opponent." Sam picked up a Chinese star and threw it at her.

She leaned to the side and the star raced by her.

"Offense. Strike first, strike hard." Sam shook his head. "Don't just dodge the star. Think of an attack before I have a chance to throw it."

"Yes, sir." Her defense strategy worked only for someone who played by the rules. Sam didn't acknowledge this because there were no rules in a street fight. She'd spent years drilling every move with the thought that the rules were fixed. Now she faced matches that had no rules. Although she understood Sam's point, she hated the *Strike first, Strike hard* mantra that he made her practice.

"Meditate on the mistakes in your last match," he advised, stepping off the mat.

Kelly kneeled and closed her eyes. Her legs ached with exhaustion and a sharp pain radiated through the side of her chest with each breath. She heard Sam invite Rick into the back office and then listened as they shuffled past her on the mat. The office door closed, muffling their voices. She wondered what Rick was saying and could make out only fragments of their dialogue—something about money.

Sam and Rick were close friends as well as business partners. Sam had been Kelly's sensei since she'd started karate at thirteen. Eight years later, she still didn't know a lot about him. His father was a second-generation Chinese American and his mother was born in Mexico. He had a dragon tattoo on the inside of his forearm, many stories of his martial arts training and, at thirty-two, claimed he was happily settled with a sweet wife, a baby girl and his own karate dojo, or at least claim to half ownership.

Rick was the other half-owner of the karate school. He wasn't a martial artist and Kelly had known him to make only rare appearances at the dojo. The school was only one of several of his business investments. After a long career with the FBI, he had retired to run his own private investigation service and to manage his other investments. While Sam seemed to be made for the relaxed fit of a karate Gi, Rick seemed to be cut out for a starched shirt and black business suit. Recently, Rick had become a more frequent visitor at the dojo.

The dojo was a second home for Kelly. She lived in San Francisco during the school year and returned to Ashton every summer to teach the children's classes at the dojo. Teaching karate provided a welcome break from studies at Bridges University and the summer wages were at least a small offset to tuition. This summer she'd also taken on a side job.

Rick needed someone to deliver packages and run errands for his PI business. He offered Kelly twice her teaching wage and she agreed to his terms of secrecy. Initially, her work with Rick was easy and too profitable to turn down. Within a few weeks, he asked her to consider working on more challenging projects than dropping off packages and typing up his investigation records. He needed an assistant and wanted to set up a training program to groom her for investigative work. The lure of a high-paying job was impossible for her to turn down and Rick had promised that by the end of summer she could easily afford tuition for her last year at the university.

Kelly shifted on her knees, trying to ignore the cramp that was forming in her quads as she meditated. She strained to catch some of the conversation behind the closed office door, but the voices were too muffled. Her early-morning lesson had been commissioned by Rick. He was paying Sam to teach her more offensive fighting than was traditionally taught in the dojo.

From throwing knives at watermelons and slashing pumpkins with a broad sword, Kelly was quickly learning how to attack with every weapon in the dojo. Still she'd lost every match against Sam and wasn't looking forward to any experience that really tested her skills. Aside from the training with Sam, Rick had also given her lessons in breaking into buildings and trailing cars. She hadn't decided if she liked the new training and wondered why an investigator would ever really need any more fighting skills than she already had. So far the paychecks from Rick were over twice what she earned teaching the children's karate classes so she wasn't ready to argue.

Sam came out of the office first. "Hey, Kelly, lock up the dojo when you leave and make sure the mirrors are clean."

As soon as the back door slammed behind Sam, Rick stepped out of the office. He held her car keys in his hand. "These keys are to your Volkswagen, right?"

"Yes, sir." She always kept her keys in the office because her karate uniform had no pockets. Sam must have given the key ring to Rick. But what would he want with her keys? The key ring had four keys—for her car, the dojo, her brother's house in Ashton and a spare key for her apartment in San Francisco.

"Good." He slipped the key ring in the front pocket of his slacks. "So how's your training with Sam going?"

"Good." She sighed and stood up. Her knees were stiff from meditating after the long workout. She didn't really see how the extra training would benefit Rick. "Though I don't really see why you've arranged for the extra lessons. I already know how to fight, and it's not like you're hiring me to be a bouncer at a bar."

"No." Rick smiled and the wrinkles made deep crevices on his face. Kelly thought he looked older when he wasn't wearing a suit. He continued, "You're a black belt who likes to sport fight. I want someone who can handle street fights. If I send you out to investigate someone, I need to know that you can get a job done and report back to me. I don't want to have to pay you just so you'll get killed in some dark alley."

"You almost sound concerned about me," she countered.

"It's just business." His lips were tight when he smiled. "Speaking of business, I'd prefer it if you stopped hanging out with cops."

"What are you talking about? Gina?"

"Yes, Gina Hernandez." He paused. "I followed you to her house last night."

"You're tailing me now?" She wished she had noticed him and wondered how long he'd followed her. "So, did you follow us to the club as well? Were you dancing off-stage and I just didn't notice that either?"

"No. I don't dance." He chuckled. "At least not at your type of club."

"Rick, I don't see why Gina is a problem." Gina was a rookie cop with the San Francisco Police Department and Kelly had just started dating her.

"She's a cop who will want to be involved with your work." Rick crossed his arms. "What have you told her about your work with me? Does she know about the deliveries you made or the transcription notes?"

Kelly started, "I told her you were a PI and you were training me. I didn't give details—"

"Remember, in this job you can't have any witnesses for anything you do for me." He cleared his throat. "And I don't need the cops to follow my business. Our clients trust that we work independently."

Kelly wondered how much Rick knew about her involvement with Gina. She hadn't mentioned her name because she guessed he'd disapprove of any association with cops. Although she wondered how much he knew, she wasn't about to ask. Gina wanted to be an investigator and talked about this all the time. "You know, she could probably help you more than I could. She'd be a good investigator."

"She's a cop. I don't want her involved in any project I give you. Don't tell her anything," Rick said. "Understood?"

"Yes, sir." Kelly stared at the ground. She hated how he had assumed authority over her personal life when she'd only been working with him for a few months. It really wasn't his business who she slept with. "I won't talk to Gina about my work, sir." Kelly responded with the formal tone that had been drilled into her during hours of martial arts training. She couldn't read Rick's emotion. At times, he seemed to trust her and even respect her. Then again, he'd just as often treat her as a slow employee who needed to be coddled.

"By the way, have you finished the transcription notes from the Dakota insurance case?" he asked, heading for the back door. "I added one more interview tape to your stack on Friday."

"I'm halfway through the last section of your tape." Transcribing Rick's notes was slow work and she wished she could type faster, or that he would pick up a more interesting case than insurance fraud.

"Well, then, I'll see you in the office tomorrow."

Rick opened the back door and Kelly called to stop him. "Sir, what about my keys?"

He paused. "Oh, I almost forgot. There's a wire hanger in the office and a flat-head screwdriver. I want you to practice breaking locks. I showed you the basics last week—let's see if you were paying attention. By the way, your old car should start if you jam the screwdriver past the ignition lock."

He left the dojo then, deaf to Kelly's quiet cussing. The door slammed and she swore louder. It was true that he'd shown her how to crack a lock. Once. After one lesson, she wasn't ready to pick anything short of a bike lock.

After cleaning the mirrors, she gathered her karate gear, snapped the door lock from the inside and then closed the door. She wasn't sure exactly how she was going to unlock the dojo in the morning, but Sam would kill her if she left the place unlocked. On Monday morning, she was always the first one in the dojo to set up for the karate camp kids. Hopefully Alex, her brother, would be able to help her with the lock. He boasted that he could break and fix almost anything with a couple of trusted tools.

Her blue Volkswagen Jetta was parked behind the dojo. She untwisted the wire coat hanger that Rick had left in the office and slid the wire between the window and the door. After several attempts, the wire snagged on something and the lock snapped up when she wiggled the wire. She squeezed the handle and the door popped open, almost magically. She sank into the front seat and stared at the ignition. Hot-wiring her own car seemed like a dumb idea and she doubted Rick's advice about the screwdriver. Unfortunately, she didn't have a spare key or any other ideas.

She positioned the screwdriver in the keyhole and then cussed Rick again. Once the screwdriver broke the lock casing, the regular key would never work again. She climbed out of the driver's seat and slammed the door shut.

A phone booth was one block down from the dojo on Main Street. Of course she'd left her cell phone at home today, of all days. She tried calling her brother first. Alex didn't answer the phone and she remembered he had plans to go surfing. Next she tried Gina. As she waited for Gina to answer, she remembered that she was at work today. Kelly hung up the phone. She had only Gina and Alex's numbers memorized. Her parents were on vacation and none of her friends were listed in the old phonebook chained to the booth.

Reluctantly, she headed back to her car. She grabbed the screwdriver and jammed it in the ignition, then pushed past the first catch-point and heard one metallic click. She pushed a little harder and the screwdriver was stuck. Wrenching it to the right, she heard the engine rumble, just like always. Awed by the power of a screwdriver, she backed out of the parking place. The screwdriver stuck in place, just as effective as her key would have been. An old Jetta had at least a few advantages over the newer thief-resistant models, she thought.

She pressed her foot on the gas and grinned as the engine roared in response. Only a few months ago, she'd been an ordinary broke college student and now she was ready for a career in auto theft. Grinning at this idea, she thought of the lectures and essay exams still to come in her last year at the university. None of her studies was as exciting as spy work with Rick, but she couldn't quit school. Breaking into one old VW didn't mean she had a guaranteed career.

Chapter Two

Kelly parked in the driveway and glanced at her watch. It was only mid-afternoon and since it was Sunday, she guessed that Alex would still be at the ocean. He'd probably stay until sunset. He was always hoping to catch the last good wave before dusk. Nearly every weekend he drove to the beach with his surfboard tied to the tool rack of his truck and the radio tuned in to the baseball game.

Fortunately, Alex never locked the doors. He owned the worst house on the block in a premier Ashton housing tract, just off Main Street. His theory was that no one would be stupid enough to burglarize the biggest eyesore in the neighborhood. Furthermore, as he had stated often, Ashton had so little crime that the local paper resorted to reports of petty theft and traffic violations just to fill the police report section.

After dropping her sweaty karate uniform in the washing machine and starting a load, Kelly headed for the shower. She found a business card for a local house painter taped to the bathroom door. This was Alex's second hint today. His first hint had been a receipt from Home Depot taped to the front door and a stack of paint cans in the entryway. She had almost tripped on the cans as she headed to her karate lesson that morning. Guiltily, she pulled the painter's business card off the bathroom door and tossed it in the trashcan.

Alex had promised to give her free rent in exchange for painting his house. She fully intended to keep her end of the deal, but she had discovered that the second job with Rick was taking up more time than she had planned. Between teaching the karate camp, running Rick's errands, the extra workouts with Sam and dates with Gina, the last thing she had time for was house painting. Kelly stared at the shower longingly, then headed to her bedroom to change into an old tank top and shorts.

Armed with paint cans, a roller, two paintbrushes and a mixing tray, she surveyed the house, trying to decide where to start. She settled on the south-facing wall near the garage. The paint can lid popped open with a turn of her pocketknife and a layer of oil drowned the yellow paint sludge below. Two of the divas on the Ashton suburban housing board wheeled their baby strollers along the sidewalk, passing Alex's house slowly. Their gossipy voices were full of obvious disdain as they critiqued the yard.

"Look, there's another dead spot." One of the women pointed her long nose at a large brown splotch in the grass as they passed the mailbox.

Her companion eagerly nodded in agreement. "What a sight!"

In downtown Ashton, brown spots on the lawn were an instant mark of condemnation. The other reason Alex's place had been chosen to be the sacrificial lamb at the annual housing board meeting was the house's exterior, twenty years overdue for a Mary Kay makeover.

With a wave that would have made a homecoming parade queen jealous, Kelly batted her eyelashes and called a greeting to the two women as they passed. "Hello, ladies. It's a beautiful day, isn't it?"

They returned the wave with matching artificial smiles and nods of agreement before continuing down the block at a more hurried pace. Alex had nearly married a woman who would have fit in perfectly at the Ashton housing board meetings. He had been engaged to Laura, a self-absorbed woman addicted to Nieman Marcus catalogue orders and Saks Fifth Avenue credit cards. Fortunately, Alex had come to his senses, called the engagement off and kicked Laura out of the house not long ago. Kelly didn't hide her satisfaction at his decision.

As soon as Laura was out of the house and Alex's hope for a wife dashed, the housing divas had descended on him. Since he was a bachelor with no wife to coerce into action, they exerted their force by issuing a housing pink slip. He had to have the slip signed once he'd fixed the sprinklers, fertilized the lawn and repainted the house. After cursing out the housing board, leaf blowers, the PTA, strip malls, dog-walkers, minivans and every other mark of suburbia he could think of, Alex started soaking his lawn and had selected the most obnoxious house paint he could find—Daisy Yellow. He'd burned the housing board's pink slip and offered Kelly free rent in exchange for painting the place.

When classes at the university ended, Kelly sublet her apartment in the city and moved into Alex's spare room. She usually spent her summers in Ashton with her parents so she could teach at the karate camp. Unfortunately, this year her parents had sold their house. They were cruising the countryside in an RV and sending postcards from every notable landmark that they passed, including Paul Bunyan's monument, a corn maze in Iowa and Mount Rushmore.

Shoving a wooden stick deep into the paint, she slowly stirred until it reached a consistency that spread on the wood siding with ease. As her shoulders cooked in the afternoon sun, she coated the glowing yellow acrylic over the south-facing wall. August was probably the worst month to paint in the valley. Sweat evaporated before it had a chance to cool your skin and roses dried even as they grew on their stem. Eyeing the coastal mountain range on the western horizon and longing for the stench of San Francisco's fog, she counted the strokes necessary to cover each foot of the wall. Only thirty miles and a big bay separated her from the cooler San Francisco temperatures. She imagined an ocean breeze while wiping the sweat off her forehead and then turned back to the paint bucket. The wood drank in the paint greedily and four or five brushstrokes just concealed the old patches of mustard.

She finished the southern wall and moved her supplies to the next area. A silver Corvette pulled up to the white picket fence and parked behind her Volkswagen.

Gina shouted out, "Hey, chica—what the hell are you doing painting today? Are you crazy?"

Kelly shrugged. "I don't think I'm crazy. People paint houses all the time."

"Not when it's over a hundred degrees. That yellow paint looks like fried eggs." Gina climbed out of her car and hit the button to arm the alarm. "Damn, it's hot."

Kelly always thought it was strange that Gina would bother with alarms in Ashton. She guessed it was a cop thing. "Yeah, it's a little warm."

"Time for a painting break. You look ready for a shower."

"Not yet." Dipping the brush into the paint, Kelly started painting the second wall.

"Not yet? Why would you want to keep your hot Latina lover waiting?" Gina joked, swaggering up to the front porch. Still wearing her police uniform, she had no doubt just come from the station. Although she lived in Ashton, Gina commuted into the city to work at the SFPD. She claimed that police work in the suburbs was too boring and the city's higher crime rates lured her to take a position across the bay.

Kelly smiled as she watched Gina's approach. "You're looking hot in that uniform. But I just got started here. I'm not ready for my distraction." Not quite yet, anyway, she added silently. Several drops of yellow cascaded off the bristles to dot the porch planks.

"Oh, so now I'm just a distraction?" Gina rested her hands on her hips and threw back her shoulders in a challenge.

Kelly nodded, then laughed to let Gina know she was joking.

She wondered how Gina could pull off the serious cop image with her youthful feminine look. She always had to stifle a laugh when Gina tried to act tough. Gina's dark brown hair was pulled back in a girlish ponytail and her light brown skin was smooth as an apple over high cheekbones. She kept her fingernails trimmed in symmetric crescent moons and her eyelashes darkened with mascara. Occasionally she sported dark red lipstick but without it her lips had enough color to attract attention and Kelly encouraged her to leave it off. She preferred kissing naked lips.

Gina slipped her hand under Kelly's tank top and rubbed her back. "You're already wet and I just got here. Not a bad distraction, huh?"

"I'm not wet. I'm drenched in sweat." Kelly shook her head. "I feel disgusting."

Gina winked. "I don't mind sweat."

"You're gonna scare the neighbors in that uniform," Kelly replied. Ashton wasn't like San Francisco. In the suburbs, someone would notice car alarms, police sirens and women making out on the front porch. People routinely spied on their neighbors and were eager to judge everything.

"Good. I like scaring the neighbors." Gina grinned and raised an eyebrow suggestively. "And you're too hot for me to keep my hands off. Come on, I know you like women in uniform."

"You never stop flirting, do you?" She watched Gina undo the first few buttons on her shirt to expose a white undershirt beneath the coarse blue uniform material. "Feel free to borrow some of my clothes if you want to change."

"Maybe I'll stay like this, just to make a scene." Gina leaned close to kiss Kelly's neck and circled her arms around her waist. "This town is too damn quiet." She brushed her fingertips up Kelly's arm and teased, "Wow, you really have that paint stroke mastered. So smooth and determined . . ."

"Please, Gina." Kelly shrugged off Gina's arm and continued to coat the wood in bright yellow swatches while Gina watched her every movement.

"I think I could stand here all day," Gina said, feigning a breathless sigh.

Kelly laughed. "Don't tell me that's your plan."

"Well, I was thinking of soaking your tank top in water, and then, yes, I'd like to just stand here and watch you work that paintbrush." Grinning, she added, "Unless you're ready for a real break. You, me and that tiny shower of yours . . ."

"When I finish this can," Kelly replied. The paint was half gone already.

"Oh, I almost forgot." Gina headed back to her car, beeped the automatic lock button and pulled a bag out of the passenger seat. She skipped back to the porch and held out a paper bag stamped with a sourdough bakery logo. "Hungry?"

"No, I already ate. But grab something to drink and come back out here to keep me company. I'll be finished with this wall soon," she promised. "By the way, Alex made some lemonade, if you're interested. Otherwise, raid the fridge for whatever you can find."

"Your brother made lemonade? How domestic. He'd make the perfect husband."

"Well, he made the lemonade, but he drinks the beer."

Gina smiled. "He's got good taste." She opened the screen door and disappeared into the house.

Kelly watched the door close behind Gina and realized she was looking forward to an afternoon distraction. Alex wouldn't be home from the beach for at least a few hours. Dabbing her finger on the porch where a few drops of paint had already started to dry, Kelly wondered what Gina would pick out of her closet to wear. They didn't have the same taste in clothing. Outside of her uniform, Gina preferred fitted designer-brand attire that accentuated every appealing curve of her body. Kelly's clothing was uniformly baggy, often wrinkled and only coordinated because nearly everything she owned was in varying shades of gray or blue. Kelly didn't like standing out and tried to slip unnoticed through crowds.

Gray fit in with the city fog. In Ashton, bright colors were in fashion and the sun was always shining, almost as obnoxiously bright as the daisy yellow house paint. Although Ashton was less than a half an hour from San Francisco, the suburbs lacked everything that made city life exciting, including the crime rates, as Gina had noted. Despite this, Kelly always looked forward to coming to Ashton each summer. This was supposed to be her last summer teaching the camp. Her senior year began in a month and she'd need a real job by next summer. Rick had already suggested that she work as a private investigator after graduation but Kelly hadn't decided if she wanted a full-time job in Rick's business. At twenty-one and almost out of college, she still wasn't ready to make a commitment to a career.

Gina emerged wearing Kelly's gray surf shorts and a white undershirt. Her hand was wrapped around a light brown bottle. She pointed at the beer and asked, "Alex won't mind, right?"

Kelly shook her head. Gina settled on the porch swing and popped off the bottle cap. For some reason, seeing Gina in her clothing was very sexy. It was good to see her relax. "How was work?"

"Slow, even for a Sunday." Gina took a sip. She leaned back on the swing and stretched out her legs. "I passed out a few speeding tickets and called a tow truck on some idiot who was parked in a red zone with his lights on." She sighed. "You know, I've always hated traffic cops. I wish I could just skip this part of the training and work on criminal investigations."

Kelly shook her head. "I don't think investigating criminals is as exciting as you make it sound."

Gina sighed. "Compared to watching a radar screen, it is." She unwrapped the deli sandwich and surveyed the fat slices of sourdough. "I have tomorrow off. What do you think about taking a drive somewhere? I've heard Lake Tahoe is nice this time of year."

"I have to work," Kelly admitted. "But Lake Tahoe does sound nice, clear skies, mountains and an ice-cold lake . . ."

"You could take a few days off from the karate camp. One of the other guys at the dojo could work a few days for you."

"Yes, but I'm working with Rick, too."

Gina sat up at the mention of Rick. "Speaking of that guy, did you tell him I wanted a moonlighting job?" She paused. "Sometimes I think I'll go crazy if I spend the rest of my life handing out speeding citations. God, I'd love the chance to work with an investigator."

"I'll mention it the next time I talk to him," Kelly said, knowing she wouldn't bring it up to Rick again but not ready to confess Rick's answer. She had known that Rick wouldn't want Gina's help. He had already mentioned that private investigators had to limit any information leaks to the police. Gina's first allegiance would be to her precinct, not to Rick's PI service. "But you know, you haven't been a cop for that long. Maybe you'll learn to like ruining people's day with a ticket. There are a few people out there that I wouldn't mind writing a ticket for."

Gina laughed. "There's more to being a cop than that. And honestly, I hate giving most people tickets. Some assholes deserve it though, you're right."

Letting the yellow paint seep down the crevices at the baseboard, Kelly changed the subject, "Hey, have you heard from Vicky lately? I was listening to the radio this morning and the news announcer said the military might be sending some of the soldiers home earlier than they had expected. I wondered if you've heard how she's doing?"

Vicky was Gina's ex-girlfriend and had been stationed in Iraq for the past six months. Previously Gina had said that Vicky's original orders for a six-month tour had been extended to a nine-month stay.

Gina shook her head. "She's probably sweating in some desert. The last letter I got from her said she was smack-dab in the middle of the 'sandbox.' She couldn't tell me any details."

Kelly watched the paintbrush wick up the last few drops at the bottom of the can. "Did you mention you had started dating other people?"

"No. She'll think you seduced me."

"Me?" Kelly shook her head and smiled. Vicky and Gina had

19

separated a few months before Gina and Kelly met, but the terms of their relationship were unclear. Once Vicky was notified that she was being sent to Iraq, Gina had broken up with her. But Gina had admitted to Kelly that she still had strong feelings for Vicky.

"Why are you grinning? You did seduce me," Gina said.

"Hey, I just knocked on your door. You're the one who invited me inside that first night."

Gina laughed. "Well, it's a good thing Vicky is in Iraq and I already broke up with her then, isn't it? She doesn't need to know the details."

"Details? Such as, you said you were still in love with Vicky the first time you flirted with me?"

"I wasn't flirting. You wouldn't leave me alone at the bar."

"You wouldn't stop staring at me."

Gina smiled and shrugged. "Maybe I was sizing you up."

"Tell her you had no choice but to fall for me. I swept you off your feet with my dashing good looks and charming personality." Kelly laughed. "In fact, I'll tell her myself. I'm sure I could just slip a little note into one of the weekly letters that you send to her."

Gina stared at her silently. She looked like she'd just been caught lying. "How'd you know I still send her letters?"

Kelly had found out about the letters last week from Tasha and Beth, their mutual friends, but she hadn't planned on letting Gina know that she was aware of her correspondence with Vicky. She regretted slipping the information now.

"Relax, Gina. I don't mind if you send her letters. She's stuck in Iraq and needs to stay in touch with her friends. I think it's great that you keep up the correspondence." Kelly finished the first coat on the west-facing wall and moved to the other side of the doorway to begin tracing the borders of the windowsill. Vicky was supposed to spend nine months in Iraq. If that plan held, she'd be back in Ashton in three months. But three months was a long time, Kelly reminded herself. It was too far away to worry about what would happen when Gina's first love came home.

"Who told you I was writing to her?"

"Gina, let's just drop it." She glanced over at Gina, who was staring at the women coming down the sidewalk. The Ashton housing board ladies were wheeling by Alex's mailbox with their strollers. Kelly waved at them and they flashed their artificial smiles for the second time that afternoon. "Don't worry, they're harmless," Kelly said under her breath. "They're just our local Mary Kay team back from a stroll in the park."

Gina nodded. As soon as the women and the strollers passed, she slipped her hand over Kelly's wrist and pulled the paintbrush away from the wood. "I should have told you I was still sending letters to her—"

"I understand."

"Let me finish, okay?" Gina said. She was obviously irritated that Kelly had found out about the letters. "Look, I wouldn't want you to be writing to your ex all the time. But this is different. She's had a tough time. Hell, she's been living in a war zone. She needs friends. And that's all I am to her now."

Kelly nodded. She was sorry she had mentioned the letters now. Gina's hot temper ignited quickly.

"It's been months since we broke up and there's nothing between us now."

"Fine." In a lower voice, Kelly added, "Nothing except an ocean and a few continents."

"Kelly, you know what I mean. We're just friends."

"And she's halfway around the world. Being 'just friends' has got to be easier when she's in Iraq. What happens when she's back in Ashton?"

"I liked you from the first moment we were introduced. Maybe I was thinking about Vicky before I met you but that's over. I was perfectly ready for you to seduce me." Gina shook her head. "Let's forget about ex-girlfriends. We both have had our share of drama."

Kelly nodded. She had started seeing Gina before breaking up with her own girlfriend. But all of that was in the past.

"I think you're ready to put down your paintbrush and take a shower with me."

21

"What makes you think that?" Kelly tried to ignore Gina's gaze and continued to paint. She loved Gina's forwardness.

"Call it intuition."

Gina pulled the paintbrush away from the wall and plucked the bristles, sending a flurry of paint droplets onto Kelly's arm. Her shirt was already splattered with yellow. Kelly dropped the paintbrush into the can and dipped her finger into the paint. "You know, I have more ammunition. Do you really want a paint fight?"

Backing away from Kelly, Gina jumped off the porch and held up her hands. "Wait, I changed my mind. I don't think we should waste your brother's paint." Her hands settled on her hips and she grinned slyly. "And, if it's an option, I'd rather have a water fight in your shower."

"Well, there could be worse compromises." Kelly smiled. She wiped the paint off her fingers and opened the screen door.

Inside the temperature was just as warm, despite the loud fan that blew through the family room. They headed down the hall to the spare room behind the garage. Kelly had already discovered that Alex's spare bedroom and the adjoining bathroom had a few flaws, one of which was that the shower stall really did not fit two people. She really didn't mind the lack of elbow room when it meant that two people found it necessary to shower in constant contact with each other.

They slipped out of their clothing and stood naked on the cool bathroom tiles as the water reached a comfortable lukewarm temperature. Gina slid into the stall first and waited for Kelly to join her. Within a few minutes they were covered in soap bubbles and Kelly started scratching at the dried paint on her arms.

"I think you got more paint on yourself than you got on the house. Next time we have a paint fight, let's use latex." Gina drew a line with her fingertips down Kelly's chest. "We could get paint all over ourselves."

"Plucking hair off certain places along with the latex paint doesn't sound like fun," Kelly replied, loosening a flake of paint attached to several fine arm hairs.

Gina laughed. "You use lotion first. Lots of lotion."

"Is that why your skin is so damn smooth?" Kelly teased.

She nodded seriously. "I have a can of glow-in-the-dark latex. Think of all the possibilities."

"Ouch. I don't want to."

Gina leaned forward and kissed her. The warm water sprayed on their faces as they explored each other's bodies. Gina traced a line of kisses down Kelly's neck and over her breasts, murmuring encouragement as Kelly massaged her back, kneading the knots between her shoulders. The muscles relaxed under the touch of her hands and Kelly continued to rub lower along Gina's spine, down to the rise of her butt and forward to her hips and inner thighs. She pushed Gina back against the wall of the shower stall. With her hips pressed against Gina's, she trailed her hand down to part the folds between Gina's legs. Gina found Kelly's lips and moaned with pleasure as Kelly thrust her finger inside her. She pushed deeper, fingers drawing slow circles between her legs as the water pelted their bodies.

Chapter Three

The next morning Kelly arrived at the dojo early. Picking locks was more time-consuming than it seemed and she'd discovered that her morning schedule was several minutes delayed without her keys. The last thing she wanted was for one of her karate camp students to show up while she was still working the lock. Fidgeting with the wire, she cussed out loud. The wire snagged something, but the handle still refused to turn. She cursed Rick again, wishing he could hear all of the names she'd called him since he'd taken her keys yesterday. Not only was she starting the day locked out of the dojo, but it was Monday, which meant she would have several new students added to the camp roster, a longer day of teaching and a meeting tonight with Rick.

Alex would know what to do, she reasoned. He would probably have the lock picked on his first try. Anything mechanical was like putty in his hands. But she didn't want to call her brother every time she needed help. Anyway, he was usually at the construction site working by seven a.m.

After Gina left last night, Alex had trudged in late from his surfing trip. He agreed to teach Kelly the finer points of picking locks in exchange for a spaghetti dinner. When he had asked why she wanted to learn this skill, her excuse was that she'd lost her keys and needed to know how to break into the dojo the next morning. He pulled out his toolbox and taught her several locksmith tricks, then patiently stayed up half the night while she fumbled with every lock in the house.

At exactly eight, the lock finally clicked. Kelly turned the handle and opened the door. Every Monday morning the dojo had the same odor—sweaty socks. She sniffed the familiar stench and then walked through the empty studio to hang out the Open sign. As she positioned the sign, she spotted a boy staring up at her from the other side of the window. She didn't recognize him at first but thought he looked familiar. A woman stood next to him, and Kelly suspected this was his mother. Her face had an annoyed "I'm waiting" expression and Kelly guessed she wouldn't like the woman.

As soon as Kelly opened the door, she realized where she'd seen him before. He was the kid she'd seen at the park last week chasing after the soccer ball. Hopefully he wouldn't recognize that she was the witch-in-training with her Bo staff—er, broom handle. In an overly cheerful tone, Kelly greeted the boy, and then glanced up at the woman who stood next to him. "Good morning!"

The woman nodded coolly. She introduced the boy as her son, Thomas, and continued, "Today's our first day of karate camp and we're so excited."

"I bet," Kelly said, winking at Thomas. "Well, you're the first one here, but this place is gonna be jumping with kids in a few minutes." She smiled and Thomas gazed solemnly at her with overwhelmed brown eyes. "Come on in and get ready. I'll show you how to tie that belt."

Thomas shook his head. She figured he was five or six years old. His white belt was draped around his neck and he clasped his mother's pant leg with one hand while sucking the thumb of his other. His big brown eyes reminded her of a chimpanzee or a baby

25

monkey and she quickly decided to call him Monkey for the dura-
tion of his time in karate camp.

After a few attempts, Monkey's mom finally got him to let go of
her pant leg and they both entered the waiting room. More students had started to arrive and the boy's eyes were beginning to
glaze over in fear. Monkey locked tightly onto Kelly's hand when
his mom finally announced she was leaving. He seemed ready to
cry at any moment. Kelly showed him how to bow and quickly tied
his white belt around his waist.

She scanned the dojo, searching for someone to partner him up
with. Spotting Colin, the ten-year-old squad leader for the camp,
she called, "Colin, hurry up and get your belt on. You're late."
Although Colin had given her the most trouble of all her students
at the start of the summer, he had quickly become her favorite
challenge. "I need you out on the mat in thirty seconds."

"Yes, ma'am. Sorry I'm late," he apologized, then yanked off his
sneakers, tied his purple belt and scrambled to the edge of the mat.
He waited for Kelly's permission to bow and entered the mat.
"Ma'am, we're late because my dad spilled his coffee."

His brother, Isaac, chimed in, "It's true, ma'am. We had to stop
and clean out the minivan with McDonald's napkins." He added,
"Dad's lucky we had lots of McDonald's napkins."

Kelly nodded. "Fine. I'll let you boys off easy this time. Just
warn your dad not to drink coffee while driving."

Colin smiled. "Dad always drinks when he drives. He also
speaks French."

Isaac giggled. "Yeah, he was speaking a whole lot of *French* this
morning, that's for sure."

Kelly quickly silenced the boys as they tried repeating some of
the phrases. Isaac was two years younger than Colin and was
always the perfect student. Colin, on the other hand, had been
born causing trouble, his parents insisted. And Kelly had had a lot
of trouble with Colin in the past. At the beginning of summer, she
was ready to kick him out of the karate camp. But after she cracked
down on him, he made some improvements, and she found that
the more responsibility she gave him, the harder he tried in each

class. He had brimmed with joy when she announced he was to be the squad leader for the camp. He turned out to be the perfect drill sergeant.

Colin's father, who always seemed too busy to bother with his sons, had even stopped in to the dojo to admit how surprised he was at Colin's changed attitude at home. They were considering stopping his Ritalin. Several kids in the karate camp were on behavior drugs. Sam was convinced that a diagnosis of attention deficit disorder had simply replaced the word *hyperactive* and Kelly found she often agreed with this theory.

"Colin, meet our newest camper. This is Thomas. But in the dojo, his name is going to be Monkey." Thomas glanced up at Kelly with surprise when he heard this. She nodded at him. "Colin, can you take over from here?"

"Yes, ma'am." He turned to address Thomas. "Hi, Monkey. I'm Colin, the squad leader." He extended his hand and waited for Monkey to shake. "So, it's your first time? I've been doing this for a long time so if you have any questions, ask me." He proudly slapped his own chest.

Monkey stared wide-eyed at Colin and Kelly had trouble not laughing at the scene.

Colin continued in his authoritative tone, "By the way, you'll get used to your nickname. You aren't the only animal here. We also have Bear, Tiger, Alligator and a bunch of other animals in the dojo." He pointed out two kids who had just stepped on the mat and introduced Gorilla and Cougar.

Kelly had started renaming the new kids once she had over twenty students enrolled. There were too many names to remember. On average, there were thirty kids enrolled in every two-week session. At a quarter after eight, she lined up the class and started the morning meditation.

That evening Monkey was the last student waiting at the dojo. His mom came nearly an hour late to pick him up. As soon as he saw his mom, he ran up to her and announced that he was no longer to be called Thomas. He'd changed his name to Monkey and wanted to spend every day at the karate dojo. His mother eyed Kelly suspiciously and quickly scooped the boy into her arms and hurried out of the waiting room.

Kelly smiled as the door closed. She dialed Gina's number from Sam's phone in the office. "Hey, it's me."

"Hi," Gina answered. "Want to meet for dinner tonight?"

"Maybe. What's the plan?" She remembered her meeting with Rick was also that evening and hoped it wouldn't take long.

"Beth was talking about going for pizza with the team after softball practice. I think Tasha is coming too. We'll be at the Pizza Joint around eight."

"The Pizza Joint?" Kelly could already feel her stomach aching for a slice of the famous pizza pie combo. "You know I never turn down pizza. I'll see you there."

She hung up with Gina and left the dojo with a quick wave to Sam. After a short drive across town, she reached Rick's office, a hole in the wall sandwiched between a jewelry shop and a laundry. Rick had divided the office space to include the front reception area with a bail bonds distributor and a notary public, and a small back office where he ran his private investigation service. There was no sign posted about his service, and Kelly had learned that he did no advertising to obtain his clientele—everyone found him through word of mouth.

Rick's car wasn't in the parking lot, and the only person in the office was Jerold, the bail bonds man. She smiled at Jerold, uncomfortable as always around this man who gawked at every woman that entered the building and left his porn magazines cluttered behind his desk.

Jerold nodded a greeting when she passed his desk. "You just missed him."

"Well, I'll have fewer distractions then. I've got a bunch of typing to do tonight anyway." She was careful to not tell Jerold too much information about what she did for Rick. "Do you mind if I play some music?"

"Suit yourself. Once that door closes to Rick's office, I can't hear a damn thing." Jerold tapped his right ear. "It helps that I'm half deaf from my wife yelling at me all the time." He laughed and held his jiggling belly.

Rick's office door was locked with a combination lock and she quickly dialed the combination. The odor of dingy newspapers and lingering cigarette smoke accosted her as she opened the door. Rick smoked too much and had a habit of collecting newspapers from his neighbors. He claimed that he only took the newspapers that were left out for more than a day, and he had no problems with reading day-old news. The old newspapers stacked in boxes behind Rick's desk dated back to 1993. She flipped on the lights and headed over to Rick's desk. A note was Scotch-taped to the computer: "Finish transcription notes for the Dakota case. Meeting canceled. Will call to reschedule."

Kelly sighed. She hated listening to Rick's audiotapes and recording his notes. The work was tedious and seemed a waste of time, but the money was good. He insisted that transcribing his notes was a valuable part of her training—to copy his investigation style. She thought Rick needed a secretary instead. After tuning the radio to a jazz station, she found Rick's tape from the Dakota case and his cassette player. She donned the headsets and settled back in Rick's leather chair. The Dakota case concerned an insurance agent who had been producing fraudulent claims and stealing money from retirees. Rick had done countless interviews to identify the best witnesses for the lawyers to use in the trial against Dakota. After hearing all of the witness accounts, Kelly had only decided one thing—she was reluctant to ever buy life insurance. She adjusted the keyboard for her speed typing session. She only had another half-hour's worth of tape to transcribe and then she could relax with Gina and a pizza pie.

"Hi, stranger!" Tasha shouted enthusiastically as Kelly entered the restaurant.

"You guys got the best seats in the house." Kelly joined Beth, Tasha and Gina, who were seated at a booth by the front window. The place was always packed and good seating was limited.

"Tasha smiled at the waiter so he'd give us the best spot." Beth

29

grinned. "I have to hold her down—she'll flirt with any Tom, Dick or Jenny."

Tasha pushed Beth's shoulder. "Do I have to sit with you? Just because I'm bisexual doesn't mean I flirt any more than you do."

Beth arched her eyebrows. "Yeah, whatever."

"You need to get over your insecurities," Tasha answered sharply. She wadded up her napkin and tossed it at Beth's chest.

Beth smiled. "My insecurities are only warranted when you flirt with all the guys!"

"They've been arguing like an old married couple since we got here," Gina confided to Kelly as she sat down on her side of the booth. "Watch what you say or someone might bite off your head."

After ordering their pizza, Tasha announced she'd received a letter from the army that morning stating that her case might be dropped due to inconclusive evidence. Over a week ago, she'd received a similar letter stating that she was under full investigation and faced a possible discharge because of major code violations that had been brought to the attention of the review committee. Tasha was in the Army Reserves, stationed in San Francisco, and everyone else in her unit had already been transferred to Iraq. She was kept behind without a full explanation.

Beth worked in a hardware store in downtown Ashton and expressed an active distrust about everything concerning the military. They had been dating for over a year and Beth seemed to be continually worried that someone from the army would swoop down and attack Tasha at any moment.

"I swear, the military is too disorganized to know when the one hand is giving some poor guy a purple heart and the other hand is flipping that same guy off." Beth poked her straw at the ice cubes in her Coca-Cola. "I'm just glad someone said you were a lesbian. Otherwise, you'd be out there frying in the desert."

Tasha shook her head. "I'd rather be with the rest of my unit in Iraq than facing a dishonorable discharge."

"I think we should move to Canada. Who needs the military

breathing down their back? They hate gays anyway." Beth sighed. "Has anyone heard if the Gay Political Action Coalition is going to try another lawsuit against Don't Ask, Don't Tell?"

Tasha shook her head. "I doubt it."

"I know a discharge would suck, but I'm glad you weren't sent to Iraq along with the rest of your unit." Beth paused and then continued in a quieter tone, "Maybe the anti-gay policy is a good thing."

"Are you crazy?" Tasha countered. "It's completely ridiculous. Plenty of other countries allow gays in the military. Look at Australia and over half of Europe. A gay person can defend their country, just like anyone else."

"Yes, but I don't want you to go off defending us when you could stay here with me. I'm still worried about what the military will do if they ever find out you like women, as well as men."

Beth's concern about Tasha was obvious. Tasha's position in the military was still uncertain. If they were able to find some proof of lesbian activity, she would certainly be discharged, but from what Kelly could tell, they still had no proof. And Tasha was not a big risk to the military. She had been caught at the wrong place at the wrong time. She was under investigation by the military because she had been caught coming home late from a bar with Beth, and one of the military officers said they had proof that Tasha was a lesbian. Tasha wouldn't deny the charge and was waiting for the officer to prove his claim. She could have come up with a story and gotten off without a full investigation, but she refused to lie.

"Hey, speaking of Iraq, Gina, have you heard anything from Vicky?" Tasha asked.

"Yeah, is she still pining away for you?" Beth muttered.

Gina shifted in her seat and avoided Kelly's gaze. "No, I haven't heard from her for a while now." She glanced at Kelly, who was tired of hearing about someone she'd never met.

Beth arched her eyebrow in disapproval at Gina and Kelly. "I'd be pissed if my girlfriend was dating someone else while I was off in Iraq."

"She's my ex," Gina corrected her.

"Well, have you told her about the fabulous woman you've met?" Beth pointed at Kelly.

"No. Who tells their ex-girlfriend that they've met a fabulous new person? Well, on second thought, maybe you would." Gina eyed Beth. "Just to be vindictive."

"And you don't have any reason to be vindictive? Aren't you still a little mad that she made out with that girl from her base?" Beth asked. "I thought that affair was the real reason you broke up with her. The night before she left for Iraq, no less."

"All right, you guys, I think that's enough reminiscing." Tasha shot a pleading look at Beth to make her stop.

Gina shook her head. Kelly could tell she was pissed at Beth.

Tasha grinned. "Well, I think Kelly and Gina make a better couple anyway." She said after a moment, "Vicky was hard to trust, and I think she made out with more than just one person from that army base. But you better watch out, Gina. I wouldn't put it past her to be pissed if she comes home in three months to find you'd seduced another woman . . ."

"Ah, yes." Beth laughed. "Oh, Angelina Hernandez, the hot Latina lover seduces another naïve woman!"

Gina tapped her foot against Kelly's leg and shook her head. "I wasn't the one seducing this time."

"Oh, really?" Beth asked with interest. "Kelly, I didn't figure you for such a player. Any more surprises up your sleeve?"

Kelly felt her cheeks grow warm and ignored Beth's question. "I thought Gina was over Vicky when I met her."

"I was," Gina said defensively. "Vicky was long gone before I met Kelly. Everything worked out for the best."

"A war in Iraq and you're saying that everything worked out for the best?" Beth asked dubiously. "Well, I don't know if Vicky would agree."

Kelly wanted the conversation to end. She was annoyed that Beth kept trying to spark a fight. Of course no one thought that a war was a good thing, but this wasn't about the war at all.

"Beth, don't act like a prude. You certainly slept around when we were dating." Gina cussed under her breath.

Tasha leaned back in the booth and winked at Kelly. "Uh-oh. I think we're about to have a dyke drama fest."

"Not without pizza." The waiter had appeared and set the steaming pizza on a stand at the center of their booth. He started handing out plates and flashed a smile at Tasha. Kelly noticed the waiter's obvious attraction to Tasha, but Beth and Gina were too upset with the conversation that had abruptly ended to pay attention to the flirtatious waiter.

Neither Beth nor Gina apologized for their last statements and both pulled slices off the pan silently. While they ate, Beth and Gina remained quiet as Tasha and Kelly chatted about karate. Tasha said she was interested in learning karate and Kelly encouraged her to try out one of the adult evening classes.

Gina finished her last bite of pizza, avoiding the crust, leaned back in her seat and began, "Look, Beth, I'm sorry about what I said. I really didn't mean it. Really, it's old news now."

Beth eyed her. "We should talk about this later. But I'm sorry too. You know, we're all guilty."

Kelly stared at her plate and the onions that she'd picked off the pizza. Beth's last comment had hit home. Guilt was the one feeling she'd been trying, unsuccessfully, to shake since the duffel bag delivery she'd made over a month ago.

Rick paid her one hundred dollars for every delivery she made. The first few deliveries had been just envelopes or small packages. Of all the packages that he gave her, she had never opened one until she had to deliver the heavy black duffel bag. Unable to resist the temptation of pulling back the zipper for a quick peek, Kelly discovered a gun and a box of bullets. She made the delivery, just as requested, without asking any questions. Then she found out that the recipient of the duffel bag had been shot a few days later. And now a death was on her conscience, all because of a stupid black duffel bag that she should never have unzipped in the first place. The police had investigated the death and quickly ruled it a suicide, yet the black bag still haunted her. She doubted if she would ever get that delivery off her conscience.

She had tried to forget about the gun. Only once had she mentioned her troubled thoughts to Rick and he had shrugged her off, saying, "People kill, not guns." She wondered what else he would ask her to do. She pushed the plate of pizza remains away from her and tried to listen to the conversation about softball. Gina's team was practicing for an end-of-the-summer final series. Tasha and Beth were arguing over how many practices they should have before the series. Kelly stared at her plate, thinking about the black duffel bag and how she hated onions.

After dinner, Kelly followed Gina back to her place. Gina lived in a townhouse in downtown Ashton. Her family gave her a monthly allowance to help with the rent payments. According to Gina, her parents could afford to chip in for her rent, since they had a sizeable fortune that they were happy to waste on their five children. The Hernandez family had made their money by managing a produce distribution center for farms in the Central Valley and had moved to a posh neighborhood in southern California when Gina was just starting high school. She'd moved up to San Francisco to go to college, then dropped out of school after the second year and joined the police academy.

Although she was no longer in school, her parents continued to send her an allowance. They were apparently very proud she had become a police officer and completely unaware that she was a lesbian. When Kelly asked Gina if she planned on telling her parents, Gina had quipped, "Don't ask, and don't tell. Works for civilians just as well as the military."

Kelly parked on the street and waited by the front door for Gina to pick up her mail. A black Chevy drove slowly down the street and Kelly felt her stomach muscles tighten with uneasiness. Was he watching her? The car turned down a side street before she could see the driver or the license plates.

"What's wrong?" Gina asked as she unlocked the front door.

Kelly realized she was still staring down the dark street. "Nothing. I thought I saw someone." She shook her head. There was a glaring light on the front porch that burned her eyes. She knew that whoever had driven by would certainly have seen her standing on the porch, in the full glow of yellow.

Gina squinted down the street, then shrugged. "Looks like the coast is clear. You know, we don't really need to worry about being seen together. Who would care if I grab you and start making out here on the front porch? My neighbors are probably all watching prime-time TV—and missing the scene we could cause." She slipped her hand around Kelly's waist and tried to kiss her.

Kelly shook her head. "You're right. Coast is clear. Let's go inside anyway. I don't want to distract anyone from their prime-time cable." She remembered Rick's warning about talking to Gina. He hadn't told her not to see her—just not to talk about work.

As if reading her thoughts, Gina asked about Rick as soon as they were inside. "Did you see him today? Did you ask him about us working together?"

"Well, I told him you were interested." Kelly didn't want to lie but she wasn't ready to tell the truth either.

"Did you say that I'm willing to start on any investigation and, unlike you, I'm not afraid to shoot a gun?" Gina laughed. "He knows I'm a cop, right?"

"Yeah, he knows."

"So, what'd he say?" she asked. Gina's intense longing to do investigative work surprised Kelly. It was obvious that working with Rick would be much more than just another job for her.

"He said no," Kelly answered. She watched Gina's expression sour.

"No? Why the hell did he say no?"

Kelly shrugged. "Because you're a cop."

Gina threw her keys on the coffee table in the family room and sank down on the couch. "That sucks."

"For what it's worth, I think we would be good partners." Kelly paused and set her screwdriver next to Gina's keys. She didn't know when Rick would give her back her keys but had to carry the screwdriver everywhere now so she could start her car. "He said he wouldn't hire moonlighting cops because he's too concerned about 'information leaks.' He'd prefer if I weren't even dating you. I told him you were more qualified for investigative work than I am, but he doesn't seem to care about qualifications."

"You know what? I don't give a damn!" Gina was fuming. She picked up a coaster on the coffee table and threw it at the wall, then swore again. After a moment, Gina picked up Kelly's screwdriver. "Why are you carrying a screwdriver around?"

"For good luck," Kelly joked. "Could get lucky carrying a big tool in my pocket. Or at least I'll get—"

Gina put her finger to Kelly's lips. "Don't finish that sentence. It's too damn cheesy."

They both laughed and Kelly felt the tension ease between them.

Gina continued, "I saw the screwdriver in your pocket at the Pizza Joint and was worried you were starting some weird dyke fad."

"What's wrong starting a fad?" Kelly asked, pretending to be hurt by Gina's comment. "Some women might think a screwdriver is sexy."

"Not one this size," Gina countered. "Sorry, chica. A spaghetti noodle is more impressive. This just doesn't work for the tough-love look."

Kelly grinned. "Don't worry, I wasn't trying to be tough. Rick took my keys."

"Why?"

"Some sort of evil training exercise," Kelly replied.

"No way! Are you serious?" Gina asked with disbelief. "Forget it. I don't want to work with him anyway. I'd lose my temper if he tried to pull something like that on me. So why the screwdriver?"

"I had to jam it into the ignition to start my car and broke the key slot. Now I'm stuck carrying around a damn screwdriver until

I have enough money to pay to get the ignition fixed." Kelly sighed. She didn't want to think about her money problems. She had one month left to make enough money to pay for next year's tuition and Rick hadn't mentioned money since the last errand she'd run a week ago.

"What about the car door? Do you lock it?" Gina asked.

Kelly smiled. "I'm pretty quick with a coat hanger. And fortunately, I have an old car. The wire slips between the glass and the door. It's almost too easy."

"Great." Gina shook her head. "So, if this job with Rick doesn't work out, at least you can make some cash stealing cars."

"You'd turn me in," Kelly said.

"Or at least handcuff you and hold you for questioning." Gina grabbed her wrist and, sinking back into the couch cushions, kissed her.

Chapter Four

Tuesday passed uneventfully. There was no word from Rick about any new information to add to the Dakota case. Kelly hoped he might have a new case soon. She was tired of the insurance agency. Gina had worked the night shift, so Kelly spent the evening with Alex, watching a movie. Although they were sharing the house for the summer, it seemed she rarely had time to spend with her brother and she'd enjoyed hanging out with him.

Kelly honked her horn and waved at Alex as she pulled into the driveway on Wednesday evening. Alex was spraying a brown spot in the front lawn with his super-soaker hose nozzle. He waved his beer at her and then directed the water toward another brown spot. She stared at the brown spots that were sucking up the water and then closed her eyes, relaxing for the first time all day.

"Hey, would you like a car wash?" Alex asked, squirting the hose at the hood of her car. "Just sit tight. Your car will be clean in no time." He grinned and aimed the spray of water too close to the open window.

"Alex! Don't," she yelled, dodging the water that sprayed the front seat of the car while trying to roll up the window.

"All right, fine." He smiled. "You know, I try and do nice things for people, but no one appreciates nice guys." He shook his head, feigning a pout, and redirected the hose to water the grass. "I promise I'll leave you alone."

Not trusting that he would keep this promise, she kept her eyes on the hose. She wasn't ready to get out of the car yet anyway. That afternoon she'd taken the karate campers to the ice cream parlor. Later she'd realized that giving thirty active kids a simultaneous sugar high at the dojo was not the brightest idea. They had been unruly and rambunctious the rest of the afternoon. By the time the evening adult sparring class began, she was exhausted from managing the karate camp. Somehow, she'd managed to win her first two matches. After that, she was paired with Kevin, another black belt and her good friend at the dojo. Despite their camaraderie in class, they both drew blood during the match. He knew how to find her weak spots and she knew how to wear him down. She lost all of her matches after sparring with him.

Kelly pocketed her screwdriver and climbed out of the car. She crossed the wet lawn and Alex lifted the hose and pointed it in her direction as if he was about to squirt her.

"Yeah, right. You wouldn't spray me," she said, shaking her head.

"You're sure about that?"

"Yes. Because if you did that, I'd have to tackle you. And you don't want me to hurt you."

"Oh yeah, I'm scared now." He chuckled. "Don't worry, I'm not gonna spray you. Remember, I'm the nice guy."

"Chicken. You're scared I really might hurt you, aren't you?" Alex was almost six inches taller than her and she knew he was stronger, but that never stopped her from taking him on. "Come on, let's see it. I dare you."

He instantly pointed the nozzle at her and squeezed his thumb half over the spout, sending a spray of water at her. She turned to the side, letting the water drench her karate gi. The shower of cold water felt good and she grinned defiantly.

He turned the hose away from her. "Why are you smiling? Am I supposed to be scared?"

Lunging at him, she snatched the hose out of his hands and pointed the nozzle at him. "Now who's scared?"

He backed up a few steps and held up his arms. "Wait, how about a deal? Put down the hose and I'll make dinner."

She paused as if considering his offer then aimed the spray at the grass, inches from his bare feet. The water splashed on his toes and he stepped back quickly.

In a voice of atonement, he continued, "Think about it—grilled salmon and veggies with some garlic sourdough . . ."

"Okay, I'll take that." She smiled and handed the hose to him. "But you know, I wouldn't have sprayed you anyway. I just wanted to see that look of fear in your eyes."

Alex raised his eyebrows. "Sometimes you worry me. You seem so sweet and innocent, and yet . . . I know better." He slapped her shoulder playfully. "Go change. I'll start the grill."

Kelly headed inside and turned on the shower. Stripping off the wet karate uniform, she stepped into the shower stall just as her cell phone rang. It was lying on the bathroom counter, a green light blinking to let her know she was missing a call, in case she was ignoring the annoying ring. Dripping, she climbed out of the shower and answered the line.

"Hi," Rick said. "What took you so long to pick up? If I give you a phone, I expect to be able to reach you."

"I was in the shower," she said defensively.

"It doesn't matter where you are. If the phone rings, pick it up. Understood?"

Kelly swallowed her rising anger. She hated his patronizing tone. "Yes, sir. I'm sorry." She knew he wouldn't listen to any excuse.

He continued, "We have a meeting tomorrow night at six my office. And don't be late."

"Hey, you're the one who flaked last time," she returned, still irritated by his gruff manner.

"I had other business. I don't *flake*."

The line disconnected and she stared at the phone. "Damn, I forgot to ask him about my keys." She shook her head and climbed back in the shower. The water burned her skin until she was used to the temperature. As she rubbed shampoo into her hair, she felt a sore spot near her temple where Kevin's fist had landed. She'd have a bruise there tomorrow. Her pale skin had finally tanned after a few weeks of afternoons in the park with her summer camp kids, but a bruise would still be obvious.

Alex was in the backyard, poking salmon steaks on the grill. He looked up as she opened the back screen door. "Can you make the salad?" he asked.

She turned back to the kitchen and quickly tossed lettuce in a bowl with a few of Alex's home-grown tomatoes and sliced cucumber. She grabbed a bottle of dressing and a pair of forks then headed outside.

Alex had finished grilling and slid the salmon onto a plate. As they sat down on the back porch, he pointed at the peeling paint. "So, when are you gonna start painting the back of the house? By the way, the front looks great. I think you only need one more coat."

She shielded her eyes as she stared at the house. "Well, it looks great if blazing daisies are your style."

Alex smiled. "I bet the neighbors hate it." All of the other houses on the block were painted in muted colors—tan, gray, white or blue. With the new paint, Alex's house stood out like a sore thumb even more than it had before. "In Ashton, no one wants their house to be noticed unless it's because they've got a new Lexus in the driveway."

"I think anybody's place would look better with a shiny new car in the driveway—even this dump could use a new Lexus."

"Hey, watch it. My truck sneers at all of the Lexuses in this town." He had a beat-up Ford pickup that carried him and his tools to the construction site every day. It also carried his surfboard to the beach every weekend. Beyond remodeling the house, he had two other hobbies, gardening and surfing. He didn't tell his friends at the construction site about his garden.

Kelly thought he needed more friends. She had tried to set him up after he broke off the five-year engagement not long ago. The new girlfriend had seemed promising but he soon discovered that she was also dating a woman in the city. He broke off the relationship and swore he wasn't going to date anyone else for the rest of the summer.

A phone rang and Alex glanced at her. "I thought people turned those things off during meals." He was very vocal about his disdain for cell phones even though he had one himself.

"I would, but my boss gave it to me. Besides, just because your phone never rings doesn't mean you need to act all high and mighty about them."

He squinted at her like he always did when he suspected a lie. "Why would you need a cell phone to teach karate?"

"It's a long story." She hadn't told him about her job with Rick. He worried too much about her. "I'll be right back."

She ran inside, catching the call just after the third ring. She glanced at the screen. The number was unlisted. Rick would be pissed if she missed his call this time. Fortunately, it was Gina. "What's up? You sound exhausted."

"I am." Gina sighed. "I'm still at the station."

"I thought you worked the night shift—last night. Why are you still working?"

"I'm leaving now."

Kelly glanced at her watch. It was after eight o'clock. "What the hell have you been working on for the past twenty-four hours?"

"Can you meet me at my place? I'll be there in a half-hour."

Kelly agreed and hung up, wondering what Gina had been caught up in at work. She decided to pick up Gina's favorite ice cream on her way. Ice cream fixed most problems, or at least worked as a good mood enhancer if the problem couldn't be fixed. She grabbed a change of clothes and headed outside to say good-bye to Alex.

"You're leaving already?" Alex asked, startled as Kelly grabbed a slice of sourdough and then headed toward the back gate. "Where are you going? Did your cop-girlfriend summon you?"

"How'd you know?"

"You're a kept woman."

She winked at him. "I can't help it. When a sexy woman calls, I come."

After picking up a quart of Caramel Fudge Swirl ice cream, Kelly headed to Gina's house. Her Corvette was already parked in the driveway. Kelly knocked on the front door.

"Come in," Gina called.

Kelly opened the door and entered. "You're leaving the door unlocked now?"

Gina came around the corner of the hallway. She flipped the lock into place. "No. I just walked in and saw you pulling up."

"You must have raced home."

Gina shrugged. "I own a sports car and the engine doesn't like to drive under eighty miles an hour."

Kelly held out the bag from the grocery store.

"What's this?" Gina asked, taking the bag. She peeked inside and then smiled. "Oh, God, that looks good. Let me get spoons."

Kelly waited in the family room while Gina went to get spoons. She stared at the CDs and selected one. "So, why'd you work so long? Trying to make a good impression on your boss?"

Gina shook her head. She set two spoons and the ice cream on the coffee table, then sat down on the couch and murmured with approval as the music began. Her eyes closed as she leaned back against the sofa cushions. "I've had such a long day."

"I thought you were scheduled to work Tuesday nights. Didn't you have today off?" Kelly knew that Gina worked only one night and three day shifts each week.

Gina nodded. "I started at six o'clock last night. The accident happened at midnight. Everything has been a blur since then."

"What accident?" Kelly opened the ice cream and handed Gina one of the spoons.

Gina stared at the spoon, spun the handle around in her fingers and then jabbed it into the carton. She licked the ice cream and smiled. "I love fudge. Thank you for coming over, by the way."

"The accident?" Kelly prodded.

Gina finished her spoonful of ice cream and then asked, "Do you know where the Cliff House Restaurant is—down by the old Sutro Baths?"

Kelly nodded. "Sure, right off Ocean Beach." The Cliff House had been a famous restaurant in San Francisco for generations. It was perched on a cliff overlooking the Pacific Ocean and one of the few places in the city close enough to catch the ocean's spray. All that remained of the Sutro Baths, west of the Cliff House, was the concrete foundation. The building that had once housed the famous Sutro bathing pools had burned down years ago. Still everyone called the remaining concrete "the Sutro Baths" and in fact, the ocean flooded the area daily, recreating the old bathing pools.

"Yeah. Well, I was patrolling over there last night with Aaron when it happened." She took another spoonful of ice cream. Gina often mentioned her partner, Aaron, but Kelly hadn't met him yet. "Actually, we were parked by the beach, just south of the Sutro Baths. Aaron likes to take our coffee breaks down by the ocean, but it's not really our turf. Anyway, the waves are beautiful at night, especially if there's a full moon, like there was. And the rest of the city was dead quiet—even for a Tuesday night." She paused. "You haven't tried the ice cream. By the way, how'd you know this was my favorite flavor?"

"It's the only ice cream I've ever seen in your freezer." Kelly took a spoonful and licked it. "I like the caramel swirl."

"The fudge chunks are better," Gina argued. "Anyway, so, we're sitting on the beach in our patrol car, sipping this horrible gas-station coffee, when all of a sudden this Mazda Miata tears down the road, right in front of us. The car was going over a hundred, I'd guess. Then, before Aaron even had our patrol car on the road to chase the guy, this SUV comes barreling by us, obviously chasing that Mazda. Both cars disappeared around the curve and, as soon as we're on the road, we hear brakes screech and see the Mazda take off over the side of the cliff—nose-diving into the old Sutro Baths. Then the SUV was going like a bat out of hell to get off that road. Aaron was trying to keep up with the SUV while I was on the radio calling for backup. The SUV took one of the turns heading back into the city and disappeared, just as another patrol car came on behind us. So we were racing through the city streets, calling for other patrol cars to help. Damn SUV just disappeared." Gina sighed. "Aaron was pissed. We both were."

"What happened to the driver of the Miata?" Kelly asked.

"Ambulance said that he was dead when they found him. His neck was broken, I guess." Gina shook her head. "They found scrapes of black paint on the side of the Miata, and the SUV was black. They think the SUV must have come up alongside the Miata and squeezed it off the road right at the turn."

"And the headlines will say: 'Another case of road rage strikes our city.' I wonder what that Miata driver did wrong."

Gina shook her head. "Pissed off the wrong guy. We spent the rest of the night combing the city for the SUV. One of the other patrol cars finally found it, abandoned, near the train station. Turns out it was reported stolen earlier in the evening, about seven o'clock."

"Could you see the SUV driver at all?"

"No, I didn't see anything except the license plate once we were behind him. It was too dark, even with the moonlight. Aaron thought he saw the SUV driver's face for a moment when he first passed us—he thinks he saw a white guy with a crew cut, but that's about all we have to go on."

"That's not much." Kelly shook her head, wondering how many people would fit that description. "Did they identify the dead guy?"

Gina nodded. "He had his wallet and a briefcase in the car. His name was Marcus Edwards. Apparently he lives alone in an apartment in the city. Last I heard, they were still trying to find his relatives and had contacted his work. I don't really know much more."

"Did you have to see the body?" Kelly asked, thinking that it must have looked gruesome after a car crash down a cliff and wondering how mangled the Mazda Miata was.

"No. The ambulance took the body out of the car right away. Fortunately it was low tide, so they had no problems getting him out." Gina set down the spoon and rubbed her eyes. "I'd love to investigate this one more, but the police chief assigned one of the higher-ups to the case."

"Then why were you stuck at work all day?"

"Aaron and I had to make a report of everything. Then the guy who's investigating the accident wanted us to answer a bunch of questions about the accident. And the police chief reprimanded us for taking our break over at the beach." She shook her head and smiled. "Talk about gratitude. Whatever."

"Can you at least follow the investigation? Is the guy who's working on the case nice enough to let you look over his shoulder or at least let you know what he finds out? It could be a learning experience, right?"

"You know, they don't think about things like learning experiences at the police station." Gina shrugged. "I'll hear through the rumor mill, you know? Or six months from now, or whenever they finally close the case, I can probably get permission to review the files."

Kelly reached over and hugged her. "Thank God you survived the car chase. I hate to think of you out there racing around those cliffs."

"It was fine. No big deal." She paused and smiled weakly. "To tell you the truth, I'm glad I wasn't driving. Aaron spent all day beating himself up about the fact that he let the SUV get so far ahead of us. But that highway curves around those cliffs so tight that if he'd gone any faster or made any wrong turn, we would have ended up on the rocks with the Mazda."

Kelly shook her head. The thought of Gina's patrol car flying over the edge of the cliffs made her nauseous. She wanted to end their conversation and get Gina into bed. "You know, I mean this in the nicest way, you look beat. I think you could use a bath and a warm bed. Can I draw you a bath?"

Gina smiled. "Ice cream and a bath? Are you kidding?"

"Alex says I'm a kept woman."

"I'm sure he'd like his own kept woman." Gina laughed. "Your brother is trying to start trouble. I might have to have some words with him—just to make sure he understands his place."

Kelly grinned. She placed the lid on the ice cream and picked up the spoons. "So, what about the bath?"

"Sounds perfect," Gina answered. "Then I'd like you, in my bed, naked."

"I think that could be arranged."

Chapter Five

Kelly switched on the dojo lights and headed to the front of the studio to clean up the waiting room. She'd picked the dojo's back door lock quickly that morning and was pleased at how well her technique worked. Still, she wasn't ready to stop cursing Rick for taking her keys. A scratching sound came from the other side of the front door and she went to unlock it.

Monkey was sitting on the doormat outside. His belt was folded in his lap and he smiled sleepily. Kelly held out her hand and he grabbed it to stand. A few minutes later the other campers began filing into the waiting room and boisterous boys' voices filled the dojo. They were already full of energy at eight in the morning.

As Kelly tied Monkey's belt, she called Colin over and asked him to be Monkey's mentor for the day, again. He happily accepted this post and slung his arm around Monkey's shoulder after they bowed and entered the mat area. Colin whispered something in Monkey's ear that made the younger boy smile, and Kelly could only wonder at their secret. The first class began with flying side kicks, and Kelly settled into her usual morning routine. Only once were her thoughts distracted by the news Gina had shared last night.

That afternoon Kelly led the campers to the park for wrestling practice on the grass and water gun wars under the sunshine. They returned to the dojo to pass the rest of the afternoon lounging on the mats, lulled into half-comatose states by too much sunshine, sweat and the B-grade martial arts movies that Kelly had rented. Thursday afternoon was the one time that the TV made it out of the storage room and into the main room. Monkey fell asleep next to Colin halfway into the movie. Lion, the youngest student in the camp, fell asleep with his head balanced on Kelly's shin before the opening movie credits started. He started snoring halfway through the movie and one of the other kids started singing, "In the jungle, the mighty jungle, the lion sleeps tonight . . ." The four-year-old slept through the entire song, despite the fact that everyone in the room joined in on the chorus.

Kelly dismissed the campers just after five p.m. and the last student was transferred from her care to a Cadillac SUV at half past the hour. She waved the last one off and headed to the locker room to change, finally able to think about her plans for the evening. She hoped the meeting with Rick would be quick. Gina had asked her to go to a movie that evening. Tasha and Beth were planning on meeting them at the theater. She gathered her karate bag and gear and was just leaving when Sam called her into his office.

"You're not staying for sparring tonight?" he asked.

"No. I've got a meeting with Rick," she answered.

Sam sighed and crossed his arms. "I don't like it that he's taking you from the dojo. I have this suspicion that he's trying to steal my employee. You're not thinking of quitting, are you? I know I don't pay as well as he does."

Kelly wondered what Rick had told Sam about her job. "I love this job."

"And how do you like working for Rick?"

Kelly shrugged. "So far, he hasn't given me anything that exciting. I do a lot of typing."

"Glorified secretary?" Sam smiled. "That sounds like Rick. He'd hire someone, say that he'd train them for this great investigating job, and then stick them with office work. Well, maybe something will come along that he'll put you on. Speaking of work . . . seems like we've got a good group of camp kids this session. How's Thomas Brier doing?"

"Who?"

"Thomas Brier. He started this Monday for a two-week session. I think you call him Monkey." He paused, waiting for her nod. "Anyway, I got a phone call from his mother saying she was concerned that he was acting too aggressive at home."

"Too aggressive? No way. He's just an active six-year-old kid that's coming out of his shell."

"Well, the word she used was *cocky*."

"Karate camp is good for him. With any luck he'll get more cocky before I'm through."

"I don't know if his mother will appreciate that," Sam said.

Kelly shrugged. She didn't like Monkey's mother, but maybe there was something going on at home that she didn't know about. "Is he causing trouble? Talking back to his parents?"

"Apparently he was kicking the sofa and when she asked him to stop, he told her he was a Ninja in training and had to practice so he could protect their house from robbers."

"I can just imagine." Kelly laughed. "All right, I'll talk to him tomorrow. He'll have to find something else to kick besides his mother's sofa."

Kelly's cell phone rang just as she stepped out of the dojo. It was Rick. "Meet me at Coffee Heaven behind Uncle Lee-Hi's."

The line went dead before she could reply. Uncle Lee-Hi's was the Chinese restaurant across from the dojo. She tossed her karate gear in the backseat of her car and crossed Main Street toward

Coffee Heaven café. She ordered a mocha and sat down at a table in the back corner. Rick appeared ten minutes later carrying a briefcase and a newspaper. He nodded at Kelly and then joined her after ordering his usual cup of black coffee. The café was nearly empty. Aside from the waitress and the busboy, there were only two customers, a couple of old women discussing their evening's shopping adventure.

"Did you read this?" Rick asked, handing her the Ashton newspaper.

"Today's paper? I thought you only read the day-old news. Did you actually buy this?"

"Just read the damn thing, okay?" Rick scoffed. "My neighbors are illiterate. I don't even know why they order a paper."

Kelly scanned the front page. "Record high temperatures in the Central Valley, gas prices climb, obesity in children causes severe health risks . . . Now I remember why I don't read papers. I really think they reuse headlines on the slow news days. There's nothing new here."

He took the paper from her, flipped three pages in and pointed to a headline near the bottom of the page: "Car Crash in San Francisco Leaves One Man Dead. Few Leads in Search for Missing Suspect." The article described the accident that Gina had witnessed. Kelly felt her skin prickle. She knew the details already.

Setting the paper down, she took a sip of her mocha and then stared at the coffee mug. She didn't want to tell Rick that Gina had already told her this much and more. All he would think about was that she was still spending time with the cop. "Cars crash all the time. Why do you care about this one?"

Rick nodded. "Good question. The driver of the Mazda Miata was Marcus Edwards. He worked for GPAC." GPAC was the abbreviation for the Gay Political Action Coalition in San Francisco. "And the lawyer for that group, Nora Kinley, is paying us to investigate his death." He smiled. "Money, that's why I care."

"What a noble cause," she replied sarcastically. "Yeah, I didn't think you would really feel compassion for a random car-accident victim." She was pleased that Nora Kinley was involved in this case. Nora had hired Rick previously to investigate witnesses for a military case that she had been working on with GPAC, which had tried to set up a case against the military's anti-gay policies. Kelly had helped Rick with deliveries and other errands for the case, and she met Nora through him. She had formed a crush on her as soon as she met her. Unfortunately, Nora was straight and as Kelly acknowledged, way out of her league. Then the military case had been dropped and Rick stopped working for Nora, leaving Kelly to think that her connection to the lawyer was lost. "So, do we know any more details than what this article says?" Kelly asked.

Rick shook his head. "Not really. We know that the suspect was driving a black SUV that turned up stolen yesterday."

"That's not much to go on." Kelly decided not to add the detail that Gina had mentioned about the possible description of the suspect as a white man with a crew cut. "What about Marcus Edwards? Why does Nora want us to investigate rather than leave it to the cops."

"Leave this for the cops? You put too much faith in our police force. We don't pay them enough to carry out investigations on every hit-and-run in the city."

"Okay, I can understand that. But if it was really just a hit-and-run, why does Nora care?"

"Well, she's the lawyer for GPAC and yesterday, John Rainsfeld, the acting director of GPAC, went into the office and found that the place had been broken into. Someone crowbarred the door and overturned half the file cabinets, but he couldn't tell if anything was missing. He called Nora when he discovered that his computer wouldn't accept his password to access their system. And when he tried to get on Marcus's computer, he found that it was locked too. Whoever broke into the place just messed with their network."

"So they think the break-in's connected to Marcus's death?"

"They don't know. According to John, Nora's the only other one who'd accessed their computer system recently. She has a password, but the last time she was there was over a week ago." He took a sip of his coffee and grimaced. "Damn, this must be the end of the pot. I think I got a swig of pure coffee beans."

Kelly offered him her mocha to cut the taste but he shook his head.

"No, I like strong coffee," he replied. "My dad always said that it'll put hairs on my chest."

"I knew there was a reason why I hated black coffee."

Rick smiled and said, "You're just young. Anyway, back to the GPAC office. John decided to call Nora, after calling the cops, because he thought that it was a strange coincidence—you know, Marcus dies in a hit-and-run and then he finds the GPAC office broken into and their computer system crashed."

"Does GPAC have any enemies? I mean, other than the U.S. Army?"

Rick nodded. "A gay political group is always going to have enemies. And truthfully, I don't think the army cares about GPAC since they dropped the case against the military's gay policies. Nora said that the Conservative Veterans Association has remained a vocal antagonist of GPAC even after the military case was dropped but the U.S. Army has bigger worries."

Kelly sighed. "No kidding. They have a little conflict in a desert halfway across the world to think about." She thought of Gina's ex-girlfriend, Vicky, and then of Tasha. She couldn't understand why they'd both want to be in the army, let alone risk their lives in the war, especially knowing the military's policies against gays.

"A little conflict indeed. Anyway, your question is a good one. We need to think about what battles GPAC fights beyond military politics."

"What's the likelihood that Marcus's car accident had nothing to do with the break-in at GPAC?"

Rick shrugged. "That's what Nora wants to know."

"So, what do we do first?" Kelly asked. She was intrigued with the case and hoped Rick would let her do more than transcribe his notes and run errands.

"We meet with John Rainsfeld."

She smiled. He was including her this time. "When?" she asked. Sam would be pissed if she took time off from the dojo to work with Rick, but she was eager to do as much as she could on this case.

Rick glanced at his watch. "I've set up the meeting for this evening. We should leave soon." He opened his briefcase and took out a small notebook. "A gift. In case you want to take notes. I like the tape recorder, as you already know, but when I first started in the business, I wrote everything down."

Although it was just a drugstore notebook, she was surprised that he'd consider giving her a gift. Before she could thank him, Rick handed her two photographs.

"This is the Miata. Looks like it was a nice car, at one time."

The photos were shot from different angles to show both sides of the car. The right side had a streak of black paint, barely visible. The front end was completely smashed into the driver's seat.

"I wonder how they pulled the body out."

He pointed to the convertible top. "They cut the roof. Both doors were jammed." He took another swig of his coffee and slipped the photos back into his briefcase. "Ready?"

She wondered how he'd gotten the pictures of the car. She knew he still had connections in the FBI, and she guessed he also knew people in the police department. "I have to use the restroom," she announced as she finished her mocha. Really, she just needed to call Gina. She went to the ladies' room and dialed the number. Gina wasn't home so she left a message saying that she'd have to take a rain check on the movie and would call her later that evening to explain.

She followed Rick out of the café and down Main Street. He pointed to his car, the black Chevy with tinted rear windows. "You can ride with me or take your own car and meet me there."

"I'll go with you." She paused. "As long as I can call shotgun."

Rick laughed. "Well, there's no way I'd let you drive and I don't think anyone else will be fighting to share the front seat with me." He unlocked the passenger door and then went around to his side.

As soon as he started the car, he lit up a cigarette and took a drag. He cracked the window to let the smoke escape. "So, you're still with the cop?"

Kelly sighed, mildly irritated by his question. "She's my girlfriend."

He shook his head and took another drag. "Well, I'm sure she'll be sad when you tell her you have to break things off."

"You know, that shit will kill you," she said, hoping to change the subject.

He blew a puff of smoke out the window and turned on the radio. A smooth jazz song was playing. "You sound like Emily."

"Who's Emily?"

"My wife," Rick answered, taking another drag. "But she calls herself my ex-wife. She can't put up with my cleaning habits and she hates that I smoke. But I love her anyway."

She had assumed that he was a bachelor, or divorced, since he had mentioned before that he lived alone. There'd been no mention of a wife. "Where does she live?"

"Ashton—one block from my house. We're best friends and I keep trying to convince her to marry me, again."

"She won't be convinced?"

He shook his head. "Maybe I don't try very hard."

They drove the rest of the way in silence, with Kelly wondering what Rick's ex-wife would be like. After crossing the Bay Bridge, Rick took the first exit off the freeway. He pointed out the office building that housed the GPAC headquarters and then found a parking place after a few loops around the block. The area was a low-rent part of the city and Kelly knew the crime rates were high around here. Rick led the way into the office building, pressing the elevator for the second floor and then knocking on the door labeled "GLBT Political Action Coalition."

"How do you like that?" Rick muttered, touching the rectangular dent in the wood frame around the door. The crowbar had been wedged between the jamb and the lock. "Not bad. I bet it took about fifteen seconds to get in there."

The door opened and John Rainsfeld introduced himself. He

had just installed a new deadbolt and explained that the frame would be repaired the next morning. He ushered them into the office and pointed at two seats. "Thank you for meeting me tonight. I know you keep a busy schedule, Mr. Lehrman."

Rick nodded. "Rick is fine."

"Of course. And your partner here, I don't think I know your name?" He extended his hand to Kelly.

John was only a few inches taller than Kelly, with a thin frame and a limp handshake. A yellow tie brightened his otherwise bland attire of a blue dress shirt with black slacks. Staring at the tie, Kelly immediately thought of Alex's house paint. The color was almost identical. "Kelly Haldon."

"Good. Well, now that we're all family"—he smiled and waved his hands to include Rick and Kelly—"we can get down to business. What can I tell you? Nora told me to be prepared to answer quite a few questions as we wade through our little mystery here."

"I know you're a busy man, John. We appreciate that you had time to meet with us," Rick said, placing his tape recorder on the desk in front of John. "You don't mind if I record our conversation, do you?"

John shook his head. "Not at all." Kelly thought his answer was strained. Maybe he did mind the recorder. He glanced over at Kelly who had pulled out her notebook and pen. "I see you're doing things the old-fashioned way?" He winked. "An old-fashioned girl, are you?"

She smiled back at him. "You know, you're the first one who's ever called me that." Since she had his attention and Rick wasn't jumping to raise his hand, she decided to start asking questions. "So, what did Marcus do here?"

"He was in charge of fund-raising, primarily."

"Primarily? Any other activities?"

"Yes." John pointed out the three computers in the office, each one named after a superhero character. "Marcus had a background in computers and was in charge of our *vast* network here."

"So, he had access to all of the GPAC files?"

John paused, as if thinking over the question. "Well, only recently, actually. We just got these two new computers and set up the network. Our old computers were both archaic disasters and only linked to the printer." Smiling, he shook his head. "When GPAC first started, I set up a computer at home so we could have a Web server. Neither of the old computers had enough power to run the server. GPAC's Board of Directors never listens to me when I tell them we need a bigger office space and a bigger network budget. It was like pulling teeth to get them to agree to purchase two new computers so I decided to just keep the server at home until we move to an office with more space."

"When did you get the new system?" Kelly asked, making notes.

John pulled out his datebook and flipped through the pages. "July first. Marcus was a whiz with computers. He set up the network, the firewall, the password protections."

"Do you mind if I take a look at his computer?" Rick asked, sitting down at Marcus's desk.

John shrugged. "Go right ahead. If you want, go ahead and fix the network so I can use my damn computer. Then I can cancel my appointment with the tech nerds tomorrow morning."

Rick rebooted Marcus's hard drive and after a few minutes brought up the history of the last several commands entered into the computer. "It locked up right after printing something. Whoever got on your network used a password to disable the commands function—so the computer couldn't process any new commands."

John shook his head. "That was what I thought. But only Marcus, Nora and I have access to the system, and Nora doesn't know the network passwords."

"Are these the only two computers tied to your network?" Kelly asked.

"No." John led her over to the front desk. "Our secretary's computer ties into the same network. But that computer doesn't have access to our data files."

Kelly sat down at the secretary's desk. "This computer wasn't disabled when the other two crashed?"

John shrugged. "As far as I know, this one is working fine."

"And all three computers are tied to the same printer?" The secretary's computer could not access the last document spooled to the printer from Marcus's machine, but Kelly thought she might be able to reprint the document, since the information was saved on the printer's memory.

Rick came over and poked his head over her shoulder. "Is the printer online?" he asked, as if just realizing what Kelly was trying to do.

John went to check the printer and called over to them, "Yep, we're online. The machine says there's a document spooling." As the pages started churning out, he grabbed each one and his expression darkened. "Shit, this can't be right," he whispered, leaning against the printer table. "Someone printed out the sponsor list. The whole damn history of everyone who's ever given GPAC one cent."

Kelly joined him at the printer and glanced at the list. Not only were names and addresses listed for all who had donated money to GPAC, but the Social Security numbers were also noted with the amount of money and date of the contribution.

"Wow. Some people would be pissed if that information got in the wrong hands," she said.

"A lot of wrong hands would love to have our sponsor list." John shook his head, clutching the paper tighter. He swore at the printer, still churning out more lines of sponsors.

Kelly thought of the Conservative Veterans Association that Rick had mentioned and guessed that they'd like to have their hands on GPAC's list. She wondered if GPAC had any other enemies. Was it just coincidence that the sponsor list was printed right before Marcus's death?

John gave a bleak sigh and then sank down in his chair, crumpling the pages in his hands. Rick came over and took one of the last pages to come out of the printer. He scanned the names.

"Huh, there's a lot of people I wouldn't have guessed would be on your side."

John reached for this last page, trying to take it from Rick's hands. "That information is private! I can't have you going through every GPAC sponsor—our reputation would be ruined if this list was made public."

Rick cleared his throat and took a step back. "Look, Nora hired us to investigate Marcus's death for GPAC, which this list may very well be linked to. We don't know why it was printed, or whose hands the information is now in. But there's a good chance this information is unlikely to stay private for long if we don't figure out what happened."

John set the sheets on the printer and loosened his tie. He rubbed his forehead and after a moment finally looked over at Rick. "I'm sorry. You know, the past couple days have really taken it out of me. You're right. Of course you'll need to look over this. And we need to find out who else has the list." He handed Rick the rest of the sheets. "But you have to understand that this should never have been printed. The data files are stored so that only Marcus and I can access them."

"Or anyone who'd been given the password." Rick flipped through the list, scanning quickly, and then passed it to Kelly.

John was slow to answer. He continued to rub his forehead. "Yes, I suppose someone could have gotten the password . . . I mean, someone could have convinced Marcus to give out his password. But I just can't believe that he would have given it out. Do you think the cops should have dusted for fingerprints?"

Rick shrugged. "Well, you didn't think anything was missing, right? Chances are, Marcus printed this list himself. Maybe he was planning on contacting the historic sponsors to see if anyone would be willing to donate again."

"We never do that." John shook his head. "Our sponsors have our word that we will not send anything unless they request it. It's too risky. A lot of them are still in the closet."

"Would someone pay for this list?" Kelly wondered aloud.

"Certainly." John continued, "But we'd never sell out."

Rick shrugged. "Maybe you wouldn't, but maybe Marcus would."

"No." John folded his arms. "I just can't believe that he would do that."

"For the right price, anyone will sell their soul." Rick headed back to the secretary's computer, looking to see if any other documents had been sent to the printer recently. Kelly noticed that he deleted the print command so that another reprint wouldn't be made and turned the secretary's computer off. It appeared that only the sponsor list had been printed before the other two computers were locked from accessing the system. Rick then went over to Marcus's desk and started opening drawers, hunting for something. "You need to shut down the whole system and reboot all of the linked computers. Pull the cord on that printer as well."

John obeyed and pulled the printer's power cord. Kelly watched as Rick rebooted each of the three computers. She turned to John. "Do you think Marcus liked working for GPAC?"

"Well, he wasn't one to complain. And he was pretty good at his job. We've seen a big increase in the number of donations over the past few months because of his efforts. He seemed to know exactly who to contact." John shrugged. "I don't know if he *liked* the job, necessarily. The strange thing was, I don't think he was gay. He never mentioned boyfriends or anything. And he never talked about fashion, home decorating or cooking, even." He smiled weakly. "My gaydar wasn't flashing, if you know what I mean."

"Why'd he take the job here?" she asked. Marcus kept no photographs or any trinkets on his desk. The only unusual book on his bookshelf was a copy of *The Little Prince*, next to a travel book. Kelly flipped through *Costa Rica on a Budget*. A parched fern sat on the top shelf of his bookcase.

"That's what I never understood." John frowned. "We pay well, but it is a little strange for a straight GI Joe type to take a job here. Like I said, he'd had fund-raising experience at other nonprofits and when he applied for the job he mentioned that we were paying more than his last position. I don't really remember where he said he had last worked, but I could check his résumé. From what I could tell, he just liked the nonprofit world. And we didn't ask for his GLBT status. We like to think of this as a nondiscriminatory workplace." He smiled. "After all, we need straight allies, right?"

Kelly nodded. She didn't like his conspiratorial tone. "Did he live here in the city?"

John nodded. "Yeah, he had an apartment over in Pacific Heights. I never went to his place, but he had told me a few stories about his crazy neighbors over there. He lived alone. No pets or anything." John pointed at the fern on the bookshelf. "He told me he was waiting to see if he could keep that fern alive for a full year before he would get a pet. He wanted one of those dogs with stubby feet and long backs, you know the hotdog dogs?"

Kelly smiled. "Dachshunds?"

He nodded. "That's right. Well, I'm kind of glad he didn't get one. Since I don't think he had any other friends or relatives in the area and I don't know of anyone who'd be able to take care of a little dog, if he had one. Of course, I'll take over care of his little fern. I wouldn't want the thing to die after Marcus kept it alive for nine months."

Barely alive, Kelly thought. "Were you friends with him?"

John considered this for a moment. "Not really. I was his boss. And he kept to himself. I guess what I'm saying is that we were on good terms, but we didn't go out to the bar after work for drinks or anything. I really didn't know much about his personal life at all."

Rick stood up from Marcus's chair after a moment. "John, do you have anything with Marcus's address? A paycheck stub or your employee records? And you mentioned a résumé, do you still have it?"

"Maybe." John nodded and went over to his secretary's desk. He flipped through her drawer until he found the file on Marcus. He made a copy of the résumé and then copied down Marcus's address from his last paycheck stub.

Rick took these and nodded his thanks. "Well, I think that's all for now." He handed John a business card. "We'll be in touch soon, but if any thoughts come up before you hear from me, give me a call."

Kelly's phone rang as soon as they stepped out of the office building. She silenced the ringer as Rick glared at her. Gina's number blinked on the screen. Once they were on the road home, he handed her the paper with Marcus's address.

"So, our next step is to go to his apartment and check that place out, right?" she asked.

He shook his head. "It's *your* next step. You get to go there on your own."

She stared at the address, then folded the paper and slipped it into her pocket. She would never have considered breaking into someone's apartment before working with Rick. At least she knew that the occupant wouldn't be coming home to catch her.

"What's the matter?" Rick asked with a hint of sarcasm. "You don't look excited about your assignment. Are you scared about going into a dead guy's place?"

"I'm not scared," Kelly said, knowing that she was unnerved by the idea of burglary. "So, when should I go?"

"Tonight," Rick answered. "We don't want our evidence getting cold."

"I don't even know what I'm looking for." Kelly sighed. "He's been dead nearly forty-eight hours. Isn't the evidence already cold?"

Rick shrugged. "We'll see what you dig up."

Kelly flipped through the GPAC sponsor list, squinting in the faint light to read the names. "Wow, some of these people contributed a ton of money."

"Yes, and some of those people shouldn't be on that list."

"What do you mean?" Kelly asked.

"Robert Talcone," Rick said. "His name was on the second to last page, right at the top."

Kelly found this name and read his information. He had contributed a thousand dollars to GPAC nearly fifteen years ago. "Why shouldn't his name be on the list?"

"Well, if he's the same Robert Talcone that I'm thinking of, he's a state senator, married, and about as conservative as they come. We'll have to look up the address that is listed there and see if the senator used to live in—" He paused. "Where was it now?"

"Fresno, California."

Chapter Six

Kelly dialed Gina's number as soon as Rick drove away. After five rings, the answering machine picked up her call. She leaned against her car and listened to Gina's recorded message. After the beep, Kelly began, "Hey. I can't come over tonight. Maybe you're already in bed. Have a good night—"

"What do you mean you're not coming over?" Gina interrupted. "Why not? What's wrong?"

"Since when do you screen calls?"

Gina ignored her and asked again, "Why can't you come over? You already missed our movie date. I had to cancel on Beth and Tasha."

"I'm sorry about that . . . Look, I want to see you, but I got caught up with some work stuff. I have to finish it tonight."

"It's after ten. What work can't wait until morning?" Gina asked, obviously believing that Kelly wasn't telling her the truth.

"It's some stuff for Rick." Kelly didn't want to give any more details. Her job with Rick was already a sore subject with Gina, and Rick didn't want her to talk to Gina about it anyway.

"Stuff? What kind of answer is that?" Gina sighed. "Never mind. Look, just come over when you finish. I don't care how late it is."

She tried to argue but finally gave up. Gina was persistent and when she wanted something, Kelly knew it was easier just to cave in early. Otherwise, she could be on the phone all night. "All right, but don't wait up for me."

She started her car and headed toward the freeway. The rock music on the radio diverted her thoughts from her evening plans and she relaxed with the drive. Once she reached the city, she fished out John's note and began the search for Marcus's apartment street address. She found the apartment building, three stories tall and its stucco façade painted a nondescript gray, and parked two blocks away. The air temperature had dropped considerably from the warmth of the Ashton night and she shivered as soon as she got out of the car. She slipped on her jacket and grabbed a flashlight and a pair of gloves.

Pacific Heights was well known as an expensive neighborhood. The stunning views of the lit-up city from each hillcrest accounted for the high price tag. The steep terrain, car alarms and iron gates kept crime rates low here, at least compared to other parts of the city. Skirting the block around Marcus's apartment, Kelly eyed every passing car or pedestrian. The homes and apartments were pushed together with narrow alleyways connecting streets in a dizzying, dark, hillside maze.

The front door of the apartment building was locked. A sign directed visitors to use the call box to contact residents. She stared at the list of names and the respective glowing button for each apartment. *Edwards, M.*, was listed next to apartment number 3A.

While she was still debating which number to press, the door popped opened. A well-dressed middle-aged man stepped out, took a quick look at her, and then held the door open. Apparently he didn't see anything wrong with letting her inside.

"You might stand there all night. The buzzers don't ring inside the building—the apartment manager posted a note on everyone's mailbox saying the system broke yesterday." He smiled and continued in a sarcastic tone, "He's a real genius and didn't bother to post a sign outside where visitors could see."

"I was starting to wonder if my friends had gone deaf." Kelly slipped through the open door. "Thanks for letting me in."

She took the stairs up to the third floor. A faint odor of cigarette smoke and a buzzing fluorescent light lent a sad yellow glow to the hallway. Apartment 3A was at the end of the hallway. She leaned against the door, listening. No sound came from the other side. She slipped on her gloves and eyed the door handle and the thin keyhole. Thinking that the wire she'd been using to unlock the dojo every morning might work for this lock, she fished it out of her pocket and set it in the lock. She reached for the door handle and before she could wiggle the wire, the knob turned in her hand. With a light push, the door opened.

Kelly glanced around the large room, not ready to enter the unlocked apartment of a dead man. The place was a mess. She wondered at first if Marcus had simply left in a hurry, and then quickly decided that someone else must have been in the apartment looking for something. It was unlikely that it had been a petty thief, she thought, since a TV, stereo, music and movie collection had been left behind. The sofa had been knocked over and the pillows tossed off the seats, picture frames had been pulled off the walls, all of the drawers had been removed from a writing desk in the corner, and papers were scattered on the floor. Kelly heard another door open farther down the hallway and she quickly stepped inside, closing the door.

Squinting in the sudden darkness, with the door now shut tight behind her, she heard her heart thumping loudly and willed her feet to move off the front doormat. When she did, the flash of a red light caught her attention. Frozen in place, she reached into her back pocket for her flashlight and flipped it on. The red glare shone at her from behind a fake ficus tree. She pointed her flashlight about the room, making certain that she was still alone. The red light was coming from a palm-sized cylinder connected to a wire that ran into the wall. On the backside of the cylinder was a small trademark, "Infrared Eye."

Kelly caught her breath, realizing that the cylinder was in fact a small camera. She fought the desire to run from the place and tried to concentrate on finding something for Rick, some little piece of evidence to let him know that she'd in fact been inside the dead man's apartment. She exhaled slowly. First, she'd find out what was on the other side of the wall and if the camera was connected to anything. As she went from the front room down a narrow hall, the wooden floor creaked under her steps and she wondered how old the building was. She located the kitchen on the right and a bedroom on the left, which shared the wall with the camera wire. Kelly investigated the bedroom, also trashed by whoever had been in the apartment before her. The mattress had been pulled off the box springs and a knife had slashed through it, spreading it open like a gutted fish.

With a few slow, deep breaths, she opened the bedroom closet door. All of the clothing still hung on the hangers, and shoeboxes were piled on the floor as well as on the shelf above the hangers. For a guy, Marcus had enough shoes to make someone wonder if he was in fact gay. Dismissing this, she tried to imagine where the wire that attached to the camera would have entered the room. There were no wires here.

About to close the closet door, Kelly heard a fan buzzing overhead. She glanced up at the shelf above the rack of clothes. Why was there a fan in the closet? She pulled the shoeboxes off the top shelf and noticed a flat video screen. The image on the screen was of the front room. The fan was connected to a computer, which she guessed was recording the images that the camera received.

Kelly brought over a chair and climbed up on it to reach the computer keyboard. She scrolled through the saved images, finding that the computer saved images only when the scene in the front room changed, such as when she had stepped into the apartment. She caught her breath as her image flashed on the screen. Her first thought was to delete this image, but then she reconsidered. If her picture had been saved, maybe the camera had recorded whoever else had been there. A CD had already recorded the images, according to the computer's timer, for the past 60 hours. Was that when Marcus had last been there?

After removing the disk with the saved images, Kelly turned off the computer recorder. She would have time to go through the images and hoped she'd discover who else had been at Marcus's. The rest of her search through the bedroom turned up only an address book, a half-used journal with more sketches than writing, and a box of bank receipts. She went to the kitchen and found a paper bag to stash these items. The kitchen revealed fewer clues than the bedroom. She gathered that Marcus had not cooked much, if at all. He had only one coffee mug, one plate, one bowl and one set of utensils. Inside his refrigerator sat a half-gallon of milk, a six-pack of beer, cheese sticks and ketchup. The freezer was filled with enough frozen dinners to feed a bachelor for at least two weeks.

She scanned the front room once more, deciding that whoever had been here before her had probably taken all of the "warm evidence." The last room in the house was a small bathroom. Marcus had a very orderly arrangement to his medicine cabinet and four towels, all dark blue. The towels matched the bathmat and shower curtain. Kelly couldn't find anything else in the bathroom and was about to leave when she saw the trashcan in the corner, near the toilet. She poked through the can and found a crumpled yellow note amongst the other trash. The yellow note had Tuesday's date and the message: Hotel Savoy at 9 p.m. She slipped this note in her pocket and headed back to the kitchen, wondering who Marcus had gone to meet the night of the accident.

With the paper bag filled with Marcus's things and the CD with the camera recording, she paused for a moment in the entryway to listen for any sounds outside. After a moment, Kelly opened the door and glanced down the hallway. The pathway to the elevator was empty and all of the other doors were closed. She switched off her flashlight, closed Marcus's door and slipped quietly out into the hallway.

Kelly didn't see anyone on her way out of the apartment but didn't relax until she'd reached her car. She set the bag in the backseat and turned her screwdriver in the ignition. The engine rumbled to a start and she pulled off the curb. A pair of headlights flashed on, from a black sedan parked across the street. Trying to ignore a feeling of dread, she pressed her foot on the gas pedal and floored it. She sped around the next corner, without seeing any car behind her, and exhaled. Before she had gone far, though, she noticed that a car was indeed coming up on her tail. She made a few unexpected turns off the main road, but the car continued to follow her. It hedged close up to her bumper and flashed on its brights, casting a glare in her rearview mirror. The entrance to the freeway was two blocks up, and she debated if she should change her mind about driving home now.

Deciding the city streets would give her the best shot at losing the car, she darted out of the lane for the freeway and pumped the gas pedal. The other car picked up speed as well. They were approaching the second entrance to the freeway, but on the wrong side of the road. At the last moment, she crossed the yellow dividing lines and swerved across two lanes of the empty street to gain the onramp. The other car passed by her, missing the turn, and she breathed a sigh of relief.

Kelly dialed Gina's number once the adrenaline surge had eased. "Hey, sleepy," she started, hearing Gina's yawn. It was nearly two a.m. "I'm on my way."

"Ring the doorbell a few times in case I fall asleep again," Gina answered in a drowsy voice. "Will you tell me what you've been up to tonight?"

"I can't." The line clicked and she realized Gina had hung up on her. Kelly tossed her cell phone on the seat and glanced at her rearview mirror. The paper bag in the backseat caught her eye. She wondered if any of Marcus's things would lend any clues. The best hope for some more information in this case would come from the CD. If the camera had caught an image of whoever ransacked Marcus's house, and if this image fit the partial description of the SUV driver, they might be one step closer to finding out who had killed Marcus.

Chapter Seven

A cell phone started ringing and Kelly pulled the blankets over her head. The room was too bright and she knew it was after sunrise. Gina nudged Kelly's shoulder. "It's your phone. Are you going to answer it?"

Kelly shook her head and snuggled closer to Gina. She didn't want to wake up yet, having slept fitfully and with recurring dreams of Marcus's apartment. The ringing continued and she climbed out of bed. Rick had overreacted when she'd almost missed his call the last time and she was hoping it wasn't him now. She searched for the phone with half-closed eyes, finally finding it on the pile of her clothes in the middle of Gina's bedroom.

"Good morning," Rick said in a cheery tone. "I trust your night went well. And you have some information for us this morning?"

"Umm." She rubbed her eyes and sat down on the edge of the bed. "I found some things."

"You got into his apartment?"

"Yes. But someone else had already been there."

"Any ideas on who it was?" he asked nonchalantly.

Kelly wondered why he didn't sound surprised. Who did he suspect would have gone to Marcus's place? "I don't know. Might be able to tell you in a few hours though." She glanced at her clothes and realized she'd brought the paper bag of Marcus's things into Gina's house and neglected to hide it. Fortunately, Gina hadn't asked about it last night. She could try and cover her clothes over it now and hope Gina wouldn't suspect anything. If she had her keys to lock her car, then it would have been safe to leave the bag in the trunk. "Rick, when are you going to give my keys back?"

He ignored her question. "So, I'm meeting with Nora this afternoon. You should join us." Rick paused and Kelly heard the jangle of keys and a door opening. "I'll let Sam know that you need the afternoon off work. The meeting is at two in my office. Come in through the back door."

"What about my keys?"

"What about them?"

Kelly sighed. "Forget it. I'll see you later." She hung up and went over to her pile of clothes, surreptitiously tucking the bag under her jacket. She climbed back into bed and nestled under the covers.

Gina pulled the sheets down, exposing their shoulders to the cool air. "Who was that?"

"My mean fairy godfather," Kelly said.

"What did he want? It's a little early for a business call."

"I never can figure out his schedule." Kelly draped her arm over Gina's belly. She gazed at Gina's breasts. "Damn, Gina, I love to look at you, all naked and stretched out in bed. How long am I going to keep the other women away?"

Gina kissed her cheek. "You're changing the subject. What did Rick want? Or are you not going to tell me because it's highly classified information?"

Kelly grinned. "Yeah, real spy stuff. No, he just was calling to wake me up."

"You're a liar. And a bad liar at that."

"Look, I don't want to think about Rick right now," Kelly said, climbing on top of Gina. "I'd rather think about my sexy girlfriend who's lying naked under me."

Gina shook her head. "Doesn't he have a family or something? Why is he calling you at this time of the morning?"

"He's got a wife, or had one. I don't see how a woman would put up with him. He reeks of smoke, he's rude and condescending, and I'm not sure if I trust him." Kelly sighed. "Sometimes I wonder why I'm working with him."

"Because you like the work and he pays. What other reason do you need?" Gina shook her head. "Go back to sleep. You look like you need it."

Kelly frowned. "What's that supposed to mean?"

"Nothing, chica, except there's dark circles under your eyes and I know you haven't been sleeping enough." Gina pushed Kelly off and rolled onto her side.

Kelly closed her eyes. She draped one arm over Gina's side and hugged her. After a while, Gina climbed out of bed and Kelly's hand fell onto the warm, empty space in the sheets. She fell asleep quickly.

A hand shook Kelly awake and she glanced at her clock, suddenly worried that she'd be late for work. It was only seven o'clock. Gina was asking her something, but Kelly missed the first part of her sentence. She was obviously upset about something. Kelly rubbed her eyes and yawned. "What's wrong?"

"This." Gina held up the paper bag. "What is this?"

"A bag." It was the bag from Marcus's apartment and it took her a moment to remember why she'd brought it inside. She should have folded her clothes neatly and left them on the chair in Gina's room, with the bag hidden under the clothes so Gina wouldn't have found it. Gina hated to have clothes left on the floor and must have picked them up and then found the bag.

"You have bank statements for Marcus Edwards. Why?"

Kelly felt her throat tighten. She tried to swallow. How was she going to explain this to Gina? "I don't know. I just found them."

"Don't lie. Marcus Edwards, you know, is the guy who was killed in the car crash Tuesday night."

"I know." Kelly rolled onto her back and stared at the ceiling. She couldn't tell Gina about last night. Rick would be pissed.

"Where'd you get his stuff?"

"I found it." Kelly closed her eyes. It was easier for her to lie if she didn't look at Gina. How could she tell her about last night?

"Fuck, Kelly, just tell me the truth."

"I found it," she repeated.

Gina slammed the bag on the floor and picked up the phone on the nightstand. She dialed a number, then waited, not looking at Kelly. "Yes, can you connect me to Aaron Westmeister's desk? Thank you."

"You can't tell him." Kelly reached across the bed and pressed the button to hang up the phone line.

Gina glared at her. "Why'd you do that? Aaron's my partner. I can tell him anything."

"You can't tell anyone, Gina. Especially at the station." Kelly didn't want to talk to Gina about last night or about the bag, but she couldn't risk lying now. If Gina doubted her, she would start talking to her friends at the precinct. "You can't even tell Aaron. Not yet, anyway." She paused and sat up against the pillows. "Rick was asked to investigate Marcus's death. I got that stuff from Marcus's place. Someone else got there first and trashed the place."

Gina sank down on the bed. "Are you serious? Rick's investigating the same car crash? Our hit-and-run?"

Kelly pointed at the bag. "Why do you think I have that stuff? Something's up—it doesn't look like it was just a hit-and-run."

"I just can't believe you're investigating the car crash that I saw." Gina swore softly. "Of all the projects for Rick to pick up . . . Doesn't he have some divorce case that you could work on? Why'd he have to be hired to investigate the case I want? Who hired him?"

Kelly shrugged.

"Tell me."

"I don't know who hired him," Kelly said flatly.

"I know you're lying," Gina shot back. "Look, I'm not going to just sit here like a dumb duck while you investigate his death. *I* could be working on this case. Damn it, I should be on it, not you."

"I think you mean lame duck." Kelly turned away from Gina and stared out the window. The sun was streaming in through the blinds and she guessed it would be another scorcher today. Yesterday's temperature was over a hundred degrees. The campers would want to go for ice cream again. "You know, it doesn't really matter to me, but Rick would be pissed if he found out that I told you as much as I did. Shit, I don't even know why I brought that damn bag in here."

"Well, you're lucky you did." Gina stood up and walked over to the window. She parted the blinds and stared outside. "Maybe it was some weird intuition thing."

Kelly eyed her, puzzled. "Why's that?"

"I just went out to pick up the newspaper and noticed your car. Someone broke into it."

"What do you mean? I didn't even lock the door."

"Well, they smashed one of the side rear windows. Maybe they were trying to prove a point. There's glass all over the backseat." Gina shook her head. "Shit like that never happens in this neighborhood—hell, this is Ashton. We live in suburban utopia where no one vandalizes cars."

"Especially not a beat-up old Volkswagen," Kelly said. "Maybe they were just some bored teenagers."

"Maybe, or maybe they were looking for this bag. And who is 'they' in this case?" Gina asked, turning from the window.

Kelly shook her head. "I don't know." She thought of the black sedan that had followed her from Marcus's house to the freeway. Maybe the driver had followed her here, even though she thought she had lost him. There was no other reason to explain why anyone would break a window on an old Volkswagen in this neighborhood full of expensive cars. Her car didn't even have a CD player—it just had a radio and a broken tape deck. She tried to remember the events of last night.

Although she hadn't seen anyone follow her to Gina's house,

once she'd gotten onto the freeway, she hadn't paid close attention. The black sedan that had been parked at Marcus's place could have easily gotten on at another on-ramp and then caught up to her and followed her to Ashton. After parking on the street by Gina's place, she had grabbed the paper bag from the backseat, never leaving anything in her car anymore since it was left unlocked. She hadn't even considered that Gina might look inside the bag.

"Damn. This is over my head." Kelly stared at the bag. "I want to give this stuff to Rick. Then I'll tell him that I want to go back to typing up his investigation reports—I can handle that job."

Gina shook her head. "No. I can help you. Screw Rick. He won't have to know that I'm working with you, at least not for now. And I won't tell anyone at the station, although I'd be kicked out if they knew what I was involved with." She paused. "You trust me more than Rick, don't you?"

Kelly got out of the bed and pulled on her T-shirt and jeans. "I trust you. But I don't want either of us involved in this. Rick will be pissed off. He can tell when I'm lying. You know I have no poker face."

"Come on, we can do this." Gina opened the bag and pulled out the journal. She flipped through the pages. "Nice pictures. Looks like Marcus wanted to be an artist." She held up a portrait of a man.

Kelly felt a chill race up her spine. The picture was a perfect depiction of John Rainsfeld. Strings were attached to his hands and feet and below the picture, Marcus had written, "The Puppet."

On the opposite page another portrait depicted an old man with wrinkles around his eyes, a hooked nose and graying temples. He had a cigar in his mouth and his cheeks were puffed. This drawing was entitled "Da' Boss."

Gina flipped the page and then held up the next sketch. "Wow, this one is creepy."

A man with a full beard, dark hollowed eyes and round-rimmed glasses sat on a pile of cash. He had a Cheshire cat's grin that was more chilling than his dark eye sockets.

"This one's called 'The Closet Politician.' I don't want to think about his closet," Gina said. "You know, this guy looks almost familiar." She dropped the journal with the page still open to the sketch of the politician and walked out of the room. A moment later she returned with the newspaper. On the front of the paper, in the lower left corner, was a wallet-sized photo of the same man from Marcus's sketch. "Uncanny resemblance. It's got to be this guy Robert Talcone, right?"

Kelly shivered. She rubbed her arms hoping that Gina wouldn't notice the goose bumps. Trying to sound ambivalent, she said, "Well, looks similar." Kelly doubted she would have recognized Robert Talcone if Rick hadn't mentioned that this politician had given money to GPAC. She took the newspaper from Gina. "I've never heard of this Talcone guy."

"He's from some county in the Central Valley, I think."

Kelly nodded. "Yeah, according to this he's a state senator from Fresno County. He was a guest speaker at the Conservative Veterans Association meeting on Tuesday and tonight he's speaking at someplace called the Family Center." She folded the paper and handed it back to Gina, glancing at the time. "Damn, it's almost eight. I've gotta go." She took the journal from Gina and placed it in the paper bag. "Can't be late for my karate camp."

"You could leave the bag and I can go through it, while you're at work."

Kelly shook her head. "No. Gina, you know I'll be in trouble if Rick finds out that you've seen any of this."

"He won't," Gina said emphatically. "But you have to let me help you. Bring the bag back tonight and we'll go through every-thing."

"Maybe." Kelly knew she shouldn't let Gina help her, but she also thought that her input could be valuable. "Can you look for some info on Marcus Edwards at your work—see if he has any past we should know about?"

Gina nodded. "I'll see what I can dig up."

Kelly left Gina's house and drove directly to the auto body shop. Fortunately it was warm and the breeze from the broken back window felt good. She grabbed her karate gi and the paper bag of Marcus's things and left her car with a friend who worked at the shop. He promised to have the window repaired by noon and then offered to give her a ride to work.

She got to the dojo exactly at eight. Worried about the late start, she struggled to quickly unlock the door with the wire. She finally heard the reassuring click of metal and wiggled the handle. Before she entered the dojo, a hand landed on her shoulder. Spinning to the side, she had her hands on guard as Sam smiled at her.

"Forget your key?" he asked, puzzled. "Or are you just practicing for a career in cat burglary?"

She tried to relax but her heart was still racing. She wondered if Sam had scared her on purpose. "It would probably pay better than teaching karate, wouldn't it?" She smiled. "No. Rick took my keys last week. Why are you here so early?"

"See, I was going to ask you the same thing. Why am I here this early? Rick called this morning to tell me you needed the day off."

She could tell Sam was angry and tried to avoid looking directly at him. "It's already late. I need to open the front doors and let the kids in." She held the door open for Sam to enter. He crossed his arms and stared at her, not entering. Kelly leaned against the doorway, debating what she should tell him. "There's a meeting I have to be at with Rick and one of his clients this afternoon. I just need to leave early. If you could help me out sometime after lunch, that'd be perfect."

"Is your job with Rick your priority now?" He stared at her with an intensity that Kelly had seen before, only when he was ready to fight. "Because I need to be able to count on your being here. For the kids and for the dojo."

She considered this. What was more important—her job with Rick and the investigation of Marcus Edwards's death or the karate school and the camp? "The dojo is my priority."

"Then Rick needs to know that." Sam nodded. "And I'll help you out with the camp this afternoon, but don't schedule meetings when you have responsibilities here."

"Yes, sir." She felt the sting of his words as if he'd just slapped her. With just one glance, Sam had the ability to make her shrink.

"And you'll be in charge of cleaning the dojo after the open sparring matches tonight to make up for your missed time."

Kelly nodded. "Thank you, sir, for the compromise."

"It's not a compromise. I'm doing you a favor." He glanced at his watch. "I'll be back at noon to relieve you. Wear the kids out this morning—and check their lunches to make sure no one sneaks in any sweet snacks." He added, "I don't have as much patience as you do for six-year-olds on sugar highs."

Kelly went into the dojo and opened the front door to let in the kids. She placed the paper bag in her locker in the back changing room. Of all the hiding places that she could think of, she decided the dojo was probably the safest.

By the time Sam returned, Kelly had each student eagerly waiting for a chance to sit down after an exhausting morning of training. After inspecting their lunches, she left the campers with Sam. Her car had been delivered just before noon and the new window looked much cleaner than the old ones. She had decided to only bring the CD with the recording from Marcus's camera to the meeting with Rick. Later she would sort through the other items. She wanted time to go through everything without Rick's help. Her phone rang just as she walked out of the dojo.

It was Gina. "So, I found out that our artist friend was a military man. He fought in the Gulf War back in the nineties as a Marine. Then he came out to California and, believe it or not, was arrested once for reckless driving."

"The Marines? Anything else?" Kelly thought she remembered John mentioning that Marcus was a GI Joe type, but for some reason this hadn't registered in her mind as a military connection. Maybe that was why Rick taped his interviews, she realized.

"Nope," Gina replied. "According to the police records, he's a pretty clean dead guy."

"Okay, thanks for the help. I'll see you tonight."

Kelly drove to Alex's house trying to fit the information Gina had found into the rest of the Marcus Edwards puzzle. She wondered why Marcus would ever have taken a job for GPAC if he really wasn't gay. After a shower and a peanut butter and jelly sandwich, she turned on Alex's computer and slipped Marcus's CD into the machine. The first image was of a doorway and Kelly standing in the entryway of Marcus's apartment. She smiled at the frightened expression frozen on her face and thought how unlike a stealth investigator she was, despite her hopes.

The computer had saved the images on the file in reverse order so the next image was several hours earlier. An old man with a hooked nose and fat cheeks was leaving the apartment. Kelly instantly thought of the sketch in Marcus's journal of Da' Boss. She knew that this was the same man but had no idea why he would be in Marcus's apartment. According to the timer on the camera, he had left the apartment twelve hours after the car accident, and he had entered only five minutes earlier. Unfortunately, the camera did not show where the guy went in the apartment, only capturing the images at the doorway. Kelly doubted the old man would have been the type to ransack the place, and the old man had only stayed in the apartment for five minutes, if the timer was accurate. Also, he came and left empty-handed.

Next, a middle-aged white man with a narrow face and a crew cut appeared. He was carrying a briefcase. Kelly stared intently at him. His eyes were circled in black like he'd been sleepless or punched once on each side. Was he the one in the SUV? The image of this man entering the apartment showed that he came with nothing. The briefcase must have belonged to Marcus. He walked in empty-handed three hours after the car accident, stayed in the apartment for a half-hour, and then left with the briefcase. Thirty minutes was definitely long enough to search the place and leave it a mess, she thought. What was in the briefcase that he took?

Her cell phone rang and she glanced at the clock. "Damn, I'm late."

She picked up the phone, knowing it was Rick. "Hi. I'm on my way."

"Good, because you're already late."

"I'll explain when I get there," she said.

"I trust you have something to show for yourself."

Kelly didn't respond to this. She said good-bye and hung up the line. Rick's manners irritated her. After ejecting the CD, she switched off the computer. It was surprising that she had found as much "evidence" as she had in Marcus's place, considering two other people had been in the apartment since he had died. Why hadn't the others found the camera behind the plant?

When Kelly arrived at the PI office, Nora was already seated across from Rick. They both glanced up when she came in and Nora smiled at her, which made her catch her breath and stumble on her greeting. Having a crush on someone straight, or otherwise unattainable, was frustrating and uncomfortable. She felt childish, as if she had little control over her emotions. Once she was in the room with Nora for a few minutes, she knew she would relax, but her heart raced at first and she could say nothing intelligent.

Nora was striking as well as imposing. Kelly decided that she reminded her of a stage actor one might lust for but be too shy to carry on a conversation with. Something uncomfortable and exciting stirred in her whenever Nora looked at her. Nora moved like an experienced dancer who knew that every action was important. Her voice was what one would expect of a lawyer, projecting authority and a command of an audience's attention, but also sultry. When they had first met, Kelly had been rapt. Her sculpted hands, along with her smooth brown skin, had attracted her attention because Nora talked as much with her hands as with her lips, and her golden brown eyes had thrown Kelly off her guard.

Today, Nora wore a tan silk blouse and a straight black skirt. Although the clothing would seem traditional, or even stuffy on some people, on Nora it was sexy because of how much it concealed. There was much to wonder at, with only the first two buttons opened at her throat. Kelly imagined that Nora's eyes flirted with her from across the room, catching the light as they flickered over her. Although she was ashamed of her crush, she loved being in Nora's presence.

Thankfully, Rick didn't ask her to explain why she was ten minutes late. He pointed to a chair and said, "So, we do know that Marcus Edwards was in the Marines and well-decorated. He had no blemishes on his military record and there's never been anything to suggest he was gay, although he was unmarried."

Nora turned to Kelly. "Feel free to jump in if you have anything to add. We're just getting started."

Rick continued, "He served for ten years and left the Marines four years ago. According to his résumé, he worked in a nonprofit veterans aid organization after discharge and then came to work for the Gay, Lesbian and Bisexual Political Action Coalition, also known as GPAC." Rick glanced at Kelly. "And to my knowledge, we don't have anything on Marcus's family back in Minneapolis. His parents, as it turns out, couldn't be found because they're both dead. He had no siblings. The police identified only one next of kin, an aunt, living in Oakland. I'm trying to track down info on her." He shook his head. "Anyway, sounds like this guy was pretty much of a loner. I've never liked loners."

"Why not?" Nora asked.

He shrugged. "A loner won't worry about their actions since they've only got to be concerned about their own welfare. A lot of guys who become criminals are the loner type."

"Anything else?" Nora asked.

"Well," Kelly began, "I found out that he was arrested for reckless driving."

Rick frowned. "I won't ask where you found out about his police record."

Nora eyed Rick and then Kelly. "Something I should know about?"

"No."

"So, aside from bad driving, he has no criminal past?" Nora shook her head. "That's hardly the story of a bad egg."

"Well, what's in his police record doesn't necessarily include every criminal act he ever committed. The cops don't know everything. And even if they are aware of something . . . Well, not every felony makes it into the record, depending on your connections." Rick picked up a pen and clicked the ink cartridge. "All I'm saying is that I don't trust loners to be honest folks. I've been proven wrong before on that assumption, but not often." He nodded at Kelly, who had just set the CD on his desk. "So what's this?"

"Marcus had a camera in his apartment."

"You went inside his apartment? This is his disk?" Nora swore softly. She turned to Rick. "I hope we're not doing any breaking-and-entering here. Maybe I didn't make that clear when I asked you to investigate this."

"I didn't break anything," Kelly said defensively. "His apartment was unlocked. I just walked inside and took a look around. Someone else was there before me—the place was trashed."

"You didn't just take a look—you took evidence that could be part of a trial, except we stole it." Nora swore again.

The criticism stung Kelly. She tried to hide the blush she felt rising on her cheeks by standing up and going over to the corner coffee table. Rick had an automatic coffee maker set up. She poured a cup of coffee and added cream and two packets of sugar. Rick always made bitter coffee.

"Looks like you," Rick said with a glance at Kelly. He angled the screen so that Nora could see it.

"Great, we have evidence that she broke into Marcus's place." Nora laughed cynically. "Rick, I thought you trained her?"

Her cheeks burning, Kelly refused to look at Nora. "Go to the next saved image. The camera runs continuously but saves an image only when something in the scene changes, such as when someone opens the door and steps on that doormat."

The next image appeared and Rick sat upright in his chair. "What the hell was he doing in there? What time is this one at?"

"Twelve hours after the car accident. You'll see in the next image the time when he entered the place. He stayed for just over five minutes." Kelly pointed to the bottom of the screen with the digital clock display. "You know him?"

"Jared DiBaca," Nora answered, leaning forward in her chair to get a better look at the screen. "He's the head of the Conservative Veteran's Association—the group that's been attacking GPAC. They are the most vocal opponents to gays in the military. When GPAC announced its first lawsuit against the military's gay policy, CVA retaliated with radio announcements and newspaper ads. Then they hit up veterans for donations and drummed up allies to fight the 'evil gays' who were 'corrupting' the military."

"And why the hell is DiBaca in Marcus's apartment?" Rick wondered. "You said the place was unlocked?"

Kelly nodded. "But I think he found the place unlocked also. Someone else came in before him. Go to the next saved image."

The next image came up and both Rick and Nora squinted at the screen. After a moment, Rick asked, "Anyone know this guy?"

Nora shook her head. "What does he have in his hands?"

"A briefcase," Kelly answered. "I'm not sure, but I have an idea this guy might be the SUV driver. Apparently the cops who saw the accident gave a description of the SUV driver as being a white male with a crew cut." She paused and glanced at Rick. "Of course, lots of guys have crew cuts. But here's a guy who fits the police description and shows up in Marcus's apartment three hours after the accident. He spent a half an hour in the place. I think he was the one who ransacked it."

"Why?" Nora asked.

"Well, someone trashed the place and the only other guy on the tape, DiBaca, looks like he'd have a heart attack if he tried to topple a sofa and a dresser. This guy stayed in the place longer and left with a briefcase." She pointed to the case, barely visible at the edge of the picture. "DiBaca didn't take anything—or at least we don't see him leave with anything in his hands."

"So what did Marcus have that this guy wanted?" Nora wondered. "What would Marcus have that would make someone want to kill him?"

Rick pointed to the briefcase and then shook his head. "We need to know who this guy is before we can ask that question."

"What if the accident really was just an accident?" Kelly asked. "I mean, maybe this guy was following Marcus back to his apartment to get this briefcase. Maybe he didn't want to kill him at all."

"Unlikely. Someone ransacked Marcus's house and remember, that SUV was stolen. The police said that the SUV owner reported it stolen at a gas station in Oakland." Rick cleared his throat. "Until proven otherwise, we assume that the guy who stole the SUV drove to San Francisco, found Marcus and followed him with the intention of running him off the road."

Nora nodded. "But we can't say that this guy is the SUV driver."

"There's a strong possibility that this is our man, but no evidence yet. Next step, we need to figure out who he is. How was he connected to Marcus?"

"Any other images on the computer camera?" Nora asked.

Rick scanned through the disk. "No. Looks like the disk was put in the computer and set to start the camera recording about ten hours before the car accident—probably just before Marcus left for work."

"Why do you think Marcus had a camera set up in his apartment anyway?" Nora asked.

He shrugged. "You've dealt with him before. Would you guess that he'd be the paranoid type?"

"Not at all." She shook her head adamantly. "But I haven't worked with him much. He came to me a few weeks ago and we discussed the last military case that I had worked on with GPAC. After that, we talked about GPAC's current agenda. He mentioned the Domestic Partners Medical Benefits Act and told me that was the main reason he had come to see me." She glanced at Kelly. "Do you know about this? It's being argued in the state senate now."

"No," Kelly admitted.

"Well, the original act was proposed to help domestic partners pay for medical bills if their spouse had been previously excluded from state coverage. Some senator tagged on a provision to this act restricting the formation of new domestic partnerships. In other words, it's going to be a legal nightmare to apply for a domestic partnership if the act passes. The senate took an act that was supposed to be good for gays and made it a wolf in sheep's clothing."

"But I thought Marcus was just in charge of fund-raising for GPAC," Kelly said. "Why would he be involved in legislative work?"

"GPAC doesn't have a big staff. No one works on only one project. Marcus was in charge of fund-raising and finances for the group but he was also their lead organizer against the restrictive provision in the Medical Benefits Act."

"Who else was working with him on that?" Rick asked.

Nora shook her head. "That I don't know. To tell you the truth, since the military case was dropped, I've focused on other cases. I was surprised that Marcus came to see me at all. He said he wanted to know what the chances were that we could challenge the act if it became law."

Rick cleared his throat. "And does any of this matter to this guy?" He tapped his finger on the computer screen where the man with the crew cut was frozen near the door of Marcus's apartment.

"Any idea why Marcus would get a visit from Jared DiBaca—if he's the Conservative Veterans Association leader and they hate GPAC?" Kelly wondered.

Rick answered, "Maybe Marcus was a mole."

Nora frowned. "Are you suggesting that CVA put Marcus into a gay political group to keep an eye on the group? Well, that's an interesting thought."

"Why not? He had access to GPAC's private files and could keep tabs on everything that the group was working on. You've heard of the stories about moles for the FBI. Maybe this is a similar story."

"Marcus has been working for GPAC for too long. I can't believe that he'd been fund-raising so well for GPAC if he was a mole for CVA or any other group," Nora said.

"What if he was targeting his fund-raising at military personnel so CVA could keep tabs on the gays in the military through their donations?" Rick arched his eyebrows. "It's plausible that an ex-Marine was working for CVA."

"We have no proof of that. Of course anything is possible, but I just can't believe that about Marcus." Nora was obviously skeptical about Marcus's involvement with the CVA. Kelly wondered how well Nora had known him.

"Well, it does make more sense than a straight guy from the Marines working for a gay political group." Kelly added, "John didn't think he was gay. He has no history to peg him either way, no girlfriends or boyfriends. And after a look around his apartment, I'd wager that he was hopelessly straight—although he had a lot of shoes and his wardrobe wasn't atrocious, not one mark of interior design in the place and nothing but cheese sticks and frozen dinners in the fridge."

"Hopelessly straight?" Rick asked. "Sounds like you could have walked into my place instead of his."

"Exactly." Kelly smiled.

Nora winked at her. "Careful, he's got a sensitive side."

"Okay, let's regroup here," Rick interrupted. "We've got the bank statements to sort out still—who was paying him besides GPAC? We also need to figure out who this guy is with the crew cut." He pointed to the image frozen on the computer screen. "We also need to find any friends that Marcus might have had." He checked his watch. "You said you had another meeting at four?"

Nora nodded and stood up. "With my partner at the law firm. He's a fanatic about promptness."

"I'll keep you posted about this case," Rick said, standing also. "We have some good leads to follow."

She picked up her black leather briefcase. "Let's just try and follow them legally, from now on." Nora pointedly glanced at Kelly. She turned back to Rick and said, "We'll talk later."

As soon as Nora left, Rick sat back down and made an exaggerated sigh. "Well, I think you did a good job. Don't let Nora get to you." He took the CD out of the disk drive and set it in a manila envelope. "Was this the only thing you took from the apartment?"

"No. I grabbed a few other things, but I'm not sure if anything else is worth your time. I'm going to look through it and bring it tomorrow." She'd considered lying, but knew Rick would catch her. "So, what's my next step?"

Rick picked up the manila envelope and set it in the top drawer of his file cabinet. "I don't know. You tell me."

Kelly thought for a moment. "I'd really like to know if Marcus had any friends. I read in the paper that there was a funeral scheduled for tomorrow."

"You read the paper?" He chuckled. "Well, then you're in luck. Best way to find out if you have any friends is to die."

"Well, I guess that's one way." She wondered how many friends a loner would have. The aunt had probably been the one to arrange the funeral.

"Speaking of friends, I'm only going to say this once more— you need to stop talking to your cop girlfriend about this case."

"She's got access to police records and experience keeping secrets." Kelly thought of Gina's family, who still didn't know she was a lesbian. "I really think she could do more for us."

"I don't care. Stop discussing the case with her or I'll have to find someone else to take over your position."

Knowing that she would regret angering Rick, she agreed to his demands. "Fine. I won't talk about the case. I understand your position." But I'm still going to date her, Kelly added silently.

Chapter Eight

That evening Kelly was back at the dojo in time for the open sparring matches. She had left Rick's office that afternoon and noticed that a black sedan followed her out of the parking lot. Although she wasn't sure that this sedan was the same one that had tracked her from Marcus's house, an uneasy feeling gripped her when the car stayed two car lengths behind her Volkswagen in the stop-and-go traffic on Main Street. The driver also had flipped down the sunshades so she couldn't see his face. She memorized the license plate and planned to have Gina look it up on the police records. Kelly decided to avoid the karate school until she'd lost the tail. She drove to the Ashton Fire Department and parked, waiting for the sedan to drive by her. The tilt of the sun on the car's window obscured the driver's face as he passed by her.

She wondered if she should tell Rick about her shadow. Maybe it was just coincidence that both cars had been black sedans and maybe they weren't following her at all. Yet someone had broken her back window last night.

"Front position," Sam said to the pair of blue belts who had just finished their match. "And bow."

Panting, the two blue belts stepped off the mat and joined the line of eight other students waiting for Sam to call the last match of the night.

"Kelly, you're up," he said gruffly.

She felt his eyes on her and knew he was still displeased with her. Sam didn't like managing the camp. *It was her job.* She stood up and fastened her sparring helmet. Then she slid her mouth guard between her teeth, clenching and relaxing her jaw muscles before shaking out her shoulders.

Sam then pointed at Kevin.

She was frequently paired up with Kevin and always enjoyed their matches, regardless of who won. After bowing to Sam, Kevin and Kelly faced each other and bowed again, then shook hands. The other students waited on the edge of the mat, each probably breathing a sigh of relief knowing that they weren't in the last match of the night. The other students could finally sit back and relax as their classmates finished the long sparring session. The room was muggy with body heat.

Kelly grinned at Kevin. He'd told her that her smile at the beginning of each match made him nervous.

"Ready?" Sam asked with a quick glance at Kevin and then at Kelly. "Kelly, you're on defensive. Kevin, let's see some free fighting. Spar." His hand swept down between them and he immediately stepped back to watch their fight.

Kevin threw a roundhouse kick to Kelly's helmet and followed in with two jabs. She dodged his first attack and aimed her elbow at his shin as he threw a front kick at her ribs. He grimaced in pain as he pulled his leg back and then threw a hook punch at her head. She jumped back from the strike and grinned again at him.

She always tried to smile more when she was losing a match. It helped her check her emotions. She breathed out slowly, skirting around Kevin and trying to evade his next set of kicks. Two kicks slipped inside her guard, one tapping her belt and one striking her knee. A strike to her knee would have been illegal under other circumstances, but not tonight. Sam wasn't calling any illegal shots. Tonight, she knew, Sam wanted Kevin to push her to the point where she would want to break the rules.

After a few quick exchanges of strikes, Kevin stepped down on her foot and pummeled his fist into her belly. She tried unsuccessfully to free her foot. Her glove tapped against his head a few times, but he continued the attack. She refused to hit his head with enough force to make him stop. Sam had given him license to free fight, not her. Free fighting in their dojo meant that strikes below the belt, to the back or to the knees—usually illegal—were fair game in this fight. Kevin's favorite move was a side kick to the knee and Kelly knew that she also had to watch out for his take-down techniques. Sam had made it clear that she was still expected to use normal control even though Kevin didn't have to abide by the rules. It was a test of patience. Kevin was Sam's accomplice tonight and his fists would leave black-and-blue marks if she didn't respond to the attacks.

He threw a quick jab followed by a hook punch at her ear. Stepping out of his range, she threw a spinning hook kick at his head. He caught her foot in his hands and pulled her leg up in the air. Kelly landed on her back. He jumped down on her and slid his arms around her throat. Shifting quickly to the side, she threw him off of her chest and struggled onto her hands and knees. Before she could stand, he came at her again. She felt his foot slam into her ribs. Sam could call the match, she thought as she coughed in pain, anytime now. It was obvious that Kevin had won. He moved to kick again, but this time she rolled quickly away from him.

Finally she scrambled onto her feet and found solid footing for her shaking legs. She forced herself to smile as she looked over at Kevin, wondering if he knew she was having trouble checking her emotions. He threw another kick at her belly. She dropped her elbow on his shin to block the kick and he pulled his foot back with a grimace of pain. Wishing she could throw a counterstrike at one of Kevin's open targets, Kelly inwardly cursed Sam for this "training." As soon as her guard dropped, Kevin lunged forward with a front punch aimed at her nose. She spun to the side and his fist grazed her cheekbone. She threw a back-fist at his temple and then dodged to the side to avoid hitting him.

"Break!" Sam called to end the match.

Kevin and Kelly both came to attention, bowing first to Sam and then to each other.

Sam's hand fell on Kevin's shoulder. "Not bad. Not bad. Line up, everyone. Let's end class." He glanced at Kelly. "How do you feel?"

"Fine, sir." She coughed and loosened her helmet.

"Good." He slapped her shoulder. "Then line up."

She joined the other students standing at attention on the mat and tried to ignore the painful places where Kevin's strikes had landed. Kevin shouldered her when she got in line next to him. "What?" she mouthed.

"Nice match," he returned.

"All right, everyone," Sam called. "Come to attention and bow." He paused to eye each student. "Kneel and meditate."

The students filed off the mat after meditation and filled the waiting room. Kevin sank down on the chair next to Kelly. Dripping with sweat, he shook his head, smiling at her as the sweat beads flew off his hair.

"You're disgusting."

He laughed. "And I have you to thank for all this sweat."

"Are you going out to dinner with the guys?" she asked, pointing to the students who had gathered near the front door and were planning which entrees they would order from Uncle Lee-Hi's Chinese restaurant.

"No. I'm wanted at home. And you?"

"My girlfriend is waiting for me. She's better entertainment than a bunch of sweaty men."

The dojo emptied quickly as the dinner group gathered their sparring gear and headed over to the restaurant. Sam was in the back office working at his computer and only Kevin and Kelly remained in the dojo.

"I thought you weren't coming this week. Change of plans?" Kelly remembered that Kevin had mentioned that he might not be able to make it to sparring class anymore. He had recently changed jobs and his new one seemed to be taking up all of his time.

"I decided that I couldn't last a week without seeing you." Kevin grinned. He had been a stockbroker in Ashton for over ten years. He seemed to have had a mid-life crisis about six months ago and admitted to Kelly that he was gay. He divorced his wife a few weeks later and moved to San Francisco. Shortly after the divorce, he left his brokerage firm and took a job as a political consultant. He'd also just started dating some man in the city that Kelly had yet to meet. Now he commuted to Ashton only to visit his daughter and spar at the dojo.

"That's sweet. I wouldn't have guessed that you were into S and M," she joked. "Does your boyfriend know?"

"He knows I get beat up by some black belt every time I come here. But I haven't told him the black belt was a sexy twenty-one-year-old woman. There's some things I like to keep secret!"

"Me?" Kelly laughed. "You know, you've given me a few good bruises as well." She knew he was teasing her and was glad to have him in class, even if she was going to be nursing a few of her ribs with ice packs later that night.

"And what does your girlfriend say?"

"She doesn't know about you, Kevin."

He winked. "Good. I wouldn't want some dyke hunting me down 'cause I hit her woman."

"You're lucky I know you're kidding me, otherwise I'd give you hell for that comment."

He stretched his arms and then toweled the sweat off his face. "Well, I'm glad I came tonight anyway. I needed to blow off some steam. The politics at work are driving me crazy."

"Office politics?"

"Meridian took on a contract with a politician I detest. And wouldn't you know it—I'm his primary contact."

Kelly had wondered what Kevin did at his new job. He'd told her that Meridian was a business that provided political consultants and analysts to politicians, but she wasn't sure exactly what his job entailed. "You can't pick which politician you want to work for?"

"I've only been at Meridian for four months. I still have to ask someone for permission to pee, if you know what I mean. My boss places me with whichever politician pays them for services." He shook his head. "You know, I thought keeping pace with stock price fluctuations and following corporate buy-outs was high-pressure work. But nothing I did before compares to this level of stress. I'm working for a politician who writes anti-gay legislation in his free time and thinks the decline of marriage sanctity will poison the country."

"No wonder you were using me as a punching bag tonight. I'm glad I could help with your stress reduction."

"This sparring class is blocked off in my schedule as *Stress Management*."

"So, who is this politician?"

"A state senator—some prick from a conservative district in central California." Kevin picked up his sparring bag, now packed with all of his gear, and tossed his sweat-soaked towel over his shoulder. "And if you ask me, he ought to be kicked out of office. He's a regular slimeball."

"Are you saying he's just as bad as the rest? Or worse?"

"Touché." He laughed cynically. "Yeah, maybe they're all slime-balls. I haven't met anyone in office that I would trust. They all lie, cheat and squander. I guess Rob Talcone is no worse than average."

Her jaw dropped. "Robert Talcone?" She wondered what the odds were that Kevin was working for Talcone.

"Well, I call him other names when he's out of earshot." He rolled his eyes.

"What has he done that's so bad?"

He shrugged. "How much time do you have to listen?"

"All night." Kelly smiled. "I've got a boring life. About all I do is teach karate, get beat up by you, eat and sleep." And she'd listen all night if he could tell her why Marcus Edwards would be connected to Robert Talcone.

"Well, I know he's been involved in some shady deals with the Bureau of Land Management and the military. He also has a history with the oil industry, and there was a coastal protection act that he single-handedly killed and then accepted a large sum of money from the act's strongest nay-sayers." He sighed. "And to make matters worse, now he's attacking gay rights. There's a bill in the senate right now—the Domestic Partners Medical Benefits Act."

Kelly nodded. "Yeah, I've heard of it."

"Well, Talcone was the weasel who managed to add an amendment to that bill that nearly prevents new domestic partnerships. He's added a year-long waiting clause and a procedure to prove that the couple has been living-in-common for three years before the application can even be processed. And I'm his political consultant and, no, he doesn't know I'm gay."

"That sucks. Can you get another politician to work with—Meridian must have other clients."

"I'm stuck with Talcone for now, unless I quit. Frank thinks I should just work from the inside to take him down." Frank was Kevin's boyfriend. "I told him I was too honest for politics."

"How do you work for someone you hate?"

"People do it all the time." He shook his head. "But, it'd be easier if I got this job two years ago when I still thought I was straight."

Kelly thought of Talcone's name on the list of GPAC sponsors and Marcus's sketch of him. Why had Marcus drawn Talcone? She wanted to comb through the rest of the journal and see if there wasn't some explanation. "Wasn't Talcone just in San Francisco? I think I saw something in the newspaper about him."

"He was a guest speaker at the annual meeting of the Conservative Veterans Association," Kevin replied. "And you can bet that was a fun occasion for me. I had to write Talcone's damn speech, which was all about protecting the values and strength of

America from destruction by the *queers* and the left's radical minority. God, it's all so hypocritical."

She wondered if Marcus was tied to Talcone through CVA. "Why was he speaking to CVA?" she asked.

"He's trying to make a good impression on Jared DiBaca, the head of CVA. They've had dealings before and now Talcone wants his blessing, and that of CVA, for his anti-gay agenda. The fiscal conservatives see Talcone's proposed amendment to the Medical Benefits Act as another way to help big business save money. And the CVA will back anything that's anti-gay as long as it's sold to them in the right language."

"Have you heard of GPAC?" Kelly asked.

"Of course. GPAC has been fighting Talcone's amendment from the very beginning. Unfortunately, that group has a big bark and no teeth. I've heard they've got a big budget, but they never seem to make big headlines. I followed their case against the military's anti-gay policies, but nothing ever came of it. Last I heard, the case was pulled. I really don't think they're much of a threat to Talcone's anti-gay agenda."

Kelly decided to take a chance and asked, "Do you know a guy named Marcus Edwards?"

Kevin stared at her for a moment. "Edwards?" He shook his head. "No, why?"

"He worked for GPAC." She shrugged. For some reason, she wasn't sure if Kevin was telling her the truth. He had responded to the name as if it sounded familiar. "You know how small the gay planet is, I thought you might have heard of him."

Kevin smiled. "Well, I just got on the gay planet." He stood up and shouldered his bag. "Ugh, I stink. I need a shower. I got all sweaty fighting some fast-handed tough girl."

"Tough girl? I don't know if that's an accurate description."

"Yeah, well, you haven't been on the receiving end of one of her roundhouse kicks." Lifting his shirt, he exposed the side of his chest where a red mark covered a rectangular area over two of his ribs.

"Ouch." She hated to see any marks that she'd left and immediately felt guilty, though he had probably earned more than that one bruise during their fight. "Sorry. You're going to have a nice bruise by morning."

"And I'll have you to thank for it. Your heel is too damn bony. I get bruises there all the time from your side kicks that somehow slip under my guard." He laughed. "But I'll look tough when I hit the showers at my gym. And no, I don't tell the other guys that the bruises are from a twenty-one-year-old woman."

"Why not?"

"I have to keep up my macho image."

"Hey, Kelly, the mats need to be cleaned and there are handprints all over the mirrors," Sam said, interrupting the conversation. "I left the cleaning supplies out for you."

"Thank you, sir," Kelly replied. She took Sam's cue to start cleaning and said good night to Kevin. Kevin and Sam left together and Kelly turned on the radio when the dojo was finally clear. After getting the vacuum and cleaning supplies, she went to her locker and pulled out the bag of items from Marcus's apartment.

The address book had few clues that she could decipher. Robert Talcone was listed with a star placed next to this name. She also found two other starred names, Jared DiBaca and Leo Rausche. After seeing DiBaca's name twice, she wondered how he was connected to Marcus. Rausche and DiBaca both had San Francisco addresses. Talcone's address was in Sacramento.

The only interesting thing that Kelly could find in Marcus's bank statements was that he had been making large deposits into a savings account. His paycheck was deposited directly into his checking account and labeled as a "payroll account," but the amount that Marcus was depositing in his savings account each month was nearly double his salary. Where was the extra money coming from? If it was from CVA, then wouldn't he have tried harder to hide it? She thought he might have set up a separate account for any payoffs if he was really up to something illegal.

She had just started to thumb through his journal when her cell phone rang. She answered the line and tossed the journal back in the locker with Marcus's other things.

"Where are you?" Gina asked.

"The dojo. I got stuck cleaning after the sparring class."

"Sounds like a party." Gina laughed. "Can I join you?"

"No. I want to get out of this place. I feel like I live here." Kelly sighed. "I'll be at your house as soon as I'm finished vacuuming."

Gina opened the door and took a step back, gazing at Kelly's face. "What the hell happened to you?"

Kelly smiled meekly. "I lost a few matches. Mind if I take a shower?"

"Go right ahead." Gina let her pass and then grabbed her hand. "Any bruises I should know about before I hug you?"

Kelly shook her head and hugged Gina. "It's good to see you. Nice necklace, by the way."

"You like it?" She touched the ruby on her neck and pulled it along the silver chain. "Some hot chica gave it to me."

Kelly had found the ruby earlier that summer on a surfing trip with Alex. It had washed up on the beach and there was a small crack on one side, but after polishing, the stone shone brilliantly. She'd had it strung on a chain for Gina and had given it to her last month.

"Go take a shower. I have dinner waiting for you."

After a quick shower, Kelly went down to the kitchen where the aroma of tomatoes and chili spices brewed. "What's for dinner?"

Gina pointed to the table. "Sautéed vegetables with my mother's famous Spanish rice." She opened the oven and pulled out a plate of tortillas. "Sit down. Everything's ready."

Kelly waited for Gina to join her, then helped herself to the sizzling vegetables and bright yellow rice. She took a few bites and murmured her approval. "This is fabulous. Why do we always go out to eat?"

Gina shrugged. "I hate doing dishes."

"If I knew you cooked like this, I'd have offered to be the dishrag long ago. Did your mother teach you?"

"Both of my parents cook. My father makes the tortillas and desserts. My mother makes everything else, from rice to polenta. She can make food so good your taste buds sing, as my father says. They both love to cook and love to feed people."

"They sound wonderful . . . Do you miss them now that you live up here?" Gina's parents lived in Southern California.

Gina nodded. "They came up for Thanksgiving last year and we all cooked dinner. It was perfect. But I like living a separate life from them. You know, they'd be leaning over my shoulder all the time if they were here, telling me what spices to use and which boys to ask over for dinner."

"Why haven't you told them that you date women?" Kelly knew that Gina wasn't out to her parents. They had called once when Gina was in the shower and Kelly had answered the line. When Gina called back, she told them that Kelly was just a friend who had stopped in for breakfast. Kelly immediately guessed that her parents didn't know the truth about Gina's love life, but she hadn't brought it up then.

"My parents?" Gina seemed startled by the question. She forked a tomato chunk and a chili pepper over to her rice and then took a bite. "I thought we were talking about cooking."

A cell phone rang and Kelly glanced over at the phone she'd left on the counter. She couldn't see who was calling. "I hate when calls interrupt dinner."

"So don't answer it," Gina replied.

The ringing continued and Kelly imagined Rick waiting for her to pick up. She should have refused his offer for the free phone but it was too late now. "I have to answer it," she admitted. "Otherwise I'll have a guilty conscience."

Gina reached over and picked it up, glancing at the digital screen. "Nora? The caller ID says that Nora is calling you." Gina held her finger on the answer button. "Shall I take this call and find out what Nora wants?"

Kelly reached across the table and took the phone from her. "Hello?"

"Hi. Rick told me to call you directly. We need to meet."

"Okay. When?" Kelly glanced at Gina, sensing that she was upset at the interruption. She had told Gina that Rick's investigation of Marcus Edwards's death was being paid for by Nora's GPAC retainer. She knew that Gina would want to know the details of Nora's call and hoped that Nora would be brief.

"Now, if possible," Nora said. "The sooner the better. Can you be in the city in an hour?"

"Hold on." Kelly lowered the phone and cupped her palm over it. To Gina she said, "How mad would you be if I told you I had to leave?"

"Mad." Gina shrugged. "Just tell Nora that your girlfriend has priority tonight."

Kelly said into the phone, "Can this wait until tomorrow?"

"No," Nora answered.

Kelly mouthed an apology to Gina and then agreed to meet Nora at her office in the city. She hung up and turned to Gina. "Look, I'm really sorry, but I don't have any choice. I have to meet her tonight."

"This is bullshit." Gina shook her head. She dropped her fork on her plate where it clattered noisily. "Well, what are you waiting for? If you're leaving, you might as well just go."

"But you made dinner for me."

"Yeah, I do that for people I like. But we're finished." Gina glared at her. "Damn, you piss me off sometimes."

Kelly knew that Gina wasn't upset about ending the dinner early. Instead, she was pissed that she wasn't part of the investigation. "Gina, I'm sorry."

"What's going on with Nora?"

"Nora is Rick's client, you know that."

Gina sighed. "What's going on with the case? You haven't told me anything."

"I can't. Rick said he'd fire me if I talk to you about it. He kept

100

the things that I took from Marcus's apartment. I think he was worried that I would show you." She added this lie so Gina wouldn't ask about the bag later. "I can't afford to lose this job."

Gina swore under her breath. She stood up from the table and grabbed their dinner plates. "Kelly, how can you deal with a guy like that? Has he even given your keys back?"

"No. I think he's trying to prove a point, or something."

"He's trying to prove that you're submissive. You'll do anything he puts you up to and you don't question him. What if he's not an honest guy?" She turned on the kitchen faucet and splashed the plates. "You know what? Never mind. Forget about everything I've said. You'll ignore my advice anyway. And you're the one working for the guy. I need to stay out of it." She turned off the faucet and wiped her hands, then left the room.

Kelly finished clearing the table and washed the dishes. She found Gina in the family room, staring at the TV news. "Any good news tonight?"

Gina shook her head. "Not unless you're just about to announce that you've changed your mind and will be staying here with me."

"I can't." Kelly kissed her forehead, since Gina wouldn't look up at her, and gathered her things. She stood by the doorway finally. "I'll call if I can be back within a few hours."

"Don't bother. I'm going to bed early. I've had a long day."

Kelly felt bad for not thinking to ask Gina how her day was. She had been consumed by her own world. "Well, good night then." She waited for Gina to make some reply, but she didn't look up from the television screen. Kelly left quietly.

Chapter Nine

Nora's office was on the fourth floor, suite 402, just off Market Street. Kelly spotted her waiting at the entrance to the building and holding her leather briefcase. She suggested that they go to a bookstore across the street, rather than her office. Apparently some of the legal aides were working late on a case that her partner had just taken on. They crossed the intersection and entered the bookstore. A café was on the second floor, tucked behind rows of books and several tables for reading space. Nora didn't start their conversation until they had found a table in the back of the bookstore and ordered two coffees.

"Thanks for coming out here tonight." She unlocked her briefcase without looking up at Kelly. "Did Rick tell you I would call?"

"No."

Nora glanced at her with obvious surprise. "Really? Well, I just expected he would." She paused and then handed Kelly a folded sheet of paper. "After I met with my partner this afternoon, I went to the gym to work out. This note was taped on the windshield of my car." She shook her head. "I have no idea of who put it there—the parking garage has a lot of traffic on Friday evenings. This is a copy. I've sent the original to a friend of mine who works in a forensics lab."

Kelly read the printed note to herself. *It is in your best interest to call off investigations of Marcus Edwards' accident. Otherwise there will be future accidents involving red cars.*

Nora waited for Kelly to fold the note and hand it back to her before continuing, "As soon as I joined the law firm I bought my red convertible. I never knew it would lead to a calling card like this."

"You didn't see anyone near your car?" Kelly asked.

"There was no one unusual-looking in the parking garage." Nora shook her head. She leaned back in her chair. "Obviously the note is unsettling, but I'm trying to ignore it for now. The reason I called you was that I'm wondering who else knows we're investigating Marcus's death. The only people who know about it are Rick, John and you. Unless you've been talking to someone about this."

Kelly felt Nora's eyes on her. "Rick told you about my girl-friend?"

"He mentioned that you have a close relationship with a police officer. Gina Hernandez, right?"

"She hasn't told anyone about the investigation, I swear." Kelly wondered even as she said it if she could trust Gina not to have told her partner or someone else at work.

Nora nodded. "Well, I don't usually worry about the police. I can't see how they would be linked to anything involving GPAC or Marcus Edwards, but Rick has his doubts. He said he was going to pull you off the case."

Kelly took a deep breath and exhaled slowly. "Gina was one of the police officers who witnessed the car accident. She's the one who told me about the guy with the crew cut. Look, I know she's not talking to anyone else." She hoped this was true.

"That's a dangerous thing to believe. We can only really know ourselves. I've discovered that my fiancé is not always as honest as I trust him to be." She paused and Kelly gulped. She was surprised to hear that Nora was engaged. "I've told Rick that I want him to keep you on this case. I don't think that your police friend was our leak. But you understand that you can't talk to her again about the case?"

"Yes," Kelly replied as Nora handed her two files from the briefcase. "What's this?"

"I received this in my mail. Marcus Edwards sent them to me. The post date was Tuesday."

"Shit." Kelly cursed softly. She opened the file and then glanced at Nora. "Why didn't you tell Rick about this?"

"I just picked up my mail. He sent it to my post office box. I went there after the gym."

"Shouldn't Rick be the one to look at these with you?"

Nora shrugged. "He was busy. We're meeting tomorrow morning and I wanted to see you first."

Kelly wondered why Nora was on her side against Rick. "So, what exactly are we looking for?" She opened the first file and scanned the date and list of items.

"I don't know exactly." Nora took a sip of her coffee. "I'm hoping something will jump out at you. I've had a look through them and can't make much of it. Just a bunch of receipts and office memos." She flipped through a stack of memos in one of the files as Kelly sorted out the pile of receipts from office supplies and computer parts.

"Why would he send you all of this?"

"Like I said, I don't know."

Kelly turned one of the receipts over and saw an address that she immediately recognized. "This address is for Robert Talcone—I've seen it before in Marcus's address book."

"When did you see his address book?"

"At his apartment." Kelly hesitated, not willing to explain that this was one of the things that she had stolen. "And Talcone was one of the GPAC supporters. We saw his name on the sponsor list."

"Rick mentioned that." Nora nodded. "So why does Marcus's receipt have Talcone's address on it?"

Under the address was a sixteen-digit number—with a notation for five thousand dollars. "Do you think he was getting money from him? A payoff? Look at this." She pointed at the number. "Maybe it's a credit card number or a bank account routing number."

Nora took the receipt. "You're certain that this address is for Senator Talcone?"

"Well, no. But it's definitely the same address that was in Marcus's address book." She flipped through the rest of the receipts and then glanced at Nora. "I need to think," she announced, tossing the receipts back in the file and standing. Nora had chosen a table at the corner of the children's book section. At this time of night, it was the quietest part of the store. She wandered down the aisles, leaving Nora with the files. She was ready to be done with Marcus Edwards. Yet every time she looked at Nora she felt an uncomfortable blush about to break on her cheeks.

Picking up a copy of *The Little Prince*, she stared at the boy with a wand in his hand on the front cover. She could almost hear her mom reading the story and remembered it was one of her childhood favorites. Right now she wanted to hear the story, to be tucked under a warm blanket and just listening to her mom's voice.

"I think you should look at this. We have another address," Nora called. She held out a memo with an address. "Recognize this one?"

Kelly came back to the table. She recognized the address. "Jared DiBaca. His name was one of the three that was starred in the address book—Talcone, DiBaca and some guy named Leo Rausche." She took the memo from Nora. On the back of the memo another sixteen-digit number and an amount, this time for three thousand dollars, was printed in blue ink. "He's cheaper."

"What do you think this was for? A payment or a bill?" Nora asked.

"I don't know." She had a swell of misgiving and wished Rick was here to sort through the files with Nora. What use was she? "Maybe we could find out some more info on this guy DiBaca."

"There's plenty of newspaper articles about him. He's probably even written a book about his own military career. As I understand it, he's a highly decorated old bastard."

"No, I meant personal information. This address isn't far from here."

Nora arched her eyebrows. "I'm not going to endorse another burglary."

"Another? Marcus's place was unlocked and I just poked around. Besides, a dead man can't press charges."

"His possessions belong to someone." Nora smiled. "And crimes against the dead are still crimes. Everything depends on how the laws are interpreted."

"And how much you're paying the lawyers, right?" Kelly winked. "I should have guessed I'd get a response like that from you."

"Something's bothering you, isn't it?" Nora slipped the memo back inside the front pocket of her briefcase. "You're too quiet."

"I've been thinking about the last case." Nora had worked hard with GPAC on the last case against the military. GPAC had dropped the military case when an unexplained murder occurred. Rick had been hired to help investigate the suspects on that case and they had found no answers. This uncertainty still bothered Kelly. She didn't want Marcus Edwards's death to be another unsolved case. "Don't worry, I'll be fine." She smiled at Nora. "Can I see that memo with Jared DiBaca's address? And the one with Talcone's?" There was an answer here and she was going to find it.

Nora handed both to her. "What are you thinking?"

"The sixteen-digit codes on the two notes are the same. I wonder if we have Marcus's bank account number here." Kelly paused, trying to remember the amounts of the deposits that had been entered into his account. "I think he was being paid by them."

"By DiBaca and Talcone?" Nora asked. "Why?"

"The GPAC sponsor list? It makes sense that CVA would pay Marcus for that list, right?"

106

Nora caught on to her thought. "And you think Robert Talcone might have paid for the list as well?"

"Talcone's name was on their donation records. I doubt any conservative senator would want CVA to see his name on the queer list."

"Talcone would stand to lose a huge amount of support if he lost the CVA endorsement." She shook her head. "I still don't understand why Talcone would have contributed in the first place. He's married and conservative."

"Maybe he wasn't ten years ago. Rick looked up the information about Talcone from the GPAC sponsor list. Apparently the address on the list matches Talcone's parents' ranch. He inherited their ranch about when the contribution to GPAC was made in his name."

"We still have no good motive to explain Marcus's death as anything other than an accident. Talcone's only definite link to Marcus is the fund-raising list, right?" Nora asked.

"And what about Jared DiBaca? We need to know why he was paying Marcus." Kelly flipped the receipt over and stared at DiBaca's address. "Want to go for a drive?" She waited for Nora's response. "I think we both need some more answers."

"Okay," Nora agreed. "But we aren't going inside DiBaca's house. I'm not about to be an accomplice to a burglary."

"Fine with me." Kelly was too nervous to enter a house with living occupants, but she didn't want to tell Nora this. "Let's go. I promise nothing will happen to ruin your reputation."

"What's that supposed to mean?"

Kelly felt her cheeks warm with a blush and she was glad when Nora turned to leave without waiting for her response.

Over her shoulder Nora said, "Never mind, don't answer that."

Kelly followed her out of the bookstore. She convinced Nora that they should take her car since it was less noticeable than a red sports car. Nora looked surprised when Kelly mentioned that the doors were already unlocked.

"You know, the city isn't that safe. You really should keep your car locked."

"I would, if I had my keys."

"You lost your keys?" Nora asked.

"Well, not exactly. Rick has them. He's holding on to them."

"How do you drive this thing?" She sighed as Kelly pulled the screwdriver out of her pocket once they had both fastened their seat belts and jammed it past the lock mechanism in the ignition. The car started easily and she pulled out of the curbside parking space. "I'm going to hope that this isn't a stolen car."

"No. And in case you don't believe me, the car registration papers are in the glove box." Kelly watched with surprise as Nora opened the glove box and fished through the mess of suntan lotion, gloves, flashlight, school tuition bills, credit card applications, maps and spare change.

She finally found the registration forms. "Okay, Kelly Haldon, since you really are the owner of the 1984 beauty, why did Rick take your keys?"

"I think it's a training exercise." Kelly shrugged.

Nora folded the paper and replaced it in the glove box. "Training? What is he training you for exactly?" She held up her hand as Kelly started to explain, "Wait, forget I asked. I have a feeling it will be something illegal, and the less I know, the better."

Kelly shook her head. "It's just a training exercise." She kept her eyes on the road. Having Nora in her car was an unexpected pleasure but she wished she'd had time to clean it up a bit. The windows were lined with street grime, the upholstery had miscellaneous food crumbs in the cushion crevices and the smell of her sweaty karate gear in the backseat was embarrassing.

DiBaca's house was located just a short drive through the city, along a quiet street in the hills above the city's fog line. The house had a Mission-style stucco front complete with a guard fence that bordered the road. Kelly parked a block away and stared at the view of the city lights below. The view reminded her of Marcus's neighborhood, only a few miles from here. The dark waters of the San Francisco Bay encircled the city, and the coastal mountains to the north, beyond the Golden Gate, were bathed in blue moonlight.

"You know, I'd rather go for a walk here and enjoy the view than worry about how Jared DiBaca fits in with the investigation." Kelly sighed. "The view is perfect." She glanced at Nora and then at the rearview mirror, pretending to be surveying DiBaca's house. An awkward pause followed and she hoped Nora wasn't put off by her suggestion.

Nora adjusted the rearview mirror, angling it so DiBaca's house was visible. "Well, do you think anyone's home?"

"No." The lights were all out, at least in the front. Maybe he was sleeping. "I'll take a walk around and see what I can find." She reached over Nora's lap and opened the glove box, pulling out her flashlight and gloves.

"I thought we agreed that you weren't going inside."

"I'm only wearing gloves in case my hands get cold." And, Kelly thought, if there was an open window or unlocked door, she might slip inside for a quick peek around. It was better to be prepared for any opportunity than to miss one for lack of gloves. "Here's the screwdriver. If you have to leave me for any reason, just jam it into the ignition and turn the handle."

"This is no getaway car. Why didn't we take mine?" Nora asked, clearly frustrated.

"Because yours is bright red."

Nora shook her head. "I think Rick needs to give you a raise."

"I'd be happy if he just gave me back my keys." She smiled, feeling a warm familiarity with Nora. Her cheeks were blushing again, but it was so dark Nora wouldn't notice.

"Do you have binoculars?" Nora asked.

"You can use the scope." She reached under her seat and found the rectangular case. She took out the scope, focused the lens on DiBaca's mailbox and then handed it to Nora.

"Where'd Rick find this? The Army Surplus store? It looks like this thing has already been through a few battles. And lost."

"Probably," Kelly agreed. "But it works better than you'd think. Try it out."

Nora held up the scope and grinned. "Wow. I feel like a real spy. I kind of like seeing the world in a green light."

Kelly smiled at Nora's excitement. "The green light makes me nauseous after a while, but it's better than squinting in the dark." Rick had just recently given her the scope.

Nora scanned the house as Kelly climbed out of the car. "You don't want to take this with you?"

"No. I'll see everything in closer detail soon enough," Kelly replied. " If you have to leave me here for any reason, just leave. I'll be able to get home on my own." She closed the door and headed toward DiBaca's house. Leaving Nora behind in the safety of her car wasn't easy. Her thoughts were tied to Nora even as she circled the property line of the stucco house. She wanted to impress Nora tonight.

Aside from the porch light, the house was dark. Kelly crouched in the bushes near the front window and cupped her gloved hands against the glass to see inside. A staircase led up from the foyer to a second floor. She couldn't make out anything beyond the foyer. The front door was locked, of course. She headed to the backyard and hopped the fence on the side of the house. No open windows. The back door had a space cut out for a small dog door. Kelly hadn't seen or heard a dog anywhere. Hopefully, there was no ferocious beast awaiting her arrival on the other side of the door. She pushed back the rubber flap and peered inside. The house was quiet, save a murmuring fish tank filter. An aquarium was set up next to a big-screen TV, and a large orange guppy stared at her through the glass under a blue fluorescent haze. No one else was home, apparently. Or else, they were sleeping. Kelly glanced at her wristwatch, half-past ten.

Reaching through the dog door, she unlocked the deadbolt and then squeezed back out of the dog door. The door creaked noisily as it opened to the family room. She switched on the flashlight and took a quick inventory of the room before entering. Secured to the wall behind the aquarium was a large ship's anchor with a military insignia. A black-and-white photo of a young man in a sailor's uniform was displayed on the opposite wall. She couldn't tell how old it was but recognized the sailor's features in other pictures displayed around the room. The other pictures showed an older balding man with a double chin and a potbelly. From the more current shots, Kelly guessed he was in his early seventies and Marcus's sketch of Da' Boss made DiBaca's frozen image eerily familiar. She left the family room and headed toward the front of the house, passing a table in the hallway with a bronzed scale and a framed diploma from Stanford School of Law. A staircase led to the second floor and she glanced into two guest rooms and the master bedroom. DiBaca was married to a woman who liked to wear muumuus. She had several in varying floral patterns and DiBaca had matching button-down Hawaiian shirts. Cruise ship photos of the older couple hung between the *His* and *Hers* bath towels. Kelly searched through DiBaca's drawers, carefully touching everything only with her gloved hands. After finding nothing of interest on the second floor, Kelly went back downstairs.

She stopped in the dining room and, spotting a shelf of photo albums, pulled out an album labeled with the current year. One photo caught her eye. A group of men stationed around a golf cart, each holding his putting clubs as though he meant business, smiled at the camera. The photo's date was imprinted at the corner, June 6th. Kelly recognized DiBaca in the driver's seat of the golf cart with Talcone as his front passenger. Marcus was standing next to Talcone. Two other men were in the picture, one with his back to the camera and one she didn't recognize. The man with the crew cut wasn't there. But why was Marcus?

Suddenly the sound of an automatic garage door opener growled through the house. Kelly pulled out the golf photo and closed the album. She slipped the picture in her pocket and ran to the family room. Slipping out the back door, she stumbled on the patio step and landed in the grass just as the hall lights flickered on.

She crawled against the side of the house and crouched under the window next to the back door as the family room filled with voices. Footsteps approached the back door and Kelly froze as the door opened. No one came out.

"Honey, you forgot to lock the door again!" a woman said.

"No, Marie, I locked it. You must have gone around behind me and unlocked it to let Taffy out."

"No, I didn't. You know, Taffy comes and goes as he pleases." Holding the door open, she called, "Here, kitty, kitty."

A fat orange cat appeared at the edge of the patio. He made his way toward the door and the woman continued beckoning to him. With a glance in Kelly's direction, he stopped and hissed.

"What are you hissing at?" The woman stepped out to the first patio step and glanced toward the bushes.

Kelly closed her eyes and sank back against the wall. *Please, don't see me.*

"Oh, there's nothing there but your own shadow," she scoffed. "Come on, Taffy boy. I'm not going to wait here all night!" She stepped back inside, holding the door wide open and calling repeatedly, "Kitty, kitty."

"Just leave him out," DiBaca said. "We put that dog door in and if he's too lazy to come in for supper, maybe he doesn't need any."

"Jared, this is between Taffy and me," she replied. "You can just stay out of it."

Kelly peeked over the window ledge. DiBaca's back was to her. He slipped off his coat and slung it over the arm of the sofa, then sank down into a leather recliner. She recognized his full face and double chin from the photos. His wife was still holding the door, waiting. The cat refused to cross the threshold while Kelly still lurked at the edge of the patio.

"I'm telling you, Marie, leave him out there. Damn cat needs to work off some of his fat with a night out. Maybe he'll appreciate his milk more."

"You should talk." She laughed. "Honey, I think there may be a rat or something out there. Why don't you go check? Taffy never acts like this."

DiBaca shook his head. He switched on the television. "No, I've had enough of rats for the evening. Leave that fat cat outside." After a moment, he said, "I just can't believe Talcone had the nerve to bring up that Nora Kinley tonight."

The eleven o'clock news was just starting and Kelly wondered if Nora was still waiting for her. She hadn't planned on staying this long.

"Where was Talcone's sidekick tonight?" Marie finally left the door open and leaned against the couch. She glanced at the TV and then at the back door. "Taffy, come in, won't you?" The cat had sat down a few feet from the doorstep, stubbornly refusing to enter and intermittently hissing at Kelly.

"His sidekick? I don't know what you're talking about, Marie."

"Oh, yes you do. What's his name? Kevin, isn't it? He has a good way of shutting Talcone up when he's about to put his foot in his mouth."

"Him? Couldn't make it tonight, I guess," DiBaca answered. "Problem is, Talcone's already too far into this whole thing, and I think he knows it. You know, Marie, if Talcone doesn't keep his nose clean from now on, it'll be trouble for everyone. That lawyer has an investigation going on over Marcus Edwards's death and Talcone wants to stop her. I know he must have had a role in it. Probably only be a matter of time before he's fished out."

Kelly wondered if Marie knew her husband had been inside Marcus's house after the accident. If Marcus's computer recording had been found by the police, DiBaca would have been a suspect in a murder trial.

Marie went to the kitchen. "Wasn't that the same lawyer who was on that military case from the gay group? Didn't somebody get murdered?"

"Uh-huh," DiBaca answered, staring at the television. Kelly wondered if he'd even listened to his wife.

"Well, if I was her, I'd stay away from that gay group. Why is she going after Marcus Edwards's death, anyway?"

"It was their Board of Directors that decided to investigate his death. They left the lawyer in charge."

"How do you know that? Do you have some sort of gay connection?" Marie asked indignantly. Kelly was wondering the same thing.

"Hell, no, Marie. That's just what Talcone told me. He's the one with the connections. Probably knows somebody on their board. Two deaths in one summer, in one gay group, doesn't look too good. That lawyer, Nora Kinley, she sits in on their board meetings, according to Talcone."

Marie was at the bar, fixing two drinks. "Well, I don't see how Talcone knows all that. The only way you have a gay connection is if you're gay, right?"

"There are other ways, my dear." DiBaca laughed. "He's a politician. Anyway, his wife seems content enough."

"Since when are you the judge of contented wives?" She muttered something else that Kelly couldn't hear and in a louder voice said, "I never have liked lawyers. They always cause trouble."

DiBaca nodded in agreement. The TV news broadcaster was introducing the weather forecaster and DiBaca turned up the volume. He thanked Marie as she handed him a cocktail glass of brandy on ice. "Lawyers are like politicians. They're most of them rats."

"What are you talking about? My father was a politician."

DiBaca ignored her and continued, "But a fight among rats is always interesting. For instance, if Nora Kinley knew about Talcone's role in Marcus Edwards's life, I wonder what she'd do." DiBaca paused. A newscaster was giving a report on the military presence in Iraq. When the news clip ended, he turned Marie. "Anyway, I don't want any part in Talcone's schemes. If he starts on Nora Kinley, we'll really have a sticky problem."

Schemes? Kelly wondered what Talcone had planned. She wished she had a tape recorder so Nora could hear this.

"Honey, it's time you retired anyway. You're just supposed to be the acting director of CVA. When is your replacement going to be announced?"

DiBaca shrugged. "I don't know what I'd do with myself if I retired. And the military needs a strong role model in CVA. If we let down our guard, they'll let gays in CVA before long."

"The military can handle them with one less old-timer. And

we're too old to worry about it." She sighed and took a sip of her brandy. "Let them take over the military. Why do you care anyway?" She sank down on the sofa and rested her heels on the coffee table. Glancing at the back door, she called again, "Here, kitty, kitty. Come on in, Taffy."

DiBaca stood up finally and headed for the back door. "All right, silly fat cat, let's see what you're complaining about."

Kelly slipped around to the other side of the house. She decided to add a tape recorder to her list of new spy essentials. Like a camping list—things not to forget when spying: flashlight, gloves and tape recorder. She raced to her car, stealing quick glances over her shoulder at DiBaca's house and the quiet street lined with garbage cans.

Nora slid over into the passenger's seat. "I thought about leaving you."

"Thanks for staying." Kelly smiled. "You won't believe what I just overheard." She started the car and, as soon as they were on their way, began recounting the conversation between Jared and Marie DiBaca. She finished with, "Now, we need to see about Talcone."

Nora shook her head. "To tell you the truth, that was enough excitement for me and I didn't even leave the car. I'm going to leave the rest up to you."

Chapter Ten

The next morning Kelly woke, still fully dressed and with a fuzzy recollection of the past night's adventure. Her alarm was buzzing and as she reached to turn it off, she found the golfing picture from DiBaca's house on the nightstand. She stared at the faces, knowing there was a connection between DiBaca, Talcone and Marcus Edwards that ran deeper than this photo could prove. Who had a motive to murder Marcus? She wanted to go back to the GPAC office and poke around more, suspecting that there were still some missing pieces she could find there.

The smell of waffles filtered into her room. "Alex?" she hollered. "Please tell me you made one of those for me? They smell awesome."

He pushed open her door and grinned. "A whole plate of crisp golden waffles are waiting for you, along with an extra can of Yellow Daisy paint. I thought you could finish up the edge work this weekend."

She rubbed her eyes and glanced at the clock. "Shit, is it really ten o'clock?"

Alex nodded. "Rise and shine, sleepyhead. Your alarm's been going off for the past hour."

"I've got a damn funeral to be at in forty-five minutes." Kelly climbed out of bed and headed into the bathroom. After a quick shower, she dressed in black slacks and a maroon blouse, the closest thing she could find to classy somber attire.

She entered the kitchen and Alex handed her a banana and a plate of waffles already lathered in maple syrup and butter. "Thanks. By the way, I promise I'll finish touching up the edges of the house paint tomorrow."

"Whose funeral?" Alex asked. "And don't get syrup on your blouse. You look nice, for once."

She caught the syrup dripping off her fork with her tongue. "This tastes great. The funeral is for some guy I don't really know. Friend of a friend—it's a long story. What time is it?"

"A quarter after."

She checked her watch to confirm the time. "Shit. I gotta go." She dropped the plate on the table after another bite and hugged Alex. "Thanks for breakfast. Sorry I have to run out on you."

"Whatever—women leave me all the time."

"No," she corrected. "You usually kick them out."

He winked at her. "Okay, you're right about that. Want to go surfing with me tomorrow? You could skip the house-painting."

She paused, holding the garage door open, "Maybe. I'll see how today goes. I'm having a crazy week and painting might be just enough excitement for me." To say the least, she thought as the door slammed behind her.

The funeral service had ended by the time Kelly arrived, but she stayed for the casket lowering. She took a good look at the crowd gathered around the casket. John Rainsfeld, the secretary from GPAC, and Nora were in the front row, near an older woman who appeared be Marcus's aunt. There were several military personnel in attendance and the dynamic between the GPAC group and the uniforms was interesting. For the most part, the military showed no emotions at all, while several on the GPAC side were freely crying. Kelly did not recognize most of the other mourners, fifteen in all. Rick wasn't there. He'd mentioned that he had a meeting that morning with the client from the Dakota Insurance case to finalize the investigation. Apparently he couldn't cancel. Just as the handfuls of dirt were dropped on the casket, she turned away, not ready to approach anyone at a funeral for details about the dead man.

Kelly headed toward the cemetery parking lot and noticed a black sedan parked several spaces ahead of her car. She cut between the line of trees near the lot to avoid the black sedan, spotting a man with a hat in the driver's seat. His narrow face and deep-set dark eyes looked familiar, and she recognized him as the man with the crew cut from Marcus's camera recording. She also recognized the license plate. This was the same black sedan that had followed her yesterday. Unfortunately, she hadn't talked to Gina yet to track down the registration. Who was this guy? If he was truly the same guy that had driven the SUV and run Marcus's Miata off the road, how could he dare to come to the funeral? Maybe he too had come to see who Marcus's friends were.

When the other mourners left the grave site and headed toward their cars, she slipped alongside the group and made her way to her car without, she hoped, attracting the notice of the man in the black sedan. The black sedan pulled out of the cemetery as soon as she started her car. Kelly followed another car from the parking lot until she reached the main road and identified the black sedan again.

The black sedan pulled onto the freeway and Kelly drove behind him, carefully keeping at least one car between them the entire route. Her phone rang and she noticed Rick's number.

"Where are you?"

"I'm following that guy with the crew cut—the one who was in Marcus's apartment. He came to the funeral."

Rick was silent, for once.

"Hello?" she asked after a moment, thinking that their phones had lost the connection.

"I'm here," he answered. "Are you sure it's the same guy that was in Marcus's apartment?"

"Yes."

"Does he know you're following him?"

"I don't think so." Kelly eyed the truck in front of her. It was a Toyota pickup and the black sedan was mostly obscured by the truck's border. "I'll just see where he's going. Hey, Rick, can you check a license plate registration?" She repeated the license number from the black sedan that she had memorized now.

"Okay, I'll look this up. Be careful. I have a feeling this guy isn't someone you want to piss off."

The line went dead with this last comment from Rick. Kelly stared at the phone and considered calling him back. She suspected that he knew something about the crew cut and wasn't telling her. Just then, the black sedan pulled off the freeway, taking the exit toward the Embarcadero. Kelly followed him through the city streets with the sunshade flipped down and her seat set as low as it could go, hoping to avoid his eyes. Traffic was light and she had no problem keeping up with him. After a few minutes, she started to wonder if he was making the trail too easy. Did he know she was following him? Just then, he hit his brakes and pulled in the driveway of a very dilapidated Victorian. Kelly swerved around him and continued down the road. She pulled into a gas station, a half a mile from where the sedan had parked. After filling her tank, she parked behind the station and walked down the block toward the dilapidated Victorian. The black sedan was still parked in the driveway but the driver was nowhere to be seen. Was this where he lived or was she walking into a trap? She glanced at the house number and felt a surge of adrenaline. Marcus had starred three addresses in his book and Kelly recognized this one. The address had been listed under the name Leo Rausche.

Just then, the front door of the house opened and the man with the crew cut came out carrying a gym bag over his shoulder. He jogged down the walkway to his car and Kelly quickly turned the opposite direction, hoping he hadn't seen her. Fortunately, she wasn't alone on the sidewalk. Four kids were kicking a soccer ball against the side of a brick building and one boy sat on the bus stop bench etching something into the wood.

"Hello," she said, approaching the boy on the bench. "Do you know when the next bus comes?"

He shook his head. "It's Saturday. No buses."

"Oh." She glanced past the boy and saw that the sedan was backing out of the driveway now.

"Mean Mister Pigeon-Eater," the boy said, nodding at the car. "We don't mess with him since he shoots the pigeons."

"He shoots pigeons?" Kelly asked with disbelief.

"And my momma says he'd shoot kids too, if they pooped on his house." The boy grinned. His front teeth were missing but his smile was otherwise perfect.

"Does he live alone?"

"Nope. He lives with his momma. Old Lady Mrs. Rausche."

By now the black sedan had driven off in the other direction. "Is his name Leo Rausche?"

"We just call him Mean Mister Pigeon-Eater all the time."

Kelly thanked the boy and then made her way toward Rausche's house. He had earned the recognition of the neighborhood children and she wasn't eager to have any more dealings with him, yet she was still curious. A sign for *The Rausche Family* hung on the front door. Directly under the welcome sign was a sticker with a picture of an attack dog and a little note warning against solicitors.

Kelly waited near the mailbox, debating whether she should walk the perimeter of the narrow lot. She glanced down the street at the children with the soccer ball and the boy on the bench. An older woman was pushing a shopping cart on the sidewalk past the soccer game, moving slowly and with the obvious effort of arthritic joints. Her gray hair was done up in a puffy cloud pinned at the top of her head and the "do" added several inches to her thin, stooped frame. When the old woman was nearly on top of Kelly, she pulled the cart to a stop.

"And you must be from the Women's Catholic Society. I had a message that they were sending someone round."

"Mrs. Rausche?" Kelly asked, extending her hand.

"Yes." The old woman shook her hand and smiled. "You're very young to be working with the Society." She sighed. "But maybe that's just my old eyes. Seems that the young women look younger every day." Her eyes were steel blue, with a red tinge at the edge of the irises. Smile lines creased the corners. "You're not married yet, are you?"

Kelly shook her head. "Not yet." She wasn't going to try and pretend to be married without a ring on her hand. "I was told you might have some chores that I could help you with today." Fortunately, her mother had worked with the Women's Catholic Society for years and she knew that volunteers visited the elderly to help with housework and to socialize. "When no one answered the door, I thought you weren't at home and was about to leave. It's lucky I met you here." Very lucky, she thought.

"Yes, well, I was just out shopping, as you can see. I don't suppose you'd be able to help me. I have all of these groceries and I can't always push the cart up the steps." She pointed toward the flight of stairs leading to the front door of the house. "Could you lift them for me? You're such a sweet dear. I do appreciate it."

Kelly was taken back by the old woman's pleasant warm nature. She couldn't believe that this woman had raised a man suspected of murder. "I'd be happy to help, Mrs. Rausche."

"Oh, you don't have to call me Mrs. Rausche," she chided. "Claire will do just fine."

Kelly smiled. She avoided giving her own name and the woman didn't press her for it. She took two of the bags from the cart and followed Claire up the flight of stairs to the front door. They went through the narrow hallway to the back of the house where the kitchen was located. An old terrier lifted his head to eye Kelly as she entered the kitchen. He didn't stand up until Claire presented a bone to him. After seizing the bone from her, he settled back on his rug and started to lick it.

"He's not much of a guard dog anymore. But you should have seen him in his prime—used to get the mailman running for his dear life." She laughed. "Oh, I think I'll just sit down for a moment and let you bring the rest of the groceries inside. You don't mind, do you?"

"Not at all." Kelly set the two bags on the counter. "What else would you like help with today?"

"If you don't mind too much, the bathrooms need a good cleaning. There's a mop in the pantry and cleaning supplies under the sink." She pointed these out to Kelly. "Then perhaps we might have a game of cards?"

Kelly smiled. "Perfect. I'll just finish with the groceries first."

"You're very sweet." She patted Kelly's hand. A thin gold band encircled her left ring finger. Kelly noticed a small ruby inset in the band.

"That's very pretty. Unusual." She pointed to the ring.

"Oh yes, I suppose it is now. When I was married, nearly sixty years ago, rings like this were more common." She paused, as though a sixty-year-old memory had been triggered with the mention of the ring. "Anyway, I always thought diamonds were too plain. But you know, now they're the style."

"I like rubies."

"The fire of the heart." Claire's eyes seemed to sparkle as she said this. She twisted the ring on her finger and giggled. "That's what my husband used to say about them . . . I miss him now. He died ten years ago, this October."

"I bet he was a good man."

"Oh, yes and no, yes and no. But I miss him." She patted Kelly's hand again. "Now, don't you worry about getting married too soon. I know that's what all the young women think about—getting settled and having a ring to show off." She shook her head. "But you take your time and don't rush in with the men. Someone as pretty as you can have her pick."

Claire headed into the living room adjoining the kitchen and turned on the television. Kelly went outside to retrieve the rest of the groceries. She pushed the shopping cart behind the fence and carried the last two bags into the kitchen. The terrier didn't look up from his bone when she entered. Claire had tuned in to the afternoon news and seemed intent on listening to the weatherman's report. Kelly began putting the groceries away, trying to decide which items needed to be refrigerated and leaving the dry goods out on the counter for someone to put away later. By the time she finished in the kitchen, Claire had fallen asleep on the sofa.

"Claire?" Kelly called. "I'm going to clean the bathrooms now."

The terrier looked up from his bone to eye Kelly, but Claire didn't seem to hear her. With the mop and cleaning supplies in hand, she decided to investigate the rest of the house under the pretext of finding the bathrooms. She went through the dining room and down the hallway, searching the front sitting room. She found nothing of interest and started cleaning the hall bathroom. She returned to the kitchen to grab a clean rag and heard the old woman snoring. The dog was still licking his bone and didn't even growl at her approach. A Siamese cat appeared at the back door, scratching to be let in. Kelly opened the door, noting that Claire still didn't wake at this sound. The cat rubbed between her legs and purred loudly. Kelly abandoned the cleaning supplies in the kitchen and headed upstairs to see if she could find any clues to Mr. Rausche. By the time she reached the top of the stairwell, the cat's meows drowned out the newsman's booming voice as the program returned from a commercial break. She hoped the old woman would continue to sleep. The mewling Siamese led the way through the upstairs hall. Four closed doors faced the landing.

"Well, what now?" she asked softly.

As if in answer, the Siamese walked up to the first door and reached up for the handle. Of course she couldn't open it and was frustrated after one attempt. She sat down and stared at Kelly, then meowed again. Kelly put her ear up to the door, listening. No sound. She grasped the handle and then realized she wasn't wearing her gloves. It was too late anyway. Her fingerprints were all over the house. With a quick glance at the stairwell, she opened the door. The room had a musty smell and the curtains were drawn. She turned on the light switch. A flowery quilt was draped over the bed and a pair of house slippers were waiting on the Oriental rug. She guessed this was Claire's room.

After leaving the old woman's bedroom, she tried the next room that the cat walked up to. Kelly gasped softly as she stared inside. The first image to greet her was an American flag hanging above an arsenal of three or four guns mounted on the back wall. One shotgun was positioned just above the doorway and the strap of the gun swung at her face as she pushed the door open. The barrel of the gun had been sawed off to create a threatening stubby appearance. This room was in stark contrast to the rest of the house and smelled like dirty laundry. Kelly hesitated, feeling her heart thumping in her chest. She could hear the faint sounds of the television news still and tried to gather her courage. Claire wouldn't mind if she took a look around here.

She entered the room, careful not to disturb the clothing that was strewn across the floor. Behind the closet door she found two more guns amidst unsorted laundry and boxes of junk. She closed the door and backed away cautiously. Piles of bills were littered on the nightstand and she sifted through the contents of the top drawer. Nothing of interest, save a vintage copy of a *Mad* comics magazine. In the second drawer, she found a manila envelope. She started to open the envelope when the sound of a door slamming made her pause.

A man's voice boomed over the noise of the television broadcast. "Mother? Why'd you leave the door unlocked again?"

Claire didn't answer, or at least Kelly couldn't hear response. She quickly folded the manila envelope and tucked it down the back of her pants, hoping her shirt would conceal the bulge. With the guns seeming to attack her from every angle, she quickly escaped the room. As she closed the door, the cat meowed again.

One of the steps on the staircase creaked. Kelly opened the door to the third room on the second floor. It was a bathroom. She slipped inside and closed the door as quietly as possible. There was a window above the toilet and a fire escape just outside.

She locked the bathroom door and climbed up on the toilet. The window latch took some time to loosen and before she had it open, she heard the door handle click. Someone was trying to come in. The latch gave way and she started to climb out of the window as something heavy struck the bathroom door. The wall shook with the effort of the lock to resist entry.

She squeezed out of the window, trying to concentrate on her footing as she slid onto the fire escape landing. The bathroom door burst open just as she stepped onto the fire escape ladder. Rausche's eyes locked on hers through the narrow bathroom window. Her chest tightened as he stared her down, recognizing her as she recognized him. Leo Rausche, the man who shot pigeons and had probably run Marcus off the road, was glaring daggers at her. She turned from his sight and scrambled down the ladder. As soon as she was on the ground, she ran toward the side gate. As she reached to unlock the gate a hand grabbed her shoulder.

She spun around to face Rausche. In the same moment, he swung the barrel of the sawed-off shotgun at her head. Kelly lunged to the side and ducked as the shotgun whistled in the air over her head. He swung at her again, missed and knocked into the fence with enough force to split the weathered wood. Kelly grabbed at the fence latch again and the gate sprang open. She took one step and then dropped to the ground, hearing the attack before she could see it. Rausche had slashed at her, swinging the shotgun like a baseball bat. The gun swung over her and as he tried to recover, she lunged at him, wrapping her arm around his forearm, locking his elbow joint. He struggled against the hold and she jumped in the air and then hung on his arm, sending her full weight into the arm lock. She heard his elbow snap as the joint dislocated, and he screamed in pain. As soon as Kelly let go, he swung at her again with the shotgun in his good arm. His narrow face contorted with a horrible grimace of pain and seething anger.

Kelly caught the barrel of the gun and twisted her arm to the side. Rausche's wrist contorted in a strange angle and he cried out again, finally releasing the gun. She gripped the gun tightly and tore off down the street, slamming the fence gate closed behind her. All the dogs in the neighborhood seemed to be barking and their noise followed her down the street.

Kelly raced down the three blocks to her car. She threw the gun on the passenger seat and slid the screwdriver into the ignition, praying the car wouldn't take this moment to give her trouble. The engine gurgled happily and the VW lurched forward as she hit the gas.

She didn't consider where she was driving—it was just a matter of speed. Her heart was still pounding in her chest and no number of slow, deep breaths would calm her pulse. As she neared the entrance to the Bay Bridge highway, a patrol car switched on its lights to signal her to pull over. She had just rolled through a stop sign. She knew she should have stopped and cursed at her own stupidity. It was impossible to find a cop in the city when you wanted one because they were all too busy watching for California curtseys at the stop signs. She pulled to the side of the road and parked, then realized the shotgun was in plain view. She stared at the gun. It felt like a poisonous snake about to lunge for her throat. She shifted in her seat and watched the officer in her rearview mirror. When he lowered his head, she slid the shotgun under the passenger seat. The gun disappeared.

A blaring sound filled the Volkswagen as the cop aimed his speaker at her car. He announced, "Please remain seated. Do not attempt to exit your vehicle."

Kelly nodded and put her hands on the steering wheel, in clear view. Hopefully, she could just take the ticket and he'd let her go.

A burly officer approached her car. He eyed her through the window and then tapped on the glass. Kelly dutifully rolled the window down and waited as he scanned the interior of her car.

"Do you know why I pulled you over?"

She nodded. "I don't think I came to a complete stop at the stop sign."

He smiled. "You didn't even tap your brakes." A loud rash of static interrupted their conversation. The officer stepped away and held the radio up to his ear. He listened intently to what sounded like turkey gobbles to Kelly's inexperienced ears and then responded that he was on his way. He glanced at Kelly. "God, I hate Saturdays. It's not even dark yet and the crazy people are already out." He shook his head. "Okay, you're off the hook this time. I have to take this call." He paused to draw a line through the ticket that he had started to write. "Watch the stop signs next time."

Kelly nodded. She felt nauseous.

The officer turned and started to walk away, then turned back. "By the way, I'll double your ticket if I catch you again."

Somehow, she managed to drive herself back to Ashton. She couldn't remember the trip, but it didn't matter. She reached Alex's about seven and breathed a long sigh of relief. This was her base and she was safe now. She didn't want to touch the shotgun. She left it under the passenger seat, hoping that maybe it would disappear overnight if she left her car unlocked.

Alex was asleep on the sofa in the family room. She pushed his feet off the cushions and sat down next to him. He grumbled softly and tried to fall back asleep in the new position. She shook his shoulder to wake him.

"Hey, bro. Wake up."

Alex rubbed his eyes and yawned. "What's wrong?"

She stared at him for a moment, hating to admit the trouble she'd gotten herself into. "Nothing's wrong," she lied. "I just wanted to say that I got home okay."

"Why wouldn't you?"

She shrugged. "I don't know. Things happen."

Alex nodded. He closed his eyes again. In a few minutes he had fallen back asleep. He never snored. Kelly wanted to wake him again but instead just watched him sleep, his regular, slow breathing finally starting to ease the edge of insanity she'd battled since she'd stared at Rausche through the bathroom window.

To get her mind off this, she listened to the messages on her cell phone. The first missed call was from Gina, upset about their change of plans. Gina wondered if she would flake on the Sunday BBQ as well. Tasha and Beth were coming, Gina reminded her. Kelly deleted this message and listened to the second call. Nora had rung sometime after the funeral. She needed to talk about a letter she'd received and asked Kelly to call her as soon as possible.

She dialed Nora's number. "Hi. Sorry I didn't call sooner. What's up?"

"I received another letter. This one was left under my doormat. And there's a car that's followed me home twice now." Nora sighed. "I was wondering if you've been in touch with Rick."

"Not recently. I just got home," Kelly admitted.

"You sound beat."

"I had a hell of an afternoon." She didn't want to remember anything she'd seen, but every image was as garish as a frozen image on a television screen. "So, when did you get the second letter?"

"Today, just after the funeral. The creepy thing is, I was inside my house the whole time and had stupidly left the front door unlocked, don't ask me why. I never do that. Whoever it was could have easily walked right in on me."

"Did you try calling Rick?" Kelly asked. She didn't know what to say about the letter. Maybe Nora should send a copy of this one to the police also.

"Yes. I got a message that he was out of town for the weekend."

Kelly frowned. He'd just called her after the funeral. Maybe his meeting with the Dakota client had been out of the area. "Are you alone now?"

Nora didn't answer.

"I mean, I can keep you company if you want . . ."

128

"No, I'm fine. Just a little unnerved and Terrance, my fiancé, is in L.A. on a business trip." Nora sounded unperturbed and her usual confident tone had returned, but Kelly thought it might be an act. "But I'll be fine. The door is locked and deadbolted now."

"Okay. By the way, I have a few things I need to fill you in on. When can you meet again?"

"Monday," Nora suggested. "If the evening works in your schedule."

Kelly agreed and hung up the phone. Alex shifted in the sofa as Kelly stood up. She knew he was sleeping in the family room because it was the coolest room in the house. The heat in the bedrooms was stifling. She opened the windows reluctantly, nervous that Rausche might know where she lived and come looking for her now. She thought of him walking the perimeter of Alex's house just like she'd walked around DiBaca's house, searching for an easy entry point.

As she started to change her clothes, Kelly remembered the folded manila envelope stuck down her pants. She opened it and pulled out a snapshot. Nora, John and Marcus were standing together outside the GPAC office building. An orange grease pencil mark encircled each of the three faces. Marcus's face was crossed out. Kelly shivered. She hated to see the circle around Nora's face. The photo was taken only three weeks ago, according to the date stamped on the print.

Why did Rausche have this? Kelly caught her breath as she glanced at the backside of the photo. Someone had written: "One down . . . I know I can count on you to make sure this is finished. RT."

RT—as in Robert Talcone? Kelly wondered. Had Talcone given this photo to Rausche? Maybe Talcone was using Rausche to intimidate Nora now. But who was Rausche exactly?

The faces in the snapshot seemed to stare at her as she finished changing her clothes. She slid the photo back in the envelope and hid it in the most logical spot, between the mattress and the box spring of her bed. She called Gina then to tell her she was on her way over.

"Hi," Gina began. "So, how was Nora last night?"

"We just had a meeting. It was fine."

"Fine?" Gina's voice was laced with sarcasm. "She was fine? Or was it the meeting that was fine?"

"Look, Gina, can we just let it go for now? I've had a rough day."

"Whatever." She paused. "Kelly, I know you're a player. I'm not going to be played."

"I'm not a player," Kelly argued.

"You were dating someone else when you seduced me. Give it up." Gina laughed. Her voice was edgy. "So, who's the next girl in line?"

"No one." Kelly caught herself thinking about Nora. There was no possibility of any relationship with Nora beyond work. She was straight and engaged to Terrance. Kelly had a crush on her but that was all there was to their relationship. Just then the phone beeped to signal another call. "Gina, I'm not messing around with anyone."

"Are you going to answer your phone or just let that other caller wait? Is it your other girlfriend?"

"I think we should talk about things." Kelly paused, trying to ignore the intermittent beeping of her phone. The caller ID showed Nora's name. "I think we should talk in person."

Gina sighed. "You know, the only time someone says that they need to talk in person is if there's a problem."

"You know what? Maybe we should just take a night off." Kelly regretted this as soon as she said it. An uncomfortable silence followed. She hadn't done anything wrong, yet she didn't blame Gina for her suspicions. "I'm sorry. Forget I said that. I'm on my way over now."

Gina hung up without responding. Kelly quickly dialed Nora's phone number. The line was busy. She then dialed Rick's number and got a second busy signal. Maybe they were talking to each other, she reasoned. She drove to Gina's house and parked but didn't get out of the car. Her attention was drawn to each car that turned down Gina's street. No black sedans with tinted windows appeared. Yet she couldn't relax. She tried Nora's number again and got the same busy signal. Ten minutes later she finally climbed out of her car.

Gina's porch light was out and Kelly waited in the darkness, half expecting no answer to her knock. She watched the street and the few cars that passed, wondering where Leo Rausche and his black sedan were tonight. The door finally opened and Gina shook her head. "Why are you here? I thought this was our night off." She closed the door.

Kelly knocked again. "Please, Gina, just open up so I can say I'm sorry." She waited for some response but there was only silence on the other side of the door. She continued, knowing that Gina would be listening, "I'm sorry. I know I should tell you what's going on, but Rick said I can't talk about it."

Gina opened the door. "Why not? Kelly, we've already been through this. You told me you trusted me. So, tell me what's going on. And what happened to you? There's a bruise on your cheekbone."

"Let's forget about Rick and his little investigation for the night. There's no other woman and I'm not playing around. I've just been busy."

"How about twenty questions? Then you won't actually have to tell me anything about the investigation beyond yes, or no."

"No," Kelly said. "I can't talk about it at all. I'm sorry." She hoped Gina would understand.

"Why don't you trust me?" Gina challenged, waiting for an answer, her hands on her hips. "Do you trust me? I won't talk to anyone else. I just want to know what's going on."

"It's not about trust." Kelly knew she was too tired to argue. "It's just a job and I need the money. We can talk about anything else."

"You didn't answer my question," Gina said softly. She touched

131

Kelly's cheek in a light caress. She turned Kelly's chin to the side and touched the side of her neck. "Are you okay? There's a mark on your neck, too."

"I'm fine." Kelly felt the spot Gina had touched. It was painful but she hadn't noticed it until now.

"One of your earrings is missing." Gina tugged on her earlobe.

Kelly felt her earlobes. Usually she had hoops in each ear and now there was only one hoop on the right side. "Rough day at karate."

"You don't go to the karate dojo on Saturdays," Gina argued.

The missing earring was small and silver. It would slip into a crack or under a rug unnoticed. Hopefully, Kelly thought. "I must have lost it during my sparring class last night." She always took her earrings off before sparring. Kevin used to tease her for trying to act feminine with the little silver hoops. She knew that she had had both hoops this morning. Most likely the missing earring was due to her fight with Rausche.

Gina nodded. "You're lying."

Kelly glanced up, surprised by her quick assessment. She hadn't thought she was that easy to read. "You're right, I'm lying about the earring."

"And you're not going to tell me, I suppose." Gina didn't wait for an answer. She turned and went down the hall to the kitchen. Kelly heard the water faucet and the clang of a metal pot.

She followed Gina into the kitchen, set her wallet and phone on the counter and sank down into one of the chairs at the table. There was a plate of cheese and crackers, and she helped herself. She watched as Gina fished out two tea bags from a box of assorted teas and dropped the bags into two mugs. They waited for the water to boil, neither of them speaking. Gina hadn't asked her which tea flavor she wanted. She didn't care anyway. She wanted to tell Gina everything about the investigation but kept hearing Rick's warning in her head. Gina might leak information without even realizing it—she might talk with some friends at the station and accidentally mention something. You never knew who was listening. Rick was probably right about cops.

"Were you with Nora all last night?" Gina raised her eyebrows. Kelly shook her head. "I slept in my own bed. And Gina, don't give me that look."

Feigning innocence, Gina replied, "What look?"

"That *I caught you* look. Nothing is going on between Nora and me. She's ten years older than me, a lawyer and as I told you before, straight." Kelly stopped herself from adding, "And I'd never have a chance with her." Instead, she said, "Nothing is going on."

"Maybe not yet." Gina pulled her tea bag out of the mug. She took a sip and then grimaced.

"Careful, it's hot," Kelly said with a smile.

"Thanks," Gina replied sarcastically. "Your warning's a little late."

Kelly blew on her tea. "Gina, I really want to tell you about Marcus's case. I feel like I need to talk to someone."

Gina shrugged. "So tell me. You know I won't tell anyone else."

"I know, but . . ." Kelly shook her head. She felt Gina staring at her. "What can I say?"

"Everything," Gina answered with confidence.

Kelly couldn't say anything. She couldn't tell her where she'd lost the earring or what she'd done over the past day. Rick was right, she couldn't say anything even if she trusted Gina completely. She sighed. "I can't."

Gina shook her head. She set her tea down and stood up. "Want to try out my new hammock? It's too warm for hot tea."

Kelly nodded. "I didn't realize that you even got a hammock."

"I know. You haven't been paying attention to things lately."

The comment stung but Kelly tried to ignore it. "I'd love to try the hammock. It's a beautiful night." She slipped past Gina and headed out to the small backyard.

Gina followed her outside and pointed to the corner of the yard where the hammock was posted.

"It'd be nice to make out under the stars," Kelly said as she swung the hammock a few times. She climbed up on it and grabbed Gina's hand as she lost her balance and fell into the hammock.

Kelly's startled gasp loosened Gina's tight lips. She laughed and climbed on the hammock, straddling Kelly. "You're not very graceful. I thought you were some wonder-karate-kid. Don't they teach you balance?"

"Yes. But apparently I lose my footing when you're near me," Kelly teased. She grabbed Gina and wrestled her way on top. The hammock swayed back and forth, threatening to tip them both out. As soon as she had Gina underneath her, Kelly paused to kiss her. "Okay, enough fighting."

"Oh, I see, as soon as you win one round you think the game is over? Oh no, chica, this fight's just—"

Kelly kissed her again, stopping Gina mid-sentence. She pressed her tongue lightly into Gina's mouth then moved lower to kiss her neck. Kelly unbuttoned Gina's shirt and ran her hands over the black silk bra. She felt Gina's nipples grow firm with her touch.

Gina rubbed Kelly's shoulders. "Your muscles are tight," she observed, pressing her fingers on the knots.

"Too many push-ups in karate, I guess," Kelly replied. And narrow escapes through other people's houses, she told herself. She kissed Gina's belly as she unzipped her shorts. Kelly wanted to feel Gina's naked body. There was too much material between their bodies. Gina grabbed Kelly's hands to stop her as she started to pull off her shorts.

"Are you crazy, chica?"

"What's wrong?" Kelly asked.

Gina pointed at the two houses that overlooked her patio backyard. "I can't strip here. We'd have too many witnesses."

"Live on the edge." Kelly laughed. Gina was being overly cautious. "Hell, this is Ashton. All of your neighbors were asleep hours ago. No one will see us. And who'd be watching your backyard?"

"You never know. Someone could be watching *you*."

Kelly shook her head, then thought of Leo Rausche and his black sedan. She shook her head again. "Relax. No one is watching, not here." She slipped off her shirt. "And if they are, they'll find me with a cop and think I must be a law-abiding citizen."

Gina shook her head but didn't resist when Kelly tugged off her shorts. She only smiled mischievously as Kelly slipped off her bra. When they were both naked they relaxed back in the hammock. Gina drew circles on Kelly's belly and stared up at the stars. Kelly wanted to know what she was thinking about but stopped herself each time she started to ask. Gina shifted onto one elbow and grabbed Kelly's hand.

"What?" Kelly asked.

Gina slipped Kelly's finger into her mouth and pulled it out slowly. She shifted onto her back, rocking the hammock, and then lowered Kelly's hand between her legs.

Kelly smiled. "Nice hint." She parted the wet folds and started to stroke slow circles, dipping into the warm center each time she reached the end of her circle. She climbed over Gina, straddling her, while she continued to play on the wet lips. She kissed Gina's lips, then tugged on her earlobe with her teeth as her hand continued circling.

Gina moaned softly and squeezed Kelly's breast in her hand. She sucked the nipple between her lips and flicked her tongue on the firm tip.

Kelly's hand was circling faster. She thrust two fingers inside each time she finished a circle. Gina's clit was swollen with the attention and her hips pushed up toward Kelly's wrist with every thrust. The hammock rocked rhythmically. Kelly's bare feet dangled off the rope edge, one foot on each side of the hammock, and her hand rocked in and out of Gina's body. She had to concentrate to keep up with the spasms of Gina's pleasure and to keep from tumbling off. Gina's fingers gripped the rope, her knuckles turning pale as she squeezed tightly.

Kelly shoved her two fingers inside then lowered her head to lick Gina's swollen clit. She tasted the salty-sweet liquid and stroked Gina's clit with a gently increasing pressure. She loved Gina's taste and the soft murmurs that escaped her lips each time

Kelly pushed her fingers in. Kelly increased her rhythm, pushing deeper.

Gina cried out, then shuddered and relaxed. A moment later, her thighs tensed, squeezing Kelly's hand in a viselike grip, and she shuddered once more. Kelly pulled her hand out slowly, keeping her thumb on Gina's clit. She hugged her and relaxed, letting her weight displace the hammock mesh.

Suddenly the sound of sprinklers shattered the quiet backyard. Gina opened her eyes and shot an accusatory look at the sprinkler heads that had just popped up. The water started to coat the lavender bushes lining the back fence, as well as at the base of the hammock. Kelly slipped out of the hammock as soon as the cold sprinkler water hit her skin. Gina snatched up their clothes strewn about the wet grass and followed her back to the house.

As soon as they entered the kitchen, Gina tossed the clothes in a heap on the table. She arched her eyebrows at Kelly and then grabbed her around the waist. Kelly didn't resist as she pushed her against the fridge and kissed her.

"My turn," Gina whispered. Her hand trailed over Kelly's breasts, slipping down her belly and reaching under the line of hair between her legs. She pushed inside the moist skin. "Oh, look." She paused to pull her finger out and tasted the fingertip. "Already wet and waiting for me. So, what are you thinking about, chica?"

"Must have been the sprinklers," Kelly replied sheepishly.

Gina nodded then thrust her fingers inside again. She pushed her hips against Kelly, pinning her to the cool refrigerator door. Kelly gripped its handle and groaned as Gina pushed into her with more force. She loved the muscles on Gina's arms and shoulders that flexed with each movement of her hand. Kelly watched as Gina pulled out slightly then eased four fingers back inside, her thumb still strumming her clit.

"How do you like that?" Gina asked.

Kelly nodded. "It's all right." She was barely able to control the tremors rushing through her.

"A little more?" Gina didn't wait for an answer. She pushed her four fingers deeper and turned her wrist.

Kelly felt her body tighten around Gina's fingers as she climaxed. She squeezed her thighs to hold Gina's arm in place. Her body tingled with a wave of nerves as her wetness seeped out over Gina's fingers.

Gina smiled as Kelly opened her eyes. She kissed her, still keeping her hand inside. "Tell me what else I can do to you, chica."

Kelly pressed her finger against Gina's mouth. She didn't want to talk. Gina started to pull her hand out. She moaned once, then grabbed Gina's wrist to keep her from moving. "Don't," she whispered. She let go of Gina's wrist to caress her face. Just as she relaxed her thighs to free Gina's hand, she felt Gina's thumb press hard on her clit, sending her to a second wave of release. Kelly gripped Gina's shoulders. Gina pushed her weight on her, pinning her again on the door, and slowly pulled out her hand.

"Well, that was fun." Gina coyly turned and walked toward the living room. Over her shoulder she said, "I've never made out in the kitchen before. What room should we try next?"

Chapter Eleven

Gina's alarm clock rang at six o'clock on Sunday morning. Kelly slammed her hand on the bell, nearly breaking it. She climbed out of bed ignoring Gina's sleepy grumbles of disapproval, and dressed in the dark. She grabbed a yogurt, and left a note for Gina in the kitchen to explain why she had left: "Karate lesson at 7 a.m. Haven't forgotten about the BBQ. Maybe we can play with the hammock again?"

Sam was waiting in his office when she arrived at the dojo. He took one look at her disheveled appearance and shook his head. "Hurry up and get your gi on. We're going to practice firearms defense tactics this morning and I hope you had a good night's sleep."

"Of course," Kelly replied, smiling. Her sleep had been good, though not long. She changed into her karate uniform, noting that the bag from Marcus's apartment was still safely hidden in her locker. She had brought the manila envelope from Rausche's house to add to her stash. After snapping the lock, she headed out to the mat to stretch. Before long, Sam came out of the office. He began the lesson with the usual bow and then told Kelly to stand in front position with her eyes closed. As he talked about guns, he circled around her place on the mat, clicking a metallic lever repeatedly.

Just when Kelly had started to relax, his hand landed on her shoulder and her muscles immediately tensed. Rausche's fingers seemed to be gripping her again. Sam had the barrel of the gun against her lower back and his hand on her neck. "Don't tense up when you feel the gun on your back. And keep your eyes closed until I tell you to move."

Although she knew Sam didn't have a real gun, the feel of the metal against her spine sent a shiver through her body. She exhaled and then listened to Sam's breathing. "As soon as you feel my hand shift, you need to react."

Kelly spun to the side and wrapped Sam's arm, fighting to keep the gun pointed away from her. He overpowered her and twisted out of the arm lock, then aimed the gun at her. "Just watch the red laser." He pointed the gun at the back wall and pulled the trigger. A red laser appeared on the wall. "All you have to do is keep moving."

"I can do that." She lunged to the side as Sam redirected the laser on her. She smiled. "You know, picturing you with a real gun is frightening."

"Yeah, I decided to use the laser gun when Rick told me to take it easy on you. He said you were going to have a long day."

Before she could consider what Rick must have had in mind, Sam had the laser on her leg. "Damn," she swore softly, jumping to the side.

She paid attention, as close as she could, to every movement Sam made with the gun. The last thing she wanted to do was think about another gun after the fight with Rausche yesterday. But this wasn't a real gun. She was nonetheless fighting a gnawing fear as she waited for the red laser light to settle on her.

After several hits, she stopped in the middle of the room and bowed to Sam. "I give up. You win."

"Why are you giving up? It's just like a game of laser tag," Sam explained. "Are you injured?"

"No. But I'm losing. If that was a real gun, you would have killed me a half-dozen times."

"This is only a game. There's one gun and one target." He paused and aimed the gun directly at her. The red light was blinding. "If you're not injured, you never stop to let someone with a gun set their sight on you."

She nodded. She'd always been afraid of guns and didn't even like water guns. Unfortunately, her experience with Rausche had left her even more wary of firearms, and now there was a sawed-off shotgun in her car, the last thing she wanted to be packing. She focused her attention on Sam and after an hour of training, he seemed sufficiently pleased at her ability to avoid the red laser. They switched from gun defense to hand combat drills. At the end of two hours he finally sent her on a run. Maybe he could tell she was already exhausted because he decided not to wait for her return. "Lock up the dojo when you get back," he advised.

Rick was waiting for her when she arrived back at the dojo. She fished a towel out of her sparring bag and wiped off her sweat. "Hey, it's my Secret Agent Man."

"At your service." Rick winked. "So, how was your bout with Sam and his little laser gun this morning?"

"I survived." She filled a Dixie cup at the water cooler and sucked it down. Her plan for that afternoon was a shower and then a nap before Gina's barbeque.

"I bet you fared better with him than you did with Rausche yesterday." Rick pulled out a pack of cigarettes and tapped the box on the glass display case before pulling out a cigarette.

"What are you talking about?" she asked. "And I know you aren't going to smoke that here."

"And ruin the sanctity of the dojo?" He lit the cigarette. "So, I followed you after the funeral." He took a drag. "What happened once you got inside? Did you find anything linking Rausche with Marcus?"

Kelly set her Dixie cup on the counter and collapsed on one of the waiting-room chairs. She guessed that Rick had found out a lot on their crew-cut suspect without telling her. "When did you identify him as Rausche?"

"You have to answer my questions first." He dropped his ash in her Dixie cup and smiled.

"I didn't see you follow me there."

"You were concentrating on Rausche." He glanced at the clock on the wall. It was nearly one o'clock. "What did you find in the house? I know you didn't leave empty-handed."

Kelly remembered the shotgun in her car. She wondered if she could hide that in the dojo as well, then decided against it. "I found a photo of Marcus, Nora and John Rainsfeld. They were all standing outside the GPAC building. Someone had written a note on the back of it—initialed *RT*."

"*RT*? Maybe Robert Talcone?"

"That was my guess. Of course, *RT* could stand for something else." She was sure the initials stood for Robert Talcone. Rick seemed to agree with her and Kelly silently congratulated herself on this find.

"Anything else?"

"No, that was the only thing I took. I ran out of time. But I think that Nora might be at risk. The photo had a line crossed over Marcus's face and Nora's face was circled, as though she was the next target."

"Maybe. I'll need to see it—bring it to my office tomorrow."

Kelly thought about getting the photo now but decided she didn't want Rick to know that she was keeping things in her dojo locker.

"And Nora mentioned that you found another photo in DiBaca's house?"

"Yes. I don't know if it's useful or not. Did she tell you about the conversation I overheard?"

Rick nodded. "I'll need to see both photos when you come to the office tomorrow evening."

"And what's the next step?" Kelly asked.

"I'll tell you as soon as you need to know."

Rick didn't say good-bye. The door simply closed behind him and the dojo fell silent. Kelly bowed and entered the mat area. She stared at her reflection in the mirror. Little hand smudges littered the lower half of the mirror. The dojo needed to be cleaned before tomorrow morning. Another week of karate camp would soon begin.

Kelly passed the rest of the afternoon sorting through Marcus's bank statements again and rereading his journal. He had made several deposits into his bank account over the past two months in addition to his regular paycheck. She called Nora to check his bank account with the sixteen-digit code they had found on the back of the memos. The numbers matched. This suggested that Marcus had received money from both Talcone and DiBaca. But why? Nora had wondered. Kelly didn't have the answer. Rick's idea that Marcus might be a mole in GPAC kept recurring in her mind. If this were the case, who would have wanted him killed?

Gina had the grill fired up by the time Kelly got to her house at five. "Hey, sexy," Kelly said, kissing her on the cheek.

"Hey yourself." Gina was occupied with the grill and held her hand over the coals to check the temperature. "Can you bring me that plate of ribs?" She pointed to the table where a tray of food was arranged.

Kelly handed her the plate and then sat down, carefully avoiding the sizzle of grease that popped as the ribs were placed on the hot metal. "Where are Tasha and Beth?"

"They're on their way. Tasha just called to tell me that Beth was running late—she was trying to decide which pair of shorts didn't make her butt look fat. So as soon as she gets here, I'm going to bust out with that 'I like big butts' song." She grinned.

"She'll be pissed."

"Exactly." Gina nodded confidently. "Oh, by the way, I invited a couple friends from work too. Did you bring the salad?"

"It's in the fridge." The doorbell rang, barely audible from the backyard, even with the back door open. Gina glanced at her hands and then at the ribs. "Do you mind getting that?"

Kelly nodded and ran to answer the door. Tasha greeted her with a bear hug as soon as she stepped in the door. "Long time no see!"

Kelly smiled. "Yeah, it's been a couple days. I almost didn't recognize you," she said, teasing.

"Well, a lot can happen in a couple days. The army has revoked their charges against me. I just got a phone call from my commanding officer. He says they've reviewed everything and given me a clean slate."

"Congratulations! Tasha, that's great. Wait, does that mean you'll have to go to Iraq now? Are you going to join the rest of your unit?" She would miss Tasha and didn't want to think about her leaving for Iraq.

"I don't know." Tasha shrugged. "If I do, I'll be sure to say hello to Gina's ex-girlfriend so I can tell her how much better you get along with Gina!" Her exclamation ended with a short laugh. "Anyway, at least I'm not going to be discharged."

Beth appeared behind Tasha finally. She was lugging a large ice chest up the walkway. "Discharged or not, I'd rather you didn't leave Ashton."

Another car pulled up behind Beth's truck and Kelly watched as a burly man with perfect posture headed up to the door. Her heart sank. It was the cop who had pulled her over the day before. A skinny blond woman, also with perfect posture, stood beside him.

Beth eyed the couple and then glanced at Kelly. "Don't look so worried. They're Gina's friends from the station. If you hang around her long enough, you'll get used to seeing cops out of uniform." She laughed at her own joke and pushed past Kelly to bring the ice chest inside.

Tasha followed Beth, leaving Kelly alone in the doorway. She wished she were somewhere else. The man smiled as he approached the door. Please don't recognize me, Kelly thought. "Hi, come on in. Gina's in the backyard. You must be friends from work."

He nodded at her, then stepped inside and shook her hand. "Yep. I'm Aaron. And you must be Gina's girlfriend. Kelly, right?"

"Yes," she replied. She had to stop herself from calling him sir.

"Gina talks about you quite a bit—all good things, of course. This is my girlfriend, Brenda."

Brenda shook Kelly's hand too. She smiled the artificial smile that women use when they're warning other women not to hit on their boys. Kelly wanted to kick them both out, but they walked past her and headed to the backyard as though they had every right to be in Gina's house. Which, of course they did, and that was even worse.

She started to close the door and then stopped. A black Chevy sedan had just parked across the street. Rausche was in the front seat. He was staring at her. Kelly slammed the door and slid the deadbolt into place. She leaned against the door and tried to relax. Her hands were shaking.

Gina's wind chimes clinked softly as a breeze hit the front porch. The sheers hanging on the front windows bowed inward with the cool gust. Rausche could enter anywhere. How had he found her? Maybe he had followed Beth and Tasha. Maybe he had tailed Aaron and Brenda. If Aaron was the cop who had taken the call last night, and she guessed that could be possible, maybe Rausche was following him now. Or maybe he had followed her. He knew which car she drove and he knew who her girlfriend was. She guessed that he probably knew she lived with Alex and that she worked at the dojo as well. What didn't he know about her?

Kelly knew she had to face him. There was no way she could go out to join everyone on the patio with Rausche watching the house. She moved away from the door and pulled the sheer curtains back from the first window. Rausche's car was gone.

"Expecting someone?"

Kelly jumped at the sound of Aaron's voice. He was just coming in from the patio and must have wondered at the sight of her, half leaning out the front window.

"Well, I heard someone honk," Kelly lied.

"That's strange, I didn't hear anything from the backyard." He glanced at the street. "Maybe my hearing is going from all the damn sirens."

Kelly smiled. "Speaking of sirens . . . thanks for letting me off last night."

Aaron shook his head. "You know, I wasn't sure if I should bring it up or not. But since you mentioned it, you're welcome."

"Did everything go okay with that other call you took—the one that got me off the hook?" She chose her words carefully and hoped she didn't want to sound too interested.

"Well, we didn't find the guy—some nut running around with a gun. We found a dead dog, though. God, that was a sad sight. Apparently the guy lives with this old lady—I think she's his aunt or something. Anyway, he shot her dog. The old lady was standing in the middle of the street with this dead dog, just crying and crying."

Kelly crossed her arms. She thought of Claire and wished she could go visit her. The old terrier had just licked his bone peacefully on his pink pillow bed. Why had Rausche killed the dog? Maybe the dog had gotten in his way. "Who would shoot some old lady's dog?"

"You wouldn't believe some of the things people do. Anyway, we've got a patroller watching her house to catch the S.O.B. as soon as he comes home."

"Just for shooting the dog? I mean, I know it's sad, but I'd think the SFPD has bigger things to worry about." She hoped Aaron would keep talking about Rausche. Rausche knew too much about her and she needed to know everything she could about him.

"No, not just for shooting the dog. We searched the old lady's house and the guy's room was filled with guns. You wouldn't believe it. He had a fricking arsenal and no license for anything except a rifle. Of course, that was the one goddamned gun we couldn't find. They did a search on his personal records and I guess he was in the Marines. And according to his records he's pretty good with a rifle."

Kelly shivered involuntarily. She immediately envisioned Rausche watching her through the front windows. Would he set his first mark on Aaron or on her?

Aaron noticed the goose bumps on her arms. "You know, it's

warmer out on the patio. We should go join the rest of the party. Once the evening breeze picks up, it can be almost too cool in the shade."

"And we don't want to give our girlfriends the wrong idea by hanging out alone together," Kelly said.

Aaron laughed. "You know, that's almost not funny. Brenda is so damn jealous I have to watch my step around everyone—even lesbians!"

Throughout the dinner, Kelly kept herself on guard, watching the shadows for movement and listening for any unusual sounds. Gina didn't seem to notice that she was preoccupied with her overwhelming fear. The ribs disappeared rapidly and everyone retired to Gina's family room. Beth had rented some thriller and Kelly did her best to avoid watching it. She played with Gina's hands, took off each ring and replaced it a half-dozen times. She refilled everyone's drinks and supervised the popcorn bowl. The hosting gave her plenty of excuses to walk the length of the house and double-check each window and door lock.

After the movie ended, Tasha flipped on the news and they all listened with interest to a clip about the U.S. troops in Iraq. Kelly's cell phone rang. Unfortunately, the phone was on the coffee table in front of Gina, and Nora's name was flashing on the screen when Gina picked it up.

"Oh, look, it's your other girlfriend," Gina whispered as she handed her the phone. "Give Nora a kiss for me."

Kelly shook her head. She silenced the ringer and walked into the kitchen to answer the call.

"When did you last talk to Rick?" Nora asked, her voice sharp.

"I saw him this morning. Why?"

"I can't get ahold of him. Damn, I wish Terrance were here. He's still at his damn business conference."

Kelly could tell Nora was nervous. "What's wrong? Are you all right?"

"I'm fine," she snapped. "You know that guy with the crew

cut—Rick said he identified him as Leo Rausche. Well, he's parked outside the house."

"Have you called the police?" Kelly asked. She pictured Rausche's face as he had stared at her through the bathroom window and felt a shiver race up her spine.

"No. He hasn't done anything. He's just parked there, not doing anything at all, except giving me a headache."

Kelly glanced out at the patio where Gina was talking to Aaron. "Do you want me to come over?"

"No. I want to talk to Rick. Can you do me a favor and track him down? He's not answering his phone."

"Okay. I know he lives in Ashton. I'll just have to figure out where."

"Five-one-four Elmberry Street," Nora replied. "I'm guessing that you know the area."

"Definitely." Gina's house was only a few blocks from Elmberry Street. "How'd you pry that address from the Secret Agent Man?"

"I told him that I wouldn't pay him unless he gave me his home address."

"Money talks, I guess."

"Tell Rick that I need to hear from him." Nora's line clicked.

Kelly hung up the phone just as Gina entered the kitchen. Gina pulled a beer out of the fridge and popped off the cap. She sat down on the kitchen counter and swung her legs back and forth. "So?"

"So what?"

"Why'd Nora call? Didn't you tell her it was my turn to have you for the night?" Gina winked. She took a sip of the beer and set the bottle down. "Or are we splitting shifts with you now?"

"Very funny," Kelly responded. "We've already had this conversation. There's nothing going on between Nora and me."

"Chica, don't lie to me." Gina pushed off the counter. "You aren't nearly as attractive when you lie." She grabbed her beer and shot an accusatory glance at Kelly. As she left the kitchen, she hit the light switch, leaving Kelly in the dark shadows.

Kelly tried to call Rick. He didn't answer and she didn't wait to leave a message. After writing a quick note to Gina with an apology and a promise to meet her later, she slipped out the back door, hearing someone's laughter from the living room echo through the house. Gina would probably tell the others that she'd left because they'd had a fight. Every couple had quarrels at some point, she told herself. Gina would forgive her.

She walked the three blocks to Elmberry Street. Rick's house was a single-story ranch-style house with a long porch and a swing near the front door. A neatly manicured bright green lawn and one sycamore tree took up the small front yard. His car wasn't in the driveway, but she guessed he would park in the garage anyway. She rang the doorbell and waited on the porch, peeking through the window blinds.

A woman answered the doorbell. "Yes?"

"Oh, I'm sorry." Kelly stalled. "I know it's late to bother you. And I think I may have the wrong address. I'm looking for—" She stopped herself mid-sentence. Maybe Rick had given Nora a fake address. The woman appeared to be in her early sixties and had wrinkles creasing her cheeks as she smiled at Kelly. Flour powdered her hands and apron. Was this his wife?

"Rick?" she asked. "He's just stepped out for a moment. He told me I might expect someone. Please come in."

Kelly didn't move from the front doorstep. Why was Rick expecting her tonight?

The woman seemed to sense Kelly's apprehension. She extended her hand. "I'm Emily, Rick's wife. You're Kelly, right?"

She nodded. Flour dusted the red carpet runner when they shook hands. Emily glanced down at the carpet, following Kelly's gaze. "You know, I doubt Rick would notice if I dumped half a pound of flour on his floor. I swear that man owns a vacuum and a broom just to make me happy. He would never dream of cleaning." She turned and shuffled down the hallway, leaving a trail of flour behind her.

The kitchen smelled of apples and cinnamon. Kelly breathed deeply and smiled. "You're baking?"

"You caught me in the middle of a pie. And I've just pulled the apple cobbler from the oven." She pointed to a steaming casserole pan with the delicious aroma of baked apples and brown sugar. "Rick's trees are full of apples and it isn't even autumn yet," Emily said, dusting her hands with a fresh coat of flour and picking up the round circle of dough. She pressed the edges carefully over a mound of sliced apples in the pie tin and poked a few fork holes in the crust for an air vent. The pie was carefully placed in the oven and Emily went to the sink to wash her hands. Once the process was complete, she glanced at her watch. "I'm sorry he's taking so long."

"That's okay," Kelly responded politely. She was frustrated with Rick already and didn't want to wait for him tonight. But the smell of the apples and Emily's warm welcome made her relax.

"Well, Rick told me he'd be home by now, but he's often late. And I don't think he knew just exactly when you'd be coming by."

"How'd he know I was coming here at all?" Kelly asked.

Emily shrugged. "You know, I stopped wondering how he knew these things long ago." She laughed. "We've been married thirty-four years and separated for twelve of those years. I've learned to keep my nose out of his business if he keeps his nose out of mine."

"But you live together now?"

"No. I live just down the street. But if I don't come over at least once a week, Rick would live on fast-food burgers and frozen dinners. I've just sent him to the store now for some ice cream. I'm wondering what else he'll come home with." She smiled warmly. "Can you join us for dessert?"

Just then the garage door opened and Rick called out, "Hey, Em, did you ask for vanilla or French vanilla ice cream? I couldn't remember."

"French, but it doesn't really matter," she answered. "I put extra cinnamon in the cobbler anyway."

Rick came in, carrying two plastic bags. He nodded at Kelly as if he had fully expected to see her sitting at his kitchen table. "Smells good." Emily kissed him on the cheek as Rick placed the ice cream in the freezer. He set the items from the other plastic bag in the cupboard before turning to Kelly. "And which do you prefer—vanilla or French Vanilla?"

Kelly shrugged. "Chocolate usually, sometimes butter pecan, but then again, when I'm in the mood, it's hard to beat a smooth French."

Emily laughed. "I like her."

"Difficult. All women are difficult." Rick emphasized the last syllable by dropping his car keys on the counter. "Well, I bought the plain vanilla so I guess I've struck out on all accounts. You are, of course, staying for the apple cobbler, aren't you?"

Kelly shook her head. "I just stopped by to talk to you for a minute. Did you hear from Nora?"

Rick nodded. "Of course you'll stay for dessert. You won't have anywhere to be until later this evening. And we have plenty to discuss."

"Speaking of things to discuss, can we talk about my keys?" Kelly was frustrated by his patronizing tone. She hated to let him have control of their interactions.

He ignored her question about the keys and instead said to Emily, "Is that ginger I'm smelling? I love when you add ginger to the pie."

"You know I always put extra cinnamon and ginger in for you."

"Hmm, I like the ginger." He eyed Kelly. "So, do you like sleeping under the stars?" He didn't wait for her answer. "You're going to camp out in Nora's backyard tonight."

"Why?" she asked. She knew Rick hated questions, but that didn't stop her.

"Because I'm concerned about Rausche's presence." Rick cleared his throat. "I just talked to Nora and I don't think it's safe to have her stay in her house alone. Unfortunately, Terrance isn't back yet from his business trip."

Kelly wondered if Rick had mentioned Nora's fiancé to remind her of his presence. She didn't think it was unfortunate that Terrance was gone. "Why can't I just spend the night inside Nora's house?" She tried to keep her tone measured and hoped that her feelings for Nora weren't transparent. A night in Nora's house wouldn't be a bad thing at all. "I just don't see the point in camping out in the backyard."

"You don't always need to see the point of things when you do them." He smiled. "Think of this as part of your Sunday training program—a deprivation drill."

Emily looked up from the pile of dishes that she was hand-drying and asked, "Deprivation from what?"

Rick nodded at Kelly. "From sleep, of course."

Damn, Kelly thought. He knew about her crush on Nora. Then again, how could he not know . . . he always seemed to know everything before anyone told him.

Flicking on the headlights, Kelly looked at the gas gauge and waited for the meter to register as the engine warmed the car. The line steadied just under the last mark. She'd only put ten dollars' worth in the other day and knew the engine couldn't squeeze another fifty miles out of the tank. Halfway to Nora's house, she stopped for gas. The last thing she needed was to be on empty if she had to make a quick getaway tonight.

Before parking, Kelly scanned Nora's neighborhood. It was after midnight and most houses were dark, save the porch lights. Only two cars were parked on the street, a white van and a silver SUV. Apparently, most people parked their cars in their garages or driveways. She'd seen only one other person on the walk from her parking spot to Nora's backyard—a middle-aged white guy walking his Akita. The dog had growled as Kelly passed them, but the man didn't even look up at her. He had told the dog to heel and continued on his way as though Kelly didn't even exist. She wasn't surprised. She'd never attracted notice from strangers or stood out in a crowd. For the first time, her job with Rick had proven that being too plain could be a good thing. The man probably would never be able to identify her any more precisely than as a young white woman just above average height with brown hair, not fat or skinny, not ugly or pretty. She watched the man and his dog until they turned down the next street and disappeared from view.

Unlike the other houses on the block, lights still shone from the windows of Nora's house. Kelly tried the back gate and found it unlocked. She edged around the perimeter of the backyard, keeping close to the border of shrubs until she found a sheltered dry patch of ground behind four or five tall bushes. The spot had a perfect angle on Nora's kitchen. She pulled out her scope and focused on the kitchen. Nora was seated at the table stirring the contents of a mug and flipping through a magazine. She had a white sweater pulled over her shoulders like a shawl.

Kelly watched Nora with a tinge of guilt. Somehow it seemed wrong to be spying. She wanted to call her just to let her know she was camping in her backyard. Maybe that was the only reason—or maybe she just wanted to hear Nora's voice. The temptation of the cell phone in her pocket was hard to ignore. The minutes crawled by. Kelly tried to get comfortable on the hard dirt but whenever she moved the bushes' prickly leaves scratched at her skin. Her butt was sore after a half-hour. Nora left the kitchen after finishing her drink. The lights on the second floor flicked on and Kelly saw her through the bedroom window. Nora returned to the kitchen and started cleaning dishes. It was nearly one-thirty and Kelly wondered why Nora was still awake.

A crackle of snapped branches diverted her attention away from the scene in the kitchen. She scanned the yard, searching the shadows for movement. Something, a slip of clothing, passed through the brush on her left and she localized the sound to the far corner fence. Two men crawled over the fence and landed in Nora's yard. Kelly slipped deeper into the cover of darkness, between the rows of hedges. The men had paused ten yards from the back door. One of the men, wearing a dark blue cap and hunting jacket, pointed at the kitchen window. With a sudden tightening in her chest, Kelly realized it was Rausche. As he moved, light reflected off the metallic butt of a handgun that rested in the holster on his hip. The other man was dressed in dark blue as well and carried a larger gun. Kelly didn't know the type, but it looked like a military firearm. He adjusted a plastic device in his ear and held a small microphone up to his lips. A black cord connected the device in his ear to the mouthpiece. He whispered something into the mouth-piece and nodded at Rausche.

The men took a few steps closer to the back door, keeping in line with the fence. Their movement through the bushes was a noisy parade and the crickets that had chirped earlier were silent now. They stopped before they reached the back door, well out of range of the lights from the yard. Nora had left the dishes to dry and gone to pick up the phone. Maybe it was Terrance. It seemed too late for anyone to call. Maybe the phone hadn't rung at all. She could be calling someone. Had she heard the men in her backyard? Kelly's phone flashed once. Nora was calling her. Fortunately, she had already turned off the ringer. She picked up the line and whis-pered, "There's two men at your back door. Get out now."

Nora turned to look at the wall behind her as she hung up the phone. A red laser light flickered against the wall and then brushed over her skin before flashing off again. Kelly wondered if Nora had seen the light.

Kelly followed the beam back to its source. Rausche had his gun aimed at Nora. The red laser light was a focus beam attached to the gun. Nora hit the light switch in the kitchen and the room was instantly cloaked in darkness. The red laser flashed through the dark house, searching for a target. Kelly scanned her scope over the house, searching for some movement inside. A full minute passed and neither of the men made a move closer. Kelly won-dered if Nora was leaving the house through the front door or out the garage.

Suddenly, the back yard lights flicked on and the two men retreated a few steps from their position by the door. Rausche waited silently, his gun aimed at the back door, while the other man was hissing some message into the mouthpiece, probably asking for further directions. Who was at the other end of that line? Who was giving these men their orders? The man with the earpiece whispered something to Rausche. Hold your fire, Kelly hoped. Rausche nodded. They were waiting for Nora to make a move.

Something white passed the panes of glass by the door. From her angle, she could make out the sleeve of Nora's sweater behind the door. She wondered why Nora hadn't listened to her. Why hadn't she left the house? Kelly already had a rock picked out. She had it in her palm, waiting. As soon as the latch on the door clicked, she hurled the rock. The back door flew open at the same moment as the rock struck Rausche's hand. The gun dropped to the ground and a blinding light shone out across the yard. It focused on the place where the two men had stood only moments before. They were hastily scaling the back fence, and the sound of their scuffling feet shattered the quiet night. Nora's flashlight beam caught the pant legs of the retreating figures as they scrambled over the fence.

Apparently satisfied that the threat was past, Nora scanned the rest of the yard slowly. Maybe, Kelly hoped, she was looking for her. The light appeared to be similar to Alex's industrial lamps used at his construction sites. The beam was strong enough to momentarily blind anyone who attempted to look directly at the person holding it. Aside from the flashlight, Nora was also holding a gun. Kelly sank lower in her hiding place, ducking her head as the beam played over the surrounding bushes. The back door closed as Nora disappeared inside the house.

An hour after the men left, Kelly began a slow circle around the perimeter of the house. Rausche's gun was gone. Somehow, he had managed to grab his gun and scale the fence within seconds of the door opening. Kelly wondered if they had been sent simply to scare Nora or if they really had intended to shoot. She doubted that Rausche would have missed if he had set out to make a hit.

Kelly went to her car to grab the picnic blanket she always kept in the trunk. The van and the SUV were both gone now. She returned to her lair behind the bushes and spread out the blanket. A cool wind had picked up and the bushes did little to protect her. She fought to remain alert. A throbbing pain had settled at the base of her skull and she had an overwhelming desire to curl up in the blanket and sleep. Her headache worsened as the night grew colder. Several times she considered calling Nora. She held the cell phone in her palm, dialed the number and then hit the off button just before the call was sent. Let me inside, she begged silently. She wanted to curl up under Nora's blankets and close her eyes for a few hours. During one of her circles around the house, Kelly found the round rock that she'd hurled at Rausche. Would Nora open the door again if she heard the rock hit her window?

After three hours passed, Kelly was convinced that Rick had designed this task as pure torture. She wondered if he had known that the two men would be in Nora's yard tonight. Maybe he guessed she was getting too attached to Nora and wanted to challenge her. She had an uneasy suspicion that he wasn't telling her everything. If Rick hadn't known that Rausche would be at Nora's house tonight, why had he sent Kelly?

That evening, Kelly had told Rick everything that she'd learned about Marcus. She described the journals and the bank statements. He seemed only mildly upset that she hadn't mentioned these items before. As she described all of the clues that she had found, she watched his brow furrow and guessed he was trying to figure out the scenario that had led to Marcus's death. But he didn't seem ready to share his ideas. She had her own theory but she wanted to find out more about Robert Talcone first. Rick also suggested this. He had also promised to call Nora and touch base with her.

As the hours passed, Kelly lost interest in planning how she was going to find out more about Talcone. The cold air had made it impossible to concentrate. She had the blanket wrapped around her, but she continued to shiver. The fog had settled in with a vengeance and the ground was wet and cold. Her teeth chattered incessantly and she longed for the warmth of the coming day. She tried passing the time by humming the lines of "Henry the 8th" over and over to stay awake. By the fifth chorus, the repetitious song grew tiresome, and she finally gave in to the fantasy of being inside Nora's house. She imagined walking up to Nora's door, finding it unlocked and then sneaking up to Nora's bedroom. After she undressed, Nora would let her slip under the covers. She could almost feel Nora's skin against hers as they drifted to sleep in an embrace. The image replayed itself each time she felt her eyes start to close.

When the first light illuminated the eastern horizon, Kelly stretched out her legs and rubbed her hands over her face. Rick's instructions were to stay until dawn. She had no intention of working overtime. The house had remained in darkness for six hours and no one had entered the backyard. Kelly hoped that Nora was safe inside. She ignored the urge to call her on the chance that she had managed to fall asleep.

Chapter Twelve

Kelly drove to Ashton with the sunrise stretching over her windshield. She squinted into the bright light and tried to focus on the road. Hopefully her karate campers would be well behaved. They were usually more subdued on Monday mornings and she hoped this would hold true today. She was too tired to have any patience with them. She called Rick and was surprised when he answered on the first ring. He asked about Nora and she told him that Rausche had paid a visit. Rick didn't sound surprised and she wondered if he didn't have some kind of ESP. He just chuckled when she suggested this, mentioned that he'd drop by the dojo later and then hung up.

Alex met Kelly in the kitchen as she walked in. "You're home late."

Kelly shook her head. "I'm making a pit stop here for some food before going to work. Had a rough night."

He grinned. "And you look a little disheveled, so I'm guessing you had a good time? Doesn't look like you got much sleep." He picked up his lunch box and Thermos. "Must have been someone other than Gina, though, because she came here looking for you."

Kelly swore softly and leaned her head against the refrigerator. "Tell me you're joking."

"Nope. She called around ten o'clock looking for you and then knocked on the door around midnight."

"I'm sorry about that. She probably woke you."

He nodded. "I didn't mind really. But I was a little concerned." He took a sip from his Thermos. "Not as concerned as I am now, though. I have a feeling you're going to be in some hot water if you really were with another woman last night." He glanced at his wristwatch and headed for the door. "Work calls. By the way, I left some coffee for you."

She nodded. "Alex, can we talk about some things later?"

"Sure. You doing okay?"

She nodded. "I'm fine. Sort of."

He set his Thermos down and gave her a hug. "Don't worry. We can have a girl-talk night anytime. I'll bring the chocolate, and you can bring the—"

Kelly laughed and pushed him toward the door. "Weren't you going somewhere? You're gonna be late."

He slammed the garage door on his way out and the noise filled Kelly with a sudden loneliness. She longed to tell Alex where she had spent the night. But he knew nothing about Rick or the private investigation service, the military case, the shotgun in her car, Rausche who seemed bent killing someone, or Nora Kinley, the lawyer she was falling for. He would have to know everything before he could understand her last night's grief. She wanted to tell him. He'd know what she should do next. Alex always knew, but this time she couldn't ask for his help.

Kelly went to the dojo early. She wanted another look at Marcus's journal. Before she had gotten far into Marcus's thoughts, the karate camp students began to arrive. She stuffed the journal back in her locker and quickly changed into her gi. Marcus's drawings were still bothering her. Why did John Rainsfeld look like a puppet? She decided to pay another visit to the GPAC office to see if there was something she'd missed.

Rick came to the dojo just after lunch. The children were practicing their sparring drills and Kelly was supervising a match between Monkey and Tiger. She called Colin over to watch the younger children spar and then went to the front lobby to meet Rick. He wanted to see the manila envelope and the picture she'd taken from Rausche's house. Kelly retrieved them from her locker while he waited.

He studied the photo of Nora, Marcus and John carefully and then flipped it over to read the back. "RT." He paused. "Look, I'd like you to meet with Nora tonight. I can't make a meeting tonight, but she's expecting one of us to check in with her around nine." He handed the picture back to her. "You might not want to show her this picture. I don't know. Use your own judgment. And before you leave, scout her property to make sure there aren't any Peeping Toms around. You don't need to stay all night this time."

"Where are you going to be, in case I need to get in touch with you?"

"Sacramento. I'm going to go talk to some friends of mine who know Talcone."

Kelly didn't argue with him. Nora had been on her mind all day and she was more than willing to spend the evening with her. "I have to get back to my students," she admitted. "If I leave them sparring alone, before long someone will be crying and someone else will have a bloody nose."

He nodded. "Yeah, I never could understand kids. I don't think I ever went through that awkward stage."

"For some reason I don't believe you." She smiled. "I can just imagine how cute you'd be as a six-year-old karate camper in a little white karate gi."

"Don't push your luck, Kelly." He winked at her and then pointed to the mat area. "I don't know if I'd trust you with my kid."

"Good thing you don't have any kids."

He grinned. "Get back to work."

By the end of the day, Kelly was looking forward to seeing Nora. She dismissed the students and then waited outside until everyone had been picked up. Monkey's mother was the last one to arrive, a half-hour late. While they waited, he told her stories of dragons and sorcerers and the castle he had built with his Legos. When his mother finally pulled up to the curb, he announced that Kelly was to come play Legos at his house. Monkey's mother scowled and Kelly quickly admitted that she had her own dragons and sorcerers to keep her busy that evening. Monkey gave an over-exaggerated sigh and then took too long to climb into the car.

Kelly drove home and showered. Before she finished dressing, her phone was ringing. Gina's name blinked on the caller ID screen. "Sorry, Gina," she said, dropping the phone. "I don't have time tonight." She felt a rush of guilt as the ringing continued and she stared at the phone, debating excuses she could tell Gina. Finally the voice mail picked up.

Alex had made dinner and Kelly joined him out on the patio. They sat on the fence facing west so they could watch the sun sink low on the horizon. Kelly didn't try to explain anything about her work with Rick. When Alex asked about her day, she only told him about the karate camp. She left before the sun had set and didn't tell him where she was headed. He didn't ask where she was going. She didn't want to lie to him and would have explained everything if he'd only asked.

At five minutes to nine, Kelly knocked on Nora's door.

The drapes near the front window moved an inch or two and Kelly guessed that Nora was being cautious. The door opened and Nora greeted her warmly.

"Please come in," she said as though Kelly had only come to her home as a guest for tea.

"Thank you," Kelly said, matching the formal tone. Nora was dressed in a business suit and heels with her hair pinned neatly in place. Kelly wondered if she'd just gotten home.

"Rick said you'd be by."

Kelly nodded. She glanced around the house. It was spacious—too spacious, with windows everywhere and not enough drapes. Kelly imagined someone outside peering in at Nora through every vulnerable window. "He wanted me to show you a few things."

Nora led Kelly down a long hallway to the family room. Kelly followed silently. She hated feeling awkward around Nora. Just relax, she coached herself, and think of some conversation starter. Truthfully, there was no way she'd ever be of any romantic interest to Nora. Still, her crush was there, undeniable, and she was fumbling like an uncoordinated giraffe every time Nora looked at her.

Nora sat down on a leather couch and stared expectantly at Kelly. The room was dark, save one lamp on a table at Nora's side. The lamp cast a soft orange glow about the room. One steaming mug sat on the coffee table.

"Can I get you anything?" Nora asked. "I've just made some coffee."

"Thank you, but no." The moment was as warm as Thanksgiving dinner, yet she had to ruin it. She couldn't chitchat with Nora. Kelly pulled the photo out of her pocket and handed it to her. "I found this picture at Leo Rausche's place. From my short interaction with him, I'd say he's, well, not a nice guy. And he was one of the guys who was at your house last night."

Nora didn't even flinch as she studied the picture. She touched the grease marks that circled her face on the photo and then flipped it over and read the note on the back. "Who do you think RT is?"

"Robert Talcone, maybe."

"Rick told me about Leo Rausche. You said he was one of the guys on my back porch. Who was the other one?"

"I don't know. Do you have the golfing picture that I took from DiBaca's house?" Kelly asked.

Nora nodded. She left the room and returned a moment later. Pointing to each face in the photo, she stated, "So there's Robert Talcone, Marcus Edwards, Jared DiBaca, and these two other men we still don't know. Neither are Rausche, right?"

"I've seen him up close and too personal. I'd recognize him anywhere now and he's not either of those guys."

"And what about the other guy who was with Rausche last night? Was he either of these guys?"

Kelly shook her head. "I don't think so."

Nora sighed. "I hate golf. Do you golf?"

Kelly smiled. "No. I don't play sports that require balls."

"Really? That's strange. You've ruled out softball and basketball then too. Even soccer." Nora turned the golfing picture over. There was no writing on the backside. She set the photo on the coffee table, covering up the other photo with the grease-marked faces. "Actually, I might agree with you. I've always hated those sports. I used to run track in college . . . we won our division all four years that I was on the team at Harvard."

For a moment, Kelly felt overwhelmed with the realization that she had no idea who Nora Kinley really was. She'd gone to Harvard. She lived in this big house with dark walnut wood everywhere and too many windows. Beyond GPAC and the investigation of Marcus's death, Kelly knew nothing about her. And her fiancé was always gone. "Where's Terrance tonight?" Kelly thought she shouldn't ask personal questions, but the question slipped out anyway.

"At his condo in Pebble Beach. He had a business meeting in Monterey and decided to spend a few days visiting his mother." Nora leaned back on the sofa cushions and stretched out her legs. She yawned. "God, I'm exhausted. I haven't slept in two days." Nora picked up the photos and took another look at the grease-marked one. She shook her head. "You know, I think they're just trying to scare me."

Kelly was surprised at Nora's reaction to the picture. If her own face had been circled next to a dead man's crossed-out face, she'd be on the phone to the police instantly. Then again, what would the police do? "Have you ever met Robert Talcone?"

"No. Are you wondering if RT has a personal claim against me? I doubt it. I think this is all about GPAC." Nora shook her head. "But I don't understand why, exactly. If we say that Marcus was

162

working as a mole in GPAC and was being paid by either Talcone or DiBaca, why would he be killed?"

"Well, that's just one theory. Maybe he wasn't a mole." Kelly had brought Marcus's journal to show Nora and she flipped to the sketch of John Rainsfeld with the puppet strings. "What if there's another explanation? What if John knows more than he's saying?"

Nora shivered and crossed her arms. "What do you mean?"

Kelly flipped through the journal. She had spent hours poring over every page and was starting to believe that Marcus knew something about GPAC and about John Rainsfeld that might have led to his death. She still couldn't put her finger on what he was trying to tell her with the pictures. "I think there's a better theory to link Talcone, DiBaca, Rausche, Edwards and Rainsfeld."

"I don't know." Nora closed her eyes. "But I need more than another theory right now. I keep thinking that someone is going to break into my house to attack me."

"I don't think you should stay here alone," Kelly said.

"Where should I go, then? To some hideout?" Nora's eyes watered with this suggestion. She laughed nervously and quickly rubbed the moisture out of the corners of her eyes. "No, I'm fine here."

"You could go stay with Terrance in Pebble Beach."

Nora looked away from Kelly. "I can take care of myself, but thanks for your concern. The last person I want to run to right now is Terrance. He's got this attitude that I can't take care of myself as it is. Anyway, I'm not really worried."

"Well, I am," Kelly admitted. She wanted to ask Nora what had happened between her and Terrance. But she didn't want to pry. "I know you can take care of yourself, but . . . Rausche isn't a nice guy."

"Yeah, you already mentioned that. I have this image of a mobster and waking up at the bottom of the ocean wearing concrete slippers." Nora laughed. Her tone was deceptively light.

"What about that letter you received? Do you think Rausche was behind that?"

"Maybe." Nora stood up and headed to the kitchen. She returned with a chocolate chip cookie and offered half to Kelly.

163

"No, thanks." Kelly shook her head. "Look, I'm sorry for bringing that picture. I don't think you really needed to see that."

"Don't try and act protective. That's the last thing I need."

Kelly cleared her throat and stood up. She went over to the sliding glass door behind the sofa and pulled the drapes closed. "There are too many windows in your house."

"I like the light that they let in."

"But someone else can look in on you. Like I did last night."

Nora caught hold of Kelly's hand just as she was passing the sofa. "Thanks for staying last night." She continued with a hint of sarcasm, "I'm not going to thank you for this photo that you've brought me though."

"Sorry."

"Would you mind staying tonight?" Nora didn't look at her. "There's no way I'll be able to sleep. And I hate watching the late-night infomercials alone. I'll end up ordering some fake gold tennis bracelet just so I can talk to someone."

Kelly smiled. She wasn't about to turn down the offer to spend the night with Nora, although she knew nothing could happen between them. Nora had given her no signs of interest and, Kelly reminded herself, she was straight. "I don't mind staying. But if we're both here, one of us should try and get some sleep. We don't need to watch infomercials together."

"Thanks," Nora said. She squeezed Kelly's hand.

"I'll take the first guard shift," Kelly volunteered.

Nora sighed. Still holding Kelly's hand, she stood up and glanced around the room. Kelly stood up too, feeling slightly awkward to be standing so close to Nora.

"Okay. I think all of the doors and windows are locked, but you might want to double-check. I'm going to take a shower." She let go of Kelly's hand, finally, and then kissed her cheek. "You're sweet for staying." She turned and headed down the hall.

Kelly felt herself blush. Sweet. She didn't really want to be sweet. She sank down on the couch and closed her eyes. The soft scent of Nora remained in the room, an unusual blend of fresh-cut wood scents saddled with jasmine. Kelly heard the shower start. She got up and took a tour of the house, checking each door and window lock and pulling every drape that could be drawn.

She replaced Rausche's photo in the manila envelope, thinking that it was better if Nora understood that she was really in danger, but she doubted her decision to show Nora the photo. It was unnerving just to see Marcus's crossed-out face, let alone the circle around Nora's. Rick probably hadn't mentioned the photo to Nora, figuring that there was no reason to upset her more. But Rausche was not someone to be taken lightly, she reminded herself. Rausche's gun-laden bedroom and his glowering face were still fresh in her mind.

Nora emerged from her bedroom wrapped in a white terry-cloth robe. The terry cloth made a stunning contrast to her brown skin. Her hair was pulled back from her face and Kelly fought the urge to stare at her neckline. She couldn't stop herself from imagining what was concealed under the robe. The scent of lavender wafted into the room.

"There's a blanket in the cedar chest behind the sofa." Nora handed her a pillow. "Do you mind sleeping on the sofa? The television remote is hiding under the lamp on the end table."

Kelly nodded. "Thanks."

"I'm sorry I don't have a guest room to offer you. Terrance and I are still debating furniture styles for the extra rooms."

Kelly's thoughts snapped away from Nora's robe as soon as she heard Terrance's name. Nora is engaged, she reminded herself. "No problem. I'll be fine on the sofa. And if I find the remote, I'll spend the night watching the infomercials. I've always wanted a gold tennis bracelet. Maybe platinum—do you think they come in platinum?"

Nora suggested channel 37. "They have the best deals in the last ten minutes of the sale." She started to leave and Kelly caught hold of her hand.

"Good night."

Nora nodded. She glanced at Kelly's hand and then stepped

toward her. In the next moment her lips were on Kelly's. Kelly expected her to pull away, but she didn't. They both held the kiss for a moment too long—a moment too long for good night. They finally separated. The passion that Kelly had held at bay since she'd first met Nora surfaced with a dizzying rush. This time she didn't blush. She met Nora's gaze with unashamed lust, but she couldn't speak.

Nora stared at her. "I don't know what—"

Kelly shook her head. She didn't want Nora to try to explain what had occurred.

"Good night." Nora turned and left the room.

Kelly sank onto the couch and cupped her head in her hands. She heard the sound of Nora's bedroom door closing. Solid mahogany wood shut her out of Nora's world. She wanted desperately to open the door. Why had Nora kissed her?

Chapter Thirteen

The next day Sam came in at noon. Kelly had just finished the last morning class and the children were taking their lunch break.

"You're here early," Kelly said, eyeing Sam suspiciously. "Are you feeling okay? You know it's Tuesday afternoon?" Sam usually took Tuesdays off.

"Yes." He smiled. "And I'm here to relieve you."

"Why?"

Sam pointed to his office and Kelly followed him inside. He shut the door. "Rick called me an hour ago. He said you had plans this afternoon and needed some time off."

Kelly swore under her breath.

"Don't worry about it. Rick's making this worth my trouble."

She wondered how much Rick had offered to convince Sam to give her the afternoon off. "Did he say what the plans were?"

"He's still keeping you in the dark."

She nodded. "I hate being the last one to know what's going on."

Sam shrugged. "Rick will keep you guessing every step of the way. You can't relax when he's your boss."

"You have no idea."

Sam shook his head. "Nothing that I can talk about anyway." One of the children shrieked and Kelly immediately moved to see what was the matter. Sam pointed at the door and said, "You need to leave. I'll take care of the little camp gremlins."

Kelly gathered her things and changed out of her uniform. She avoided the front room where the children were eating so she wouldn't have to explain why she was leaving. Rick called as soon as she stepped out of the dojo.

"So, when do I get to find out what's going on around here? Sam just showed up to take over my classes. Apparently you guys had some sort of arrangement that I know nothing about."

"You need to be at the Memorial Rose Garden by four o'clock. It's a few blocks east of the Capitol," Rick replied.

"The Capitol? In Sacramento?" She tried to temper her voice. She didn't want Rick to know how upset she was and that she hated not being in control.

"Yes. Do you need directions?"

Kelly didn't answer. She wanted to tell him not to call her away from the dojo again. But something stopped her each time she tried to stand up to Rick. "You know, Rick, I like to plan things."

"Well, it's only noon. You have four hours to plan the rest of your day." Rick paused. Kelly heard the clicking of a keyboard and wondered what he was typing. "By the way, I've left bridge toll money and a little extra spending cash in an envelope in your car. Don't spend it all in one place."

Sacramento was an hour's drive from Ashton, without traffic. Kelly sighed. "Fine. Why am I going to the Capitol?"

"You need to be at the Memorial Rose Garden. It's the park just east of the Capitol. You'll understand why you need to be there soon enough."

"Where will you be?"

He clicked off without saying good-bye. She was frustrated at her inability to challenge him. But she needed the money and didn't want to jeopardize the job by talking back. She searched her car for the envelope he had mentioned, finally finding it in the glove box. Five crisp hundred-dollar bills and a few Susan B. Anthony coins for the bridge toll. She pocketed the money, thinking that five hundred was almost enough to pay the rest of her tuition for the fall semester. If she wanted to, she could tell Rick she was ready to quit. But she knew she wasn't ready. She was just getting used to the job.

"All right, now the fun begins," she said, flipping through the cash. She climbed in the car and pulled out a map to plan her trip to Sacramento.

Kelly arrived in Sacramento early and decided to take a tour of the Capitol. The last time she'd been inside was with her fourth-grade history class. A decade later, she doubted the place had changed much but it was too hot to stand around waiting outside. The tour was a waste of time until an unexpected meeting she had on the Capitol steps. While she was waiting in the shade for the tour leader to finish, Kelly noticed two men coming up the steps. One of the men glanced over at her and Kelly realized with a start that it was Kevin, her sparring partner. He continued past her without stopping. The other man he was with was Robert Talcone. She was sure of it. Robert Talcone was leading the way, taking two steps at a time. They reached the first landing and Kevin looked over his shoulder at her. She knew Kevin would want to know what she was doing at the Capitol and why she wasn't teaching that afternoon. She was glad when they finally disappeared inside the building.

At four o'clock, Kelly made her way to the Memorial Rose Garden. The afternoon sun had heated the park to well over a hundred degrees and the full-bodied aroma of roses filled the air. A rumble of drums came from a gazebo on the far side of the park as a brass band started to play. Kelly made her way to the gazebo, keeping close to the line of trees. The military marching band was playing "God Bless America" for a group of assembled gray-haired military men.

Kelly guessed that there were nearly a hundred veterans and thirty or forty others in plain clothes. She spotted Talcone in the front row. Rick was with a group of men in FBI caps standing to the side of the stage. Talcone went over to the podium after the band finished and stooped over the microphone. "I'd like to thank . . ."

Kelly scanned the crowd. DiBaca was in the third row. She didn't see any other familiar faces. The FBI men were dispersed through the crowd now that Talcone had started speaking. Rick edged closer to the line of trees where Kelly had taken up her position. She waited for him to acknowledge her but he didn't even look in her direction.

After thanking the Conservative Veterans Association for organizing the ceremony, Talcone explained that the group was gathered for a dedication of the new memorial to honor all soldiers California had lost on foreign soil. A bronze statue depicted a soldier shackled to a stone pillar. The soldier's helmet covered his face. Was he dead or sleeping on the job? On the plaque at the base of the statue, *Dedication To Our State* was etched in bronze.

A few other speakers followed Talcone, each adding a special thanks to Talcone, who, they claimed, had spearheaded the fund-raising efforts for the memorial. The band played again, this time the national anthem, and everyone in the crowd stood to salute. A flag was carried down the center aisle and the speakers followed the flag out, signaling the end of the ceremony. Kelly headed back to the rose garden as the crowd began to disperse. Before reaching the roses, she spotted Kevin on the side of the gazebo. He was talking to some bald guy in a sharkskin suit. She made a quick pass to their left and slipped behind a few trees nearby.

"Not bad, you know, for a beginner."

"Beginner? Paul, I write speeches for vote-hungry politicians in my sleep," Kevin bragged.

Paul smiled. "So, now we learn the real reason that Mrs. Slater

170

kicked Mr. Slater out of the happy homestead. I thought it was because she found out about your boyfriend."

"No, Mrs. Slater liked my speeches." Kevin paused. "But since you brought up the subject, yes, she didn't like my boyfriend. And I think we might as well be open about things. Boone was the man I left her for. And he dropped me off his call book a week later. So be careful with that boy. I'm glad I settled in with Frank. Boone was trouble."

Kelly was surprised at Kevin's admission. He had never mentioned any other boyfriend except Frank and she'd assumed that he was the only one. One of the veterans wheeled by the gazebo and Kevin extended his hand to the old man in a wheelchair. "Thank you so much for coming, sir," he said. "It was our honor that you could attend."

The old man scoffed about honor and continued on his way.

Paul laughed as soon as the old man was out of earshot. "You should be the politician. Do you ever stop shaking hands?"

"I'm just a political analyst and part-time speechwriter," Kevin insisted. "But it doesn't hurt to keep the old vets happy. Talcone needs them on his side."

"And are you on his side?" Paul winked. "I thought you were ready to jump off Talcone's bandwagon after that last stunt. When are you going to decide which side of the fence you like to sit on?"

"Hell, I need this job as much as you do," Kevin admitted. "It helps that he's running a little scared with his pay book wide open."

"He ought to be running scared," he said. "He's nearly pissed off his entire gay contingency, and two men on his wagon are both closet gays."

Talcone was heading up the path toward the gazebo with an FBI agent on his side. Kevin saw him first and tapped the other man's shoulder. "Here's the big boss now. Let's say we drop the gay buzzword from our conversation."

Paul nodded. "Just as a last thought—Boone's coming up tonight. We're going to make it a long weekend in Tahoe. I'd love it if you joined us for a threesome."

Kevin opened his mouth and then closed it again. Talcone was near enough to hear them now. "You know, Paul, I never mix business with pleasure," Kevin said, "but that wouldn't even be pleasure." He finished with a set grin.

Talcone reached the gazebo and Paul quickly stepped forward to congratulate him on the speech. He licked up the praise without thanking Kevin, who had apparently written the speech. Paul then mentioned another engagement he had that evening and left the gazebo. Kelly guessed that Paul was a political consultant or speechwriter like Kevin. She watched him walk toward the rose garden and then focused her attention back on Talcone and Kevin.

"So, Kevin, you ready for another power meeting? We've got a dinner planned with DiBaca and one of his old friends." Talcone turned to the FBI agent. "I always love an attractive escort, but can I release you now?"

The agent shrugged. "Hey, I was just keeping you company. Have a good afternoon."

Talcone watched the agent disappear in the same direction that Paul had gone. "Damn, those guys are like flies on shit. They act like they're doing you a favor by following you around everywhere. I don't need a goddamn FBI tail to use the john."

"Speaking of the FBI . . . You know who was here today?" Kevin asked.

Talcone shook his head.

"Rick Lehrman. Didn't your guy Rausche say that Rick Lehrman was working with that lawyer, Nora Kinley?" Kevin continued, "Do you think they're still investigating Edwards's death?"

He shrugged. "It doesn't matter. She'll move on to other cases soon enough. We just need to pull the right strings. Rick Lehrman doesn't have a vendetta against me. He's just a man with a PI business to run and she'll drop the investigation before he figures anything out." Talcone sighed. "And it won't be me who burns for Edwards's accident. If anyone gets fingered, it'll be Leo."

"What about paper trails?"

"You're always so worried about everything. Don't worry about it. You make me stressed." Talcone paused. "I need you to focus on

172

my legislative battles. We'll have the whole mess with GPAC cleaned up soon enough. Rausche is taking care of the lawyer and the PI will cease and desist as soon as the money stops flowing in. We've got to keep the veterans on our side and then the fiasco with GPAC can be swept under the carpet."

They headed off and Kelly watched them leave, suddenly wondering how well she really knew Kevin Slater. She would never see her sparring partner in the same light again. As soon as they were out of sight, she jogged down the tree-lined path heading the opposite direction. She reached her car just as her cell phone beeped. Rick had sent a text message:

"Nora's house tonight."

Alex was stretched out on the sofa in the family room when Kelly finally got home at seven. "Hey, Alex."

He didn't budge and Kelly quickly realized he was sleeping. The television was on and a beer was in his hand. He was still wearing his dirty work clothes and smelled like sweat. A sports newscaster was recapping the best plays of a golf tournament. She found the remote and turned off the television. Seeing the golfers had reminded her of DiBaca and Talcone and she didn't want to think about the investigation now. The golf cronies, as Nora had called them, were starting to become real entities and Kelly was frightened of where the investigation was leading. She picked up the phone and dialed Gina's number.

A strange voice answered with a California Valley-girl accent.

"I'm sorry, I think I may have the wrong number." Kelly didn't recognize the woman who had answered the phone and her artificial Valley-girl greeting was annoying. She tried to recall the number she had just dialed. Maybe she had hit the wrong key. "I was trying to reach Gina Hernandez. I think I may have misdialed."

"Oh, no, you've got the right number." The Valley girl's tone was too happy, too pleasant. "Gina's in the shower. Can I have her call you back?"

173

"Um . . ." Kelly stalled. Who was this woman? It wasn't Beth or Tasha. Gina had never mentioned any other friends. At least, not in the past few weeks since they'd started dating. "No, that's okay. I'll call later. Have a good night." She hung up the phone and stared at her watch. It was just after seven. Who would be at Gina's house now, and why would Gina be taking a shower if she had a guest? Kelly tried to ignore a swell of jealousy.

Alex sat up and rubbed his eyes. "Hey, look who's here. Good, I won't send out a search party tonight."

"No need for a search party." Kelly sank down on the sofa next to him. She grabbed a pillow and squeezed it in a tight hug. "I need a nap."

"Maybe you should take a shower first." Alex shifted away from her. "You stink."

"Me? Have you smelled yourself?"

He shook his head. "I always smell like flowers."

Kelly ignored him and curled into a ball on the sofa. She heard her phone ring a few minutes later but ignored it.

Alex tapped her shoulder. "It's Gina. Do you want to talk to her?"

Kelly shook her head and closed her eyes. She didn't know who the other woman was, but somehow she knew that Gina had made out with her. She didn't need to ask.

Alex positioned the cell phone between Kelly's shoulder and her ear, then apologized. "She wouldn't listen to me when I told her you were sleeping."

"Hey, Kelly?" Gina's voice echoed through the phone.

"Yeah," Kelly answered. She was mad at Gina and had no interest in talking to her. Although she had no proof that Gina had had sex with that other woman, she knew it was the case and wanted to get off the phone. "Gina, I'm sorry, but I'll have to call you back. I don't feel well." She hung up without waiting for Gina's response.

Kelly showered and changed her clothes. She had already called Nora to tell her that she would be coming to her house later that evening. Before she had finished dressing, her cell phone rang again. Gina's number flashed on the screen. She hit the silence button to ignore the call. Gina was going to be pissed. Fortunately, she didn't care what Gina thought tonight. Somehow she knew that the Valley girl who had answered Gina's phone was more than just a friend.

Two minutes later the phone rang again. This time Kelly answered it, worried that there might be some emergency.

"We need to talk," Gina said.

Kelly sighed. "Yeah, I know. But I'm too mad at you to talk."

"You have to let me explain."

"I don't have to. Not now." She hung up and pulled on a clean shirt, trying not to think about Gina. She was too upset.

Alex handed her a paper bag as she headed toward the garage door. Kelly eyed the bag. "What's this?"

"I made cookies. I figured that most women-troubles would be improved with chocolate."

Kelly smiled. "Thanks, Alex. I'm on my way to deal with one of the women now. Wish me luck."

"If you have more than one woman on your plate, you don't need any more good luck," Alex argued.

Ten minutes later, she knocked on Gina's front door. She didn't want to spend the night wondering if she'd jumped to the wrong conclusion. There was a blue truck she didn't recognize parked in Gina's normal spot. A U.S. flag sticker was attached to its back window and a bumper sticker read, "Support Our Troops."

Gina opened the door. "Come in," she said after an uncomfortably long moment of silent staring. "I didn't expect you'd come."

"I can leave." Kelly could tell something was up. Gina didn't sound mad at her for hanging up the phone. They stood in the doorway, still staring at each other.

"No, its just . . ." Gina glanced over her shoulder toward the kitchen. There was the sound of dishes clattering in the sink and wash water. "Vicky's here. We just finished dinner."

"Oh," Kelly said. She glanced past Gina, down the hallway leading to the kitchen. "I wasn't planning on coming in or anything . . . I just wanted to apologize."

"For what?" Gina asked.

"I don't know." Kelly wanted to see Vicky. She had seen a few pictures of her but had never met her. Gina had dated her for several months and then broke up with her right before Vicky was sent to Iraq. She remembered that Gina had said Vicky's six-month stint in Iraq had been extended to nine months. By her calculations, she'd served seven months now, so why was she home early?

"Don't bother apologizing then. It doesn't really mean anything if you just say sorry." Gina shook her head.

Kelly shrugged. "I'm sorry for leaving your barbeque and not explaining why I had to leave. I'm sorry for avoiding your calls."

"Sure." Gina nodded. "Whatever." She still had her hand on the door as if she was waiting to close it on an annoying solicitor. "Is that all?"

"I thought we agreed to talk to each other before we messed around with other people," Kelly started. "Or did we change that rule and I just forgot?"

Gina stepped out on the porch and closed the front door. She eyed Kelly silently for a moment. "Look, Vicky just got back to California. Her dad had a heart attack and the army let her come home to see him in the hospital. He's okay now but they gave her a month's leave to stay with her family. She came over here just after you left the barbeque on Sunday. She's just staying at my place for a few days."

"That's too bad about her dad." Kelly didn't know what else to say. Everything that came to mind would sound like an attack on Gina or Vicky and she didn't want to show her feelings of jealousy. "I can't remember . . . How long did you date Vicky before she left for Iraq?"

"Six months," Gina answered. "You know, I was done with that relationship before she left. I already told you I was over her and I meant it. We're just friends now."

"Sure." Kelly didn't believe her. "Since when are *friends* and *fuck-buddies* interchangeable terms?" She turned to leave.

Gina called out to stop her, but Kelly ignored her and continued down the walkway. By the time she reached her car, Gina was at her side. She grabbed Kelly's wrist and pulled her hand off the door handle.

"Yeah, you're right, okay? I slept with her," Gina admitted. "But I don't want to lose you over this. Vicky and I are old friends. We messed around for, you know, old times—or whatever. It didn't mean anything."

"Old times? And she'll be gone again in a month anyway, so what difference does it make, right?" Kelly shook her head. "You know what? I don't give a damn. Fuck her all you want." She opened the door and sat down in the driver's seat. Gina caught the door before she could close it.

"Because you're fucking that lawyer?" Gina raised her voice. "Is that why you don't care?"

"I haven't done anything with Nora," Kelly said evenly, trying to keep control of her emotions. "Say hi to Vicky for me. And call me sometime. Maybe we can go out for coffee or something."

"Kelly, this is stupid. Don't leave like this. It was a one-time thing with Vicky and me."

"Why make it a one-time thing? She'll be here for a month. You may as well enjoy your time together." She hated the thought of Gina being with anyone else and was suddenly glad she hadn't seen Vicky in person. Now she wouldn't have any images in her mind.

"Look, I'm sorry I slept with her. She was here . . . and I thought you were with the lawyer. I was jealous."

"Well, you don't need to be jealous." Kelly pulled the door handle and glanced up at Gina. "Do you mind?"

"I just wanted . . ." Gina stopped herself. She glanced down at Kelly. "Never mind." She let go of the door and banged her fist on the roof of the VW.

"What?" Kelly asked. Gina didn't answer. Kelly shut the door and jammed the screwdriver in the ignition. She cussed Rick for taking the keys and started the engine. Gina knocked on her window and signaled for Kelly to roll it down.

"I really thought you were sleeping with Nora." Gina fidgeted with the door lock, avoiding Kelly's gaze. "I know I shouldn't have slept with Vicky." She paused. "But all I could think about was you spending the night with Nora."

"You could have asked." Kelly shrugged. "It doesn't matter anyway. Sleep with whomever you want." She shifted the car into gear and started to let her foot off the brake. Gina's hands were still on the car door.

"I want to sleep with you tonight, not Vicky."

Kelly shook her head. Gina had been in love with Vicky. She said she had broken off their relationship because Vicky had been sent to Iraq and Gina knew she couldn't handle a long-distance relationship. Later, she had told Kelly that she was over Vicky. But Kelly didn't believe her then. Hearing Vicky's voice on Gina's phone had only reinforced her doubts. Gina finally let go of the car door and stepped back. Kelly didn't look for Gina's reflection in the rearview mirror. She didn't want to think about Gina heading back inside to talk to Vicky or about Vicky sleeping on her side of Gina's bed.

Ahead, the sign marked the entrance to the freeway. Kelly didn't know where she was going. She wasn't ready to face Nora and didn't want to go back home. For some reason, she decided on going to the ocean and followed the freeway signs west.

Before long, she had reached Ocean Beach. The waves crashed ashore in a reassuring rhythm, each crest thundering against the sand without care. She walked down the beach, keeping a good distance from the foam of the breaking waves and avoiding the seaweed pods strewn over the sand. She spotted the Cliff House Restaurant and immediately thought of Marcus Edwards. His car had gone off the road not far from here. She felt as though she was close to figuring out his case but wondered if it would matter in the end. Would anyone be brought to justice for his death?

After a half-hour of staring at the waves, Kelly decided she was ready to see Nora. She drove to Nora's contemplating what she had learned from Kevin and Talcone's exchange earlier that day. She was almost certain that Talcone had been behind Marcus Edwards's death. But she still had nothing to prove this. When she arrived at Nora's place, she decided to avoid the front door. Anyone could be watching the house. Instead, she entered the backyard, scaling the fence in the same place where Rausche and his accomplice had been.

Nora answered the back door. "So, are you sure you want to come in? There's probably a soft patch of grass for you to sleep on out there, in between all of my weedy flowers and overgrown shrubs."

"Yeah, I think I'm already too familiar with your overgrown shrubs and weeds," Kelly replied, smiling.

"As you've probably noticed, I'm a terrible gardener," Nora said. "But I make a perfect iced tea. It's still warm enough to enjoy one on the back porch, if you'd like."

Kelly nodded and went into the kitchen. She picked out two tall glasses as Nora sliced a lemon. She had the pitcher of tea already chilled in the fridge and poured the sweet tea over ice before dunking the lemon slices in each glass. They headed out to the back porch and sat down on the steps facing the shrubs where Kelly had been hiding the night before.

It was just after nine and the sun had already set. Still, dusk left enough light for Kelly to make out the features of Nora's perfectly sculpted face. Kelly knew she was watching her too much but Nora didn't seem to mind. They sipped their tea listening to the crickets chirp and a songbird's call as he settled in for the night.

Nora finally set her glass down and shifted to face Kelly. She pointed to the back fence. "I can still see them scurrying over that fence. You know, I was so freaked out after seeing that man with the gun that the only thing I could think of was to laugh hysterically. But no sound came out when I tried to laugh. Then they just turned and ran from me."

"They were scared—you looked pretty tough with that big light and your gun." Kelly smiled.

"Do you think that guy was going to shoot me?" Nora asked. "He had that gun pointed at me and then he just dropped it. I don't know what happened."

Kelly shrugged. "The one guy had an earpiece and was getting orders from someone else, I think. Rick thought they were only trying to intimidate you. But I wouldn't put it past Rausche to shoot."

"I don't want to think about it. Every time I look out the window his face flashes in my mind." Nora shivered as a breeze brushed through the backyard.

"It's only been a couple days. The memory will fade." Kelly remembered Rausche's shotgun in her car and almost mentioned it to Nora. She had nearly forgotten about the gun.

Nora swatted at a mosquito that had landed on her arm. "Do you mind if we go inside?" she asked. "It's getting cool out here and a little too dark for my comfort level. Not to mention the fact that this porch light is going to be attracting more bugs soon."

Kelly followed Nora inside and then locked the back door. Without asking Nora, she started checking every window lock and lowering the shades. Nora stayed in the family room and made no comment.

When Kelly finally returned to the family room, Nora pointed to the sofa. "You can relax now." She selected a CD and put it in her stereo. Soft jazz filled the room. "Is this okay?"

"It's fine. Relaxing."

Nora nodded and then sat down on the sofa. Too far away, Kelly thought, for casual contact. She wished that she'd thought to sit closer to the middle.

"Thanks for locking up everything," Nora said. "Do I get you to tuck me in bed, too?"

Kelly didn't know how to answer. Was she serious?

Nora laughed. "You know, your eyebrows are very expressive. I can't decide what I like better—your blue eyes or your little arching eyebrows."

"I've never thought about my eyebrows much."

"I can tell." Nora reached over and traced one of Kelly's eyebrows. Then she smiled and sank back to her side of the couch. "You have that 'I'm tough' attitude but those eyebrows give you away all the time."

Kelly shook her head. She couldn't tell if Nora was flirting or just teasing. "I think we should change the subject."

"You don't like it when you're the subject of the conversation?" Nora asked. "Hmm. I'll have to get used to that, I guess. I'm used to spending my evenings with Terrance, and he's his own favorite topic."

"What about you? Can we make you the subject of the conversation?"

Nora shrugged. "I don't know why we'd want to talk about me."

Kelly thought for a moment. She had so many things she wanted to ask but wanted to start with something easy. "Okay, I have a question. Do you even know how to shoot that gun that you were waving around?"

"Yes, ma'am, I do." Nora smiled. She reached under the sofa and pulled out the gun. "How do you like my hiding place?"

"I was wondering why you sat so far away from me . . ."

"Well, if you must know, I sat down here just so I could make sure there was no monkey business." Nora laughed. She checked the safety on the gun, aimed at the stereo and pulled the trigger back, halfway. "Yep, I'm not a bad shot, if I do say so myself! Terrance and I used to go out to the shooting range all the time. He has a good assortment of guns—all locked up in storage, don't worry." After turning the gun over in her hands a few times, she tucked it back in the hiding spot under the sofa.

"Were you really thinking about the gun when you sat down on that side of the sofa?" Kelly asked. She wasn't sure why Nora would have joked about the monkey business, unless she really was flirting.

"Well, I was a little worried about sitting too close to you." Nora arched her eyebrow. "Who knows what I might be tempted to try if a big sofa cushion wasn't separating us."

181

"Damn, I knew I should have sat down in the middle instead of letting you point me to the far end." Now that Kelly knew Nora was flirting she felt suddenly at ease. One thing she could handle was flirting. For the moment, it didn't matter that Nora was straight. She shifted to the center and looked away from Nora, whistling softly with the jazz tune and trying to act suave.

Nora laughed and shoved Kelly back to the other side. "I'm not ready to have you that close."

"Mind if I get some more iced tea?" Kelly asked.

"Make yourself comfortable here."

"But not too comfortable, right?" Kelly smiled. "Do you want anything?"

Nora shook her head. Kelly stood up and headed toward the kitchen. As she passed Nora's spot, she felt something brush her arm. It was Nora's hand. She brushed down Kelly's arm and then took ahold of her hand. Kelly felt herself blush as Nora explored her palm with a soft fingertip. Kelly felt a rush of heat race through her body as Nora traced each line.

"My mom used to read palms—for fun, you know." Nora smiled. "You'll have a long life, a good career and . . ." She eyed Kelly mischievously. "And four kids, at least. You'll have several affairs and break your husband's"—she paused—"I mean wife's, heart."

"That's too bad. I'll have to remember not to get married."

Nora let go of her hand. "Then you'll make some girl sorry."

Kelly reached out to caress Nora's cheek. "You know, my mom used to say that you could tell everything about someone by the lines on their face, not their palm."

"What about people without wrinkles?" Nora asked.

Kelly shrugged. "You have to look close. Everyone has a few lines."

"So? Let's hear what your mom would say about mine. As long as you don't call them wrinkles." Nora winked.

Kelly studied her closely and Nora waited, motionless. Softly brushing her fingertip down from Nora's forehead to her chin,

Kelly paused at the edge of her lips. She leaned down and kissed her. As she pulled back, Kelly opened her eyes. Nora's eyes were still closed with her lips held open as though their kiss was unfinished.

"Or maybe it was in their kiss. I can't remember . . ." Kelly said.

Nora smiled. "I've heard that song."

Kelly wanted another. Her lips were begging to kiss her again. "Either way, my mom would say you are beautiful and definitely trouble."

"Oh really?"

"Yes. She'd warn me to not get involved."

Nora grabbed a pillow and swung it at Kelly. She laughed as Kelly blocked the pillows. "And what else would your mother's reading predict?"

"That you'll have a successful career, one kid, two wives." Kelly paused and smiled. "I mean, husbands, a stressful career and a vacation rental in the Cayman Islands that you'll never use enough."

Nora stopped laughing. "Wait, how'd you know I had a vacation rental?" she asked suspiciously.

Kelly pointed to the pile of mail on the end table. A letter about Nora's property dues for a place in the Cayman Islands was at the top of the stack.

"Oh, I forgot you were an investigator. What else have you found out about me?"

The phone rang and Nora picked up the receiver from the coffee table. Kelly left then to get the iced tea. She listened to Nora's conversation from the kitchen, guessing by her tone of voice that the caller was Terrance.

When Kelly came back, Nora smiled and pointed at the phone. She left her place on the sofa and went down the hallway to her bedroom. Kelly touched the pillow that Nora had tossed at her. She knew that what had just happened on Nora's sofa, whatever it was, wouldn't happen again. She heard Nora's muffled laugh through the closed bedroom door and knew Terrance still claimed a hold on her happiness. What had she been thinking? Kelly wondered with a sharp pang of loneliness. Nora was straight and their flirting couldn't lead anywhere.

Kelly wandered outside to sit on the back porch. The crickets were a soothing change from the tidbits of Nora's conversation that she could overhear. As much as she'd wanted to get inside Nora's house Sunday night, it surprised her how ready she was to get back outside now. Terrance and Nora were only temporarily separated, just as Gina and Vicky once were. After a few minutes, Kelly heard a soft tapping on the window above her head. Nora was motioning for her to come inside. Kelly knew she'd be sleeping alone on the couch again tonight and she wasn't in any hurry to leave the back porch. She shook her head at Nora and remained in her spot on the porch.

Nora opened the door. "That was Terrance on the phone."

Kelly didn't answer.

"You don't want to come in?"

"No, I think I'd like to stay out here for a while." Kelly smiled at her, hoping she was doing a tolerable job of hiding her emotions. She hated feeling rejected and didn't want Nora's flirtations now or her pity later. "I want to make a few tours around the house so we'll know if we need to be expecting *guests* later."

Nora rested her hand on Kelly's shoulder. "Thank you. I really appreciate . . . that you're here again tonight."

"Tonight . . ." Kelly stared up at the stars and the crescent moon hanging low in the night's sky. Nora needed her tonight, but Terrance would be back soon. Their lovers' quarrel would be resolved or maybe it already was. Maybe Terrance had already said the right words to win Nora back.

"Do you think you could stay here for a few more nights? It's strange . . . I've never been nervous about being alone. Until now." Nora waited for her to answer. "He'll be home on Friday."

She thought about Nora's request. Twenty minutes ago, she would have jumped at the chance to spend every evening with Nora for the next month, at least. Now she longed to be alone. If

Rausche came back while Nora was alone she'd never forgive herself for leaving. "Sure."

"What's wrong?"

"Nothing." She wanted to cry and felt stupid for this.

Nora stepped closer to her. "You know, I really don't know why I want you to stay."

Kelly leaned against the porch railing. "What are you talking about?"

"I'm not really scared to be alone. But I like having you here."

Kelly wondered what she meant. She wanted Nora to long for her company as much as she longed for hers but knew this couldn't be the case. "I don't think Rausche makes idle threats. And we still don't know who his cohorts are."

"I know." Nora looked back at the house. "I think I'll try and get some sleep." She leaned down and kissed Kelly's forehead. "Good night."

Chapter Fourteen

Just as Kelly arrived at the dojo the next morning, her cell phone rang. It was Gina. She stared at her phone for a moment and then decided not to answer. Somehow, she had begun to hate cell phones and she'd only had one for a month. If you had a phone, people assumed they could interrupt you everywhere. But she wasn't ready to talk to Gina or mull over their relationship. Fortunately, there were thirty active kids to be taught and her mind could focus on karate for the rest of the day. She tossed her cell phone in her locker and vowed to ignore it until the last camp student had cleared the dojo.

Sam approached Kelly after class that evening. She was wiping the sweat off her helmet and only looked up when she felt his hand on her shoulder. The rest of her gear was already stowed in her duffel bag.

"Nice kick combinations tonight."

She was surprised at the compliment. Although she'd scored well, she'd felt unfocused and couldn't recall a single clean technique. "Thanks, I guess."

"You guess?" he asked.

"I wasn't really feeling it tonight."

"Hmm." He sat down on a chair opposite Kelly and stretched out his legs. "Were you missing Kevin? I know you encourage each other, even though it always looks like you're trying to kill each other, of course."

"Maybe." She guessed that Kevin was tied up with work. She did miss him in class but was also relieved that she didn't have to face him after seeing him at the Capitol with Talcone.

"What else is distracting you?"

Of course, Sam could tell that Kevin wasn't the issue. Kelly immediately thought of Nora. She would see Nora again tonight and couldn't wait. "I don't know," she lied, wishing Sam would ignore her. She glanced at the other students in the dojo. Only two teenage boys, Joe and Mario, remained from the sparring class. The others had already gone home. Joe and Mario were both sixteen and would be starting their junior year of high school in less than a month. Kelly had signed them up for karate camp five years ago and they'd kept up with martial arts ever since, though they had quickly outgrown the camp. They were now comparing their new cars in loud animated voices.

As their noise escalated, Sam cleared his throat and crossed his arms. The boys seemed oblivious to his reproach. Sam picked up a rubber band lying on the floor and stretched it between his fingers. No doubt the rubber band belonged to Joe. He'd been trying to hold together his overused sparring gloves with duct tape and rubber bands for the past month. Sam focused the rubber band at Mario, who was currently describing his car's turning radius. The rubber band tagged Mario's ear and elicited a screech of surprise. Both boys stood up immediately and stared at Sam.

Sam smiled. "Why don't you guys take your conversation outside?"

Mario quickly responded, "Yes, sir." He snatched up his karate gear and goaded Joe to move faster. After a moment, they were both bowing and scrambling out of the dojo.

"They're like putty in your hands."

Sam nodded. "I'm still working out a few kinks. But boys will be boys, you know. And they are coming along."

When Joe and Mario had been students in the karate camp, Kelly had struggled constantly to keep them in line. She was happy when they finally advanced from the youth class to the adult class and were no longer her responsibility. Although they were old enough for the adult sparring class, they often acted like they still belonged in the children's group. Sam, however, had a way of controlling them that amazed her. They respected him unequivocally.

Sam turned his attention back to Kelly as soon as the door closed behind the boys. "Where were we? Oh, I almost forgot. Kevin left a message for you." He went to the office and returned with an envelope. "He said that he couldn't make it to class tonight, but he wanted me to give you this."

Kelly opened the envelope and took out a folded note that read, "Please meet me at Uncle Lee-Hi's after the sparring class." The address was printed below Kevin's signature. She handed the note to Sam. "Looks like I have a date. Should I tell him I prefer women?"

"I think he knows." He glanced at the note. "Anyway, you're not his type."

"I don't know. This sounds like a dinner date." She added, "Not that I've had much experience getting dinner invitations from handsome men."

"Maybe not men." He smiled. "I have no doubt that you get around. Rick mentioned something about it the other day."

"What? Do you guys sit around and discuss my dating history?"

"Oh, more than that."

"You know what, I don't want to know any more." She picked up her sparring gear and headed to the locker room. After changing into a pair of jeans and a clean T-shirt, she went to Sam's office. "Do you want me to pick you up any food from Uncle Lee-Hi's?"

Sam turned off his computer and closed his datebook. "No. My wife has egg rolls waiting for me at home. Although, my uncle makes better egg rolls."

"I won't tell your wife that you said that." Sam's uncle was in fact the notable Uncle Lee, owner and manager of the Chinese restaurant across the street. Sam often got free food from him and Kelly had shared many of his dinners. The egg rolls were delicious, she thought, her mouth watering.

"So, why are you meeting Kevin tonight?"

Kelly shrugged.

"Is that why you were distracted during the sparring class? Were you expecting him?"

"No. I have no idea why he wants to see me." She thought about Talcone and the conversation she'd had with Kevin about his work with the politician. She was suddenly nervous about their meeting and wondered if somehow Kevin had figured out that she was investigating his client. She knew that he had seen her at the Capitol and he also knew that she was working with Rick Lehrman. But did he know that Talcone was being investigated?

"I grilled Rick about the work you're doing with him. I'm not training you to break into people's houses." He sighed. "Nothing illegal."

Kelly nodded. "Of course, nothing illegal," she repeated. "And for the record, I didn't break into anyone's place."

"Well, you have a bag of some dead guy's personal items in your locker. I asked Rick and he said you've gone into a few homes, uninvited." Sam shook his head. "Don't bring that shit to my dojo."

Kelly swallowed. She was upset that Sam had gone through her locker contents and had talked to Rick behind her back, but she didn't blame him. Still, he was overreacting. "I'm sorry, sir. I'll have the locker cleaned out by tomorrow."

He nodded. "Lock up when you finish vacuuming. And don't

forget to clean the mirrors. Your Windex missed some kid's paw prints the last time you cleaned." He left the office and disappeared into the locker room. He continued in a muffled voice, "I ought to fire you for the criminal record you're about to get, but I'd fire you first for being sloppy." A moment later he emerged. His uniform had been exchanged for a pair of jeans and a T-shirt. In street clothes, Sam appeared much less fearsome than in his black gi and well-worn black belt.

Since she started working with Rick, she'd wanted to ask Sam one question. She'd stopped herself each time she tried. "Sir?"

Sam had his hand on the front door. He paused, waiting for her to continue.

"Why don't you work for Rick?" She suspected that Sam had once worked in Rick's PI service. Rick had mentioned that he'd used Sam for some prior business but refused to discuss it further. She guessed that their business relations extended beyond the dojo.

"Good question. He sure pays well." Sam sighed. "I have a wife and a baby girl waiting for me at home."

Kelly finally went to her locker to check her phone messages. Gina had called twice and left one long message. She promised that there was nothing going on between her and Vicky. According to the message, they had discussed the past issues and were ready for a friendship and nothing more. Kelly didn't return her call. She had nothing to say to her.

Uncle Lee-Hi's was famous for slow service as well as the best Chinese food in Ashton. Kelly waited at the front counter for the hostess, who'd just disappeared around the edge of the wall-sized fish tank to seat a couple for dinner. From the front counter, none of the dining area was visible. The last time she'd been in the dining area was with her family to celebrate Alex's high school graduation. Since then, she'd only come to the front counter to pick up take-out orders. Staring at a bowl of mints placed next to the cash register, she heard her stomach growl.

The hostess finally returned. "Just one for dinner?" she asked in a pleasant voice.

A group of well-dressed patrons passed the front counter and Kelly felt suddenly out of place. No one came to Uncle Lee-Hi's to dine alone, let alone wearing jeans and a T-shirt advertising a karate school. "No, I'm hoping to meet a friend. Do you know if Kevin Slater may have left his name?"

The hostess glanced at the clipboard and shook her head. "Would you like to wait at a table for him?"

Kelly shook her head. "I think I'll just wait here, if that's okay."

She nodded and turned her attention to the cash register and a stack of receipts. Kelly didn't recognize this hostess and knew that she hadn't worked here long. An older Chinese woman came out from the dining area, murmured something to the hostess and then glanced up. Kelly recognized Mrs. Lee, the wife of the restaurant owner, and wondered if she'd remember her.

"Oh!" Mrs. Lee exclaimed as soon as she recognized Kelly. "No one told me you were here!" She hugged her and glared at the hostess. "Sam wants egg rolls, of course?"

Kelly shook her head. "He said he didn't want anything tonight. I'm here to meet another friend."

"Sam's wife—good cook, but Sam doesn't eat enough. He's too skinny." Mrs. Lee shook her head at this. "He needs more of my egg rolls. I'll be back." She disappeared behind the fish tank, leaving the hostess and Kelly alone again. Kelly stared at the guppies to avoid the look from the hostess. She hadn't meant to get her in trouble and hoped that Mrs. Lee wouldn't be upset for long. Nearly every time that Kelly came to pick up food, Mrs. Lee gave her an extra order of egg rolls to take to Sam. She was always very sweet. The fish darted between the broad kelp leaves and coral as though they knew that fish was served here nightly.

"Hello?"

Kelly glanced up from the tank and met Gina's eyes. She stared at her without speaking for a moment too long. Gina wasn't alone. No one dined at Uncle Lee-Hi's alone, she reminded herself. She knew that the woman holding Gina's hand was Vicky.

"Kelly?"

"Hello," Kelly said quickly. What was the luck that Gina and

Vicky would dine here tonight? "Good to see you," she said, forcing a smile through tight lips. "Sorry, I was distracted by the guppies." She extended her hand toward the woman at Gina's side. Somehow, she had regained control of the situation despite the awkward meeting. "And you must be Vicky. I'm Kelly. Nice to meet you."

Vicky nodded and shook her hand.

"Gina speaks very fondly of you," Kelly added. She could tell by Vicky's expression that Gina had not mentioned their relationship.

Mrs. Lee returned to the front counter. She handed Kelly a small brown paper bag and said, "Tell my nephew he should come by here more often. Sam used to have dinner here with us at least twice a week. Now we never see him."

Kelly thanked her. She was glad for the interruption and hoped that Gina wouldn't think she was having dinner here alone. "Sam's very busy. I'm sure he wishes he could eat here every night. I know I do."

Mrs. Lee smiled at this compliment. A waiter motioned to her from the other side of the fish tank and she motioned for the hostess to go help him, then excused herself to go back to the kitchen.

Gina's tense demeanor and silence were more apparent as soon as the hostess had left them alone. Kelly smiled at Vicky. "Did you enjoy your dinner tonight?"

She nodded. "I love this place. You know, romantic setting and great food . . . It must be nice to have friends in high places. Free take-out." She gestured at Kelly's bag and then glanced at Gina. Gina stared at her hands, avoiding eye contact. Vicky continued, "And who's Sam? Is he your boyfriend?"

Kelly shook her head. Gina definitely hadn't told Vicky about their relationship. "No. Sam's my sensei."

"Your sensei?" Vicky asked. She didn't wait for a reply. "I guessed you were in the martial arts by that shirt. How exciting! You're not wearing a belt, so I'll have to ask, what rank are you? My brother took karate lessons for a few months last summer. He liked it a lot."

"Most people do." Kelly smiled. She didn't want to talk to Vicky about karate or anything else, for that matter. She stared at Gina, hoping she might look up and say something. "But it's not that exciting. Nothing like being in the army, I'm sure."

Vicky cocked her head to one side, clearly surprised. "You knew I was in the army? I guess Gina really does talk about me behind my back!" She laughed.

"She's mentioned only good things about you."

Vicky squeezed Gina's hand and Kelly felt a rush of aversion. She didn't want to think about Gina and Vicky having a romantic dinner or holding hands, or where else they might touch each other. Gina's face had a pained look and Kelly wondered if she was embarrassed.

In a strained voice, she said, "Well, I don't want to keep you two. I'm sure you have plans for the rest of your evening."

"Of course. It was so nice to bump into you," Vicky said, still holding Gina's hand and smiling warmly at Kelly.

Kelly nodded. She caught Gina's gaze for a brief moment but couldn't read any of her thoughts. Gina let go of Vicky's hand and opened the door. They left the restaurant and disappeared into the dark night without a backward glance. Squeezing the bag until her fingernails felt like they could pierce her palm, Kelly paced the small waiting area. The last thing she needed was to have stepped into the middle of Gina and Vicky's date. She needed to get out of Ashton.

Kevin finally arrived, dressed in a business suit that seemed specifically tailored for him. He looked like an advertisement for a suit company. The hostess immediately appeared to seat them. Batting her eyes at Kevin, she was now only too eager to be helpful. He was handsome, Kelly had to admit, even without the dapper suit. His dark features and deep blue eyes, set off with lashes that seemed almost too long for a man, always attracted attention. And Kevin never seemed too modest to flirt with someone of either sex.

Mrs. Lee waited on them herself. She reminded Kelly twice to take the egg rolls to Sam and then said hello to Kevin. The two were already well acquainted, because he used to bring all of his business clients to Uncle Lee-Hi's when he still worked in Ashton. Mrs. Lee teased him for bringing Kelly as his date and then leaving her to wait for him.

He fended off Mrs. Lee's jabs with his own set of jokes. By the time Mrs. Lee had taken their orders, all three were laughing and the other guests in the restaurant eyed Kevin and Kelly suspiciously. Wontons and egg rolls arrived just after Mrs. Lee went to the kitchen. Kevin asked the waiter if the appetizers were left over from someone else's unfinished plate. The waiter looked confused and started to explain that they would never do such a thing when Kelly interrupted him. She apologized to the waiter and told him it was Kevin's way of offering a compliment for such fast service. She then glared at Kevin, who was grinning as he dug in.

As soon as the waiter left their table, she said, "Kevin, that poor kid thought you were serious."

"No one has a sense of humor anymore." He smacked his lips. "Oh, try the spicy sauce on the right. Must be a new recipe. It's delicious."

Kelly agreed. "I missed you at sparring. Were you working late?"

He nodded.

"And why are we here tonight?"

"Well, I just hate to eat alone," he whined. "I had no date tonight and I figured, a little romantic dinner and then I'll have my way with you."

Kelly laughed. "God, that's something I don't want to think about."

"Why not? I'm good in bed and you know what they say, you can never be sure you're a lesbian until you have sex with a gay man."

"You have that backward. What people say is, you can never be sure you're a gay man until you have sex with a lesbian."

"Either way, we're perfect for each other." He winked.

Chow mein, cashew chicken and vegetable stir-fry appeared in the arms of their shy waiter. He set the entrées on the table and whisked away the appetizers as Kevin made eyes at him.

In a too-loud voice, Kevin remarked, "And now the wontons will make their way to table number nine, via a shortcut through the kitchen. But we won't tell that couple at table nine that the dipping sauce just came from the gay table and might be homo-tainted."

The waiter glanced over his shoulder and smiled at Kevin before disappearing into the kitchen. Kelly jabbed her chopsticks at Kevin. "Quit flirting with him. He's barely twenty."

"But he's legal." Kevin laughed. "Anyway, do you really think he's that young? Barely twenty?"

Kelly nodded. She knew that Kevin was thirty-five years old, but his boyish looks made people assume he was much younger. "And don't you have a boyfriend?"

"That just means I have someone to come home to if I don't get lucky at the club."

She immediately thought of Gina and Vicky. Kevin's comment had stung. She wondered why Gina had said that she was no longer involved with Vicky and then taken her out for a romantic dinner. From their interactions together, it was apparent that Vicky still thought she had a relationship with Gina. Why else would they come here alone?

"Hey, I was only joking," Kevin said. "What happened to your sense of humor? Don't tell my boyfriend on me, okay?"

Kelly smiled. "Okay. But only if you tell me why we're here tonight. Otherwise I'll follow you home and spill the beans about your flirting and polygamy."

"He already knows. Remember, I was married when I met him."

"Oh, good point."

"So, aside from the good food and nice scenery"—he paused to wink at the waiter who was passing by their table—"I wanted to talk to you about our little encounter in Sacramento. And just for the record, I hate my boss and would love to see him go to hell."

Kelly was curious now. She trusted him but was surprised he'd

195

come looking for her to share information. "Yes, I was only planning to see the Veterans Memorial Rose Garden. You were a bonus."

"And I know that Rick has you working on Marcus's accident," he whispered. "So, why did you spend the day in the gardens?"

"To smell the roses, of course," she answered.

He shook his head. "Since when did you get to be so coy?"

"Why did you want to meet me?" She was going to tread lightly before giving him any information.

The waiter stopped at their table. "Can I get you anything else tonight?"

Kevin smiled. "Yes, but it's not on the menu."

"Ignore him," Kelly said. "He's a troublemaker."

"I like those types." He set their bill on the table. "Keeps me on my toes."

As soon as he left, Kelly added, "Or off your toes, in this case." She shook her head. "You know, I really can't take you anywhere."

Kevin laughed. He glanced at his watch and then eyed the rest of the food on their plates. "I think we'll need to get this to go. We can walk and talk. I've got a phone meeting at nine tonight so we'll need to put a move on it."

He paid the bill and had their food transferred to take-out boxes. They left the restaurant with waves from Mrs. Lee and winks from the less shy waiter.

Kevin started down the street. "I'm parked on Fourth Street. Where's your car?"

"Behind the dojo."

"Well, you can be gentlemanly and walk me to my car and I'll give you a ride back to yours." Kevin smiled and took her arm. "So, what you really want to know is how my boss is involved with Marcus Edwards, don't you?"

Kelly was surprised at his forthrightness. "Yes." She didn't remind him that she'd asked him about Marcus Edwards last week. She'd guessed he was lying when he'd told her that he didn't know who Marcus was.

"Before we go any further, I want to reiterate one thing. I hate Talcone. He needs to be out of office and I would love to make that happen."

"What about your job? What type of consultant gets their politician out of office?"

"I'm going back to trading stocks. I can handle the stress of Wall Street better than this. I've already told my boss at Meridian that I'm quitting and I've left a statement with our legal adviser, explaining everything that I know about Talcone. He told me I should go to the FBI."

"Then why haven't you?"

"I don't think I have the full story yet." He paused. "And I trust you more than some tool in the FBI. I know Rick has connections there and I know you work for him. My hope is that we'll get Talcone in jail where he belongs and I won't be dragged into any of this."

Kelly wondered what exactly he meant but decided not to pursue it. "Kevin, were Talcone and Marcus friends?"

"Not exactly. I know Marcus and Talcone were friends once, back in their army days. But I think they grew apart."

"What about Jared DiBaca? I saw a picture of all three of them golfing together. The picture was dated in June of this year."

"Really?" He sounded surprised. "Well, Talcone has been trying to get in good with DiBaca so he could secure the CVA endorsement on his politics. He wants their approval on the Medical Benefits Act. But I'm shocked to hear that Marcus would have gone golfing with those two."

She nodded. "Marcus had an unflattering sketch of Talcone in his journal. He called him 'The Closet Politician.' What do you know about that?"

"You mean is the conservative right's poster boy really a homo?"

"Well, he is married." She stopped herself before adding, "But that hasn't stopped some other people I can think of." Kevin probably wouldn't appreciate the jab at his failed marriage and now wasn't the time to scrape old wounds. "If he wasn't gay, then why did he donate money to GPAC?"

"As he described it to me, he went through a period of experimentation in his younger years. Once he decided that he wanted to be a politician, he got married and went into the closet."

"He told you that?" She could hardly believe that Talcone would admit he wasn't a full-blooded heterosexual.

"Yes, but only after he propositioned me." Kevin snorted. "I told him I preferred women."

Kelly laughed. "Bet you never thought you'd have to use that line again."

"I had hoped that I wouldn't."

She had a sudden thought. "Were Talcone and Marcus ever involved?"

"Do you mean sexually? No. As far as I know, Marcus was as straight as they come."

Kelly pressed further. She knew there was something more between Marcus and Talcone. "Talcone's name was on the GPAC sponsor list. I've been wondering if Marcus was blackmailing him over that."

"Ah, the sponsor list. I was waiting for you to bring that up." He glanced at a passing car. "Talcone would love to have every copy of that list destroyed. He's worried that his conservative supporters will find out about his sordid past. When Marcus was updating the computer files, he came across Talcone's name and went to him as a friend, at least as far as I could tell. I think he was concerned about whose hands the archived sponsors list would get into."

"Whose hands?"

"Marcus told Talcone that Jared DiBaca and the other coots at the CVA were waiting to get their hands on the GPAC archived records. According to Talcone, the CVA is hell-bent on flushing gays out of the military and political seats."

"How would they get hold of the list? The lists aren't public record." She remembered the memos that Nora had found with the bank tracking information and Marcus's bank statements that confirmed he'd been receiving money from DiBaca and Talcone. "Was CVA paying Marcus?"

"Talcone told me that DiBaca was paying Marcus. He freaked out when he found out about this, knowing that they'd find his name if they looked far enough back in their records. So, Talcone paid Marcus to keep the lists out of DiBaca's hands." He paused as another couple passed them. The woman looked over at Kelly and smiled, while the man nodded at Kevin. Kelly wanted to laugh at the oddity of this but merely returned the smile. The other couple crossed the street and Kevin continued, "The thing is, Talcone was kind of a nobody when he was in the military, a gay nobody. He inherited some money when his dad passed away fifteen years ago and decided to donate money to GPAC. At the time, they were known as the main political group fighting for political and military equality for gays."

"Then Talcone outgrew his gay phase," Kelly said.

"Or went back into the closet. I don't know. He got married and started a political career. Suddenly he's a conservative with a conservative agenda and he wants CVA's support."

"You know, I just don't believe that Marcus went to Talcone with the GPAC sponsor list info because of their old friendship. I think there was something else going on."

"Well, money is often the reason, of course. It is the most noble of all causes, right? Marcus probably approached Talcone with an offer to take his name off the GPAC list or to give the list and the archived files to CVA." Kevin shrugged. "The only proof I have is that Talcone paid Marcus several times. I stumbled across some records in Talcone's office and that's when I started snooping around. He even made journal entries about his meetings with Marcus. For fifty grand, Marcus promised to destroy the archived files and to give Talcone the master list. I've got a copy of a note signed by Marcus agreeing to that deal."

"You found that in Talcone's office?"

He nodded smugly. "You wouldn't believe what Talcone records. He's all about writing things down. Don't ask me why."

"Was destroying GPAC's computer system part of that deal?"

Kelly wondered aloud. "So now, no one can get the archived records."

"Not exactly. I don't think Talcone completely trusted Marcus. He had someone take care of the computer system. He's still worried that more than one copy of the sponsor list may have been printed."

Although she thought she trusted Kevin, she wasn't willing to tell him that she had seen a copy of the archived list. Kelly thought about the mess at the GPAC office and Marcus's overturned apartment. She was sure Leo Rausche had been responsible for both. "What do you know about Leo Rausche? Does he work for Talcone?"

"Ah, Leo." Kevin sighed. "It's my impression that he'll work for anyone who pays him the price he wants. He's an independent contractor, of sorts."

"Rausche went to Marcus's house after the accident. Was he looking for a copy of the list?"

"Probably." Kevin paused. "It's entirely possible that Marcus could have made a duplicate."

Kelly felt a chill race down her spine. She glanced over her shoulder to make certain they weren't being followed. "Okay, let me get this straight. Marcus printed out the GPAC archived sponsor list and crashed the computer system. Then what?"

"He had a meeting with Talcone, who was in San Francisco for a conference with CVA on his bill." They finally reached Fourth Street and Kevin pointed out his car. He unlocked her door. "By the way, I don't know how much you know about Rausche, but I'd avoid him if I were you."

Kelly climbed in the passenger seat and waited for Kevin. Rausche's face flashed in her mind. His narrow brow and dark eyes followed her, looking like a raptor about to attack its prey. She shivered and the image vanished. Kevin started the car and then made a U-turn on Main Street to head back to the dojo. "How do you know what happened at a meeting between Marcus and Talcone? Did Talcone take notes on that?" she asked incredulously.

"No. I was there." Kevin sighed. "Talcone and I were actually at a dinner meeting with a few other state senators and their respective entourages. He got a call from Marcus, who was waiting at Talcone's hotel. Talcone was upset because he had planned to meet Marcus later that evening, but I guess Marcus was early." He rolled down his window as he stopped at an intersection. Some pedestrians crossed the intersection just as their light turned green. Watching them, he continued, "Anyway, Talcone and I had driven over together, so we went back to the hotel together. At the time, I thought Marcus was just some old military friend of Talcone's and didn't understand why he wouldn't tell Marcus to wait for him."

"So this was Tuesday night, a week ago? At what time?"

"You know, I'd guess it was around eight when Marcus called. I think we were back at the hotel by nine." Kevin finally drove through the intersection just as the light turned yellow. He waved to the pedestrians like he was a friend of theirs. "Marcus met us in the lobby. He had a file for Talcone. I saw Talcone flip through the file and noticed the title 'GPAC Sponsor List' on one of the pages. Then Talcone gave Marcus an envelope and Marcus left."

"End of story?"

"Of course not," Kevin said, smiling. "As soon as Marcus left, Talcone was on the phone to this guy named Leo."

Kelly whistled softly. "My dear friend Leo Rausche."

"He's not the friendly sort."

"Yeah, I noticed." She shook her head, amazed that the pieces were finally coming together. "And Talcone told Rausche to take care of Marcus?"

"Sounds like a line from a bad movie." Kevin grinned. "Actually, Talcone just told Rausche to follow Marcus home and make sure he didn't have any duplicate files from GPAC at his house. He wanted him to check out the GPAC office as well. He never mentioned causing Marcus any harm."

"You think the car accident really was an accident?"

"No. I've met Rausche. I doubt anyone who's met that guy would believe he'd run a car off the road by accident."

She wondered when Kevin would have met Rausche, doubting that he'd stroll into Talcone's office. Unfortunately, most of what Kevin had told her was still just hearsay. She needed something solid for Nora. "Is any of this recorded? I mean, do we have any paper trail or some hard evidence to back up this story?"

"How do you think I figured this out? Talcone is meticulous about his money. He has payment accounts for everything, including payments to Marcus and Rausche. And he also has a daily planner. I'm amazed at the shit he writes down. Half the time I think he'd forget his own name if it weren't written in ten different places in that planner. I saw one of his entries just yesterday: 'Paid Leo—five G installment for other copies of GPAC list.' I'm telling you, this guy has no idea that he's writing his own prosecution notes." Kevin turned down the side street leading behind the dojo. He parked alongside her car. "Now it's your turn."

"What do you mean?" she asked.

"I don't want to be the whistle-blower on Talcone." Kevin shook his head. "I want to be out of this mess. But I don't want to be the one that calls the Feds on him."

Kelly thought about the records that Kevin said Talcone kept. "We just need an agent with a warrant to poke around when Talcone's in the office. Will he be in Sacramento tomorrow?"

Kevin nodded. "And the sooner we get an FBI agent on this, the better, obviously."

"I'll talk to Rick and he'll get it set up. Rick knows how to pull all the strings. Can I tell him that we had this conversation?"

Kevin paused and then nodded. "I'd like to have an army on my side but I guess my sparring partner and an ex-FBI agent will do."

"I know a lawyer you might want to talk to also."

"I'm counting on Meridian's legal advisor to pull me through this. Everything will work out, somehow." He smacked his fist lightly against her arm. "Otherwise, I'll just become a karate master."

Kelly said good-bye to him and then watched him drive away before climbing into her car. She started the ignition and then paused, her hand resting on the drive shaft. She could hear a man's breathing in the backseat but was too afraid to look over her shoulder.

In the next moment, his hand was on her throat. She felt her body stiffen immediately. Relax, she coached herself, knowing that she had defended herself from a similar attack before. She was frozen in fear and could only wait for his next move.

"Why did you leave your door unlocked?"

Kelly thought she recognized the stench of cigarette smoke on his hands. She couldn't mistake him now. She wrenched his pinky finger off her neck and he let go as she turned to face him. "Rick, what the hell are you doing in my car?"

"Damn, you could take it a little easier on me. I need all of my fingers." He rubbed his pinky finger.

"Then don't try to choke me again." She knew that Sam would have given her hell for not reacting to the choke sooner.

"Well, I just thought I'd test you. You know, you really should always lock your car."

"And I would," she replied, eyeing him in the rearview mirror. "Unfortunately, I have no key."

"You didn't even check the backseat before getting in. If I were Rausche, you might be dead now."

"Rausche wouldn't want to kill me." She hoped. "He wants the GPAC sponsor list."

"How do you know he's looking for the list?"

"I just finished a meeting with Kevin Slater, Talcone's consultant."

Rick nodded. "Yeah, and?"

Of course he already knew that, Kelly thought. She wondered if Sam had told him or if Rick had been following her. "He said that Talcone wants all the copies of the archived GPAC sponsor list and is paying Rausche to get them."

"Good work. What else?"

Kelly told him everything she remembered from her conversation with Kevin. She wished again that she'd had a recorder.

Suddenly her job transcribing Rick's tapes made much more sense. Rick grilled her on a few points and she had trouble recalling exactly what Kevin had said.

"Can you get an FBI agent with a warrant to investigate Talcone?"

"Not yet," Rick said, shaking his head. "I don't think we have all the pieces yet."

Kelly wondered what he thought was missing. It was possible that Rick was stalling. They had figured out who was responsible for Marcus's death, and if Kevin was telling the truth, then they had proof of Talcone's motive. What else did they need? "One thing is still bugging me," she said. "DiBaca went to Marcus's apartment after Rausche. Was he looking for the sponsor list?"

"Maybe. I don't know. Like I said, we've got some missing pieces. If Marcus was supposed to give a copy of the list to DiBaca and instead went to Talcone, maybe he missed a meeting with DiBaca," Rick suggested.

"So, DiBaca came looking for him?"

"And fortunately for Marcus, he was already dead."

"Fortunately?"

"I wouldn't want DiBaca to find me when he was upset." He laughed. "Or Rausche for that matter. Speaking of which, are you staying with Nora again tonight?"

Kelly nodded.

"Good. I don't want her left alone. Rausche might be thinking that Nora has a copy of the sponsor list. What is your next step?"

Kelly hadn't really thought of a next step. She considered her options. The only thought that came to mind was to return to the GPAC office and try to snoop around there some more. When she suggested this to Rick, he promised to get her the morning off so she could go there first thing tomorrow. He then opened the back door and waved good-bye. Kelly drove to Nora's house, trying to focus on only one thought. She needed to see Nora. Her head was swimming with all of the new information.

❧

By the time she arrived at Nora's house, Kelly couldn't decide what she wanted to tell Nora about first. She knocked on the front door, after carefully assessing the street and deciding that no one was watching Nora's place.

Nora unlocked the door and smiled at Kelly through the crack between the door and the frame. The chain was still attached. "I was just thinking about you."

"Good thoughts?" Kelly asked.

Nora arched her eyebrow. "That depends on the judge." She closed the door and the chain rattled. The second time she opened the door all the way and Kelly walked in. "Did I say you could come in?"

Kelly paused in the entryway. "Oh, I'm sorry. I thought that—"

Nora interrupted her, laughing. "Relax, I'm only joking. You look so serious tonight."

Kelly nodded. "I just talked to a friend about the case. I have news to tell you about—"

Again Nora interrupted, this time touching her finger to Kelly's lips. "Can it wait?"

"What?" Kelly asked, taken aback by Nora's touch.

"Can it wait?" Nora repeated. "What you have to tell me about the case—can it wait until we say hello?"

Kelly knew she was blushing. "Um, hi." She wasn't sure what Nora was after, but she was willing to play along. "How was your day?"

"Now see, that's better." Nora sighed. "I had a good day. How was yours?"

"Just fine." Kelly felt her blood pressure rise every time Nora touched her. Nora had moved her finger from Kelly's lips to her neck. She stared down at Nora's hand.

"Anything exciting happen—that has nothing to do with the case?"

Kelly would have to wait to tell Nora the news. After all, she had all night to spend here. She tried to remember everything that had happened that day. The dojo and Monkey suddenly came to mind. "I showed some kid how to do his first flying side kick."

"Wow," Nora replied in an indifferent tone. "Sounds exciting."

"It was, for him." Kelly smiled.

Nora stepped closer and wrapped her arms around Kelly's neck. "I'd love to see you teach sometime. But you know what I want now?" she asked softly.

"Um, no." Kelly didn't dare answer Nora's question.

Nora leaned closer and kissed her. After a moment, she let go and stepped away. Kelly stared at her, speechless.

"I'm glad you're here," Nora said. Her voice was suddenly more formal, and more like the Nora Kelly knew.

What happened? Kelly wondered, following Nora down the hall to the family room. What did Nora want from her that she was unable to ask for? The television news was playing and Nora switched off the TV. She picked up an almost empty wineglass and went to the kitchen to refill it. "May I offer you a glass? I'll admit I've already sampled this bottle and it's quite good."

Kelly shook her head. She couldn't drink tonight. "Do you have any more iced tea?"

"I do, but the wine is better."

Kelly shook her head. Nora poured her a glass of tea and brought it out to the family room. She turned on the stereo and selected a CD. A jazz song began and Nora sighed, sitting down on the sofa near Kelly. She took a sip of her wine and closed her eyes. "God, I used to love dancing to this. Ah, Miles Davis."

"You can dance to this music?" Kelly asked with surprise. "It feels too slow."

"Well, it is slow, but it's also sultry."

Kelly wondered why Nora had selected this album from the tall stack of CDs. "Do you still dance?"

"Not often. Terrance doesn't really like dancing. And honestly, I don't really like dancing with him. We do other things, you know, dinner with friends, plays or concerts. But I miss the dance clubs." She glanced at Kelly. "Do you like to dance?"

Kelly nodded. "I like fast club music. I wouldn't know how to dance to something like this."

Nora set her wineglass on the table and stood up, extending her hand. "I'll show you."

Kelly shook her head at first and Nora prodded her until she finally caved. Taking Nora's hand, she stood up and faced her. They were exactly the same height and nearly the same build. Kelly loved the striking contrast of the shades of their skin. "Okay, but you'll have to lead."

Nora smiled. "I've never tried to lead, but I'll give it a shot." She placed her right hand on Kelly's waist and set Kelly's left hand on her shoulder. She clasped Kelly's right hand and gazed into her eyes.

"I usually kiss someone when I'm this close," Kelly whispered.

Nora shook her head. "This time you have to dance." She waited for the next beat in the song and then stepped out. "Follow me."

Kelly eased into Nora's direction, trying to mirror her foot-steps. "It's kind of like swing dancing, only slower."

"And sexier." Nora glanced at her. "We're a little too far apart. See, you're supposed to dance more like this." She took a step closer and her breasts suddenly were pressed against Kelly's. She held Kelly's hips against hers as they danced.

The next song had a faster beat and Nora picked up the pace. Kelly fell into Nora's rhythm and let Nora guide her movements. Her head felt light and she found their dancing intoxicating. Every time her hips or breasts pushed against Nora's she felt a wave of excitement.

Nora paused as the song ended. She let go of Kelly and stepped back. "You're not a bad dancer. I like a quick learner."

"I blame it on years of ballet. My mom thought I looked cute in a pink tutu." Kelly laughed. "And you're a good lead."

"Thank you." Nora bowed, then curtsied. "I also wore a pink tutu." She took a sip of wine and glanced up. "You're sure you wouldn't like some?"

Kelly smiled. "Are you trying to get me drunk so I'll go to bed with you?"

"What if I said yes?" Nora laughed. She reached for Kelly's hand again. "One more dance? I like this next song."

This time, a woman's soulful voice filled the room with a rich silky tone. Kelly didn't recognize the singer and wanted to ask Nora who it was. Nora turned her in a slow circle around the family room. Kelly forgot her question about the song and instead thought of Nora's last remark. She had trouble keeping up with Nora's feet on this song. Was Nora serious? Was she intent on more than flirting tonight?

The song ended and Nora shifted her hands on Kelly. She cupped Kelly's face and then kissed her. Kelly responded, pressing against Nora and pushing her tongue between Nora's lips. Nora's hands moved under Kelly's shirt, caressing each breast. Her hands moved lower and she traced the belt on Kelly's jeans.

"Would you be uncomfortable if I asked you to take off your shirt?" Nora asked.

Kelly smiled and shook her head. This time, the drapes were already drawn in the room. No one would be looking in on them tonight. Nora bit her lower lip, waiting and watching as Kelly pulled off her shirt and unclasped her bra. She was burning to feel Nora's hands on her again. She stepped closer and started dancing again, this time taking the lead. Nora paused several times to rub her hands over Kelly's chest and to find her lips for another kiss. Now Kelly was begging to feel Nora's body. She hesitated, unsure of how far Nora was willing to take this. Finally she stopped dancing and asked, "Wouldn't you be more comfortable without that blouse?"

Nora didn't answer at first. Kelly was afraid she had overstepped some unnamed line. Then Nora began to unbutton her blouse, letting it hang open to expose her white lace bra and smooth brown skin. Kelly pulled off Nora's shirt and then undid her bra. Nora's breasts filled her hands and she massaged them with murmurs of approval from Nora. They danced to the next song, rubbing breasts whenever they could and letting the music fill their heads with desire for more contact. Kelly unzipped Nora's pants, feeling her silk underwear slide under her hands. She expected Nora to stop her, but she only continued to dance, encouraging Kelly to explore her body more.

The CD ended and Kelly glanced at the couch and then at the staircase leading upstairs to Nora's bedroom. "How far do you want to go tonight?"

Nora didn't answer. Kelly leaned toward her and kissed her. Instead of pulling away, Nora relaxed, giving Kelly every signal she needed.

When they separated, Nora gazed at Kelly. She brushed her fingers over Kelly's nipples. "Show me how far you can take me."

The cell phone rang and startled Kelly awake. She hit the ring silencer and rolled over. A moment later, a hand touched her shoulder. Nora smiled at her, then closed her eyes and snuggled up against her. "Who's calling?"

"I don't care," Kelly said. It was Gina. She'd seen her name flash on the screen and felt a moment of regret. Seven a.m. Why was she in Nora's bed? Was this the side that Terrance normally slept on? Kelly shook her head. She rolled over and kissed Nora. "This was by far the best one-night stand I've ever had."

Nora sighed. "You understand then? I was worried about what we would have to say to each other about this."

"This? We fucked." Kelly climbed out of bed and went over to the window. She raised the blinds an inch and sunlight streamed in through the crack. Kelly knew that she didn't belong in Nora's world. Their encounter had to be short-lived.

"It was more than that, at least to me." Nora sat up against the pillows and eyed Kelly. "I like seeing you naked. The sun is playing on your body like a spotlight. You're so beautiful—stunning, really. I've never had a lover like you."

Kelly shook her head. "You mean, you've never been with a woman." She didn't want Nora's compliments now. She wanted to leave the room, wanted to run from Nora's world now that she knew for certain that she would never have a place here. Nora had told her the answer last night, just after they finished making love and were curled against each other on the red sheets. "Terrance will be home on Friday," she had said. Everything in Kelly's world had collapsed at that moment. She had slept fitfully and was glad for the morning light to release her now. Nora was straight, Kelly reminded herself. She would forget her night with Kelly, or ascribe it to a moment of weakness.

"Yes, you're right, in a way. I've never been with a woman, before last night. But it's more than that." She paused. "And much more than a one-night stand." Nora came over and placed her finger on Kelly's nipple. "You know, you are my first lesbian crush."

"Crush?" Kelly shook her head. "No, I had a crush on you."

"Who's the judge on that one?"

Kelly's cell phone rang again and she saw it was Rick this time. "This call I have to take."

Nora nodded. She caught Kelly's hand and kissed her palm. "By the way, I really can't read palms. I just wanted an excuse to touch you."

Kelly watched Nora leave the room. She heard the water faucet going in the bathroom and finally answered the phone.

Rick began, "Well, it's all set. You'll have to work the morning shift but Sam is coming in at noon. I told him you'd need about three hours. By the way, I've got a friend who's working on getting a warrant to investigate Talcone's office. He's going to wait until I give him the go-ahead. Have you told Nora about your dinner meeting?"

"Not yet, but I will," Kelly promised.

"When will you see her again?" he asked. "Maybe I should just call her now."

"Well, go ahead, but I'll see her as soon as she gets out of the bathroom. I can tell her then."

"Oh." Rick paused. Kelly guessed he would understand what she hadn't said about Nora. "Fine. Have a good morning then. I'll keep you posted."

Kelly said good-bye to him and opened the window blinds fully to let the sun fill the room. She stared out the window at Nora's backyard. She found the spot under the bushes at the edge of the grass where she had spent the cold night alone. It was clearly visible from here and she wondered if Nora had watched her that night.

"So, what are you going to tell me?" Nora asked.

"You wouldn't believe what I found out last night." Kelly continued to stare out the window.

"I might believe you. Try me."

Kelly sighed. She didn't know where to begin. "Robert Talcone was paying Marcus for the archived GPAC records, mainly to keep them out of DiBaca's hands." Kelly waited for Nora's response but she was silent. "Anyway, Talcone met with Marcus the night of the accident. My friend Kevin happened to be there and witnessed them exchanging some envelopes. He didn't know what was in them. Then I guess he overheard Talcone call Leo Rausche and set him up to follow Marcus home to search his place for any more GPAC files. Apparently Talcone keeps a daily planner with notes on everything."

"Everything?" she asked, her voice soft.

"Well, Kevin didn't specify what was in the planner exactly, but it sounds like he read the planner and figured out that Marcus had first arranged a meeting with Talcone, concerning the GPAC archived files. Then Talcone set up their future meetings and had notes regarding the GPAC fund-raising files. And apparently, Talcone has detailed financial records with Rausche on his payroll, along with Marcus. Kevin is convinced that if an FBI agent takes a look through Talcone's office we'll find a motive for the murder. But Rick wants to wait. He thinks there's still some information missing about DiBaca's connections to Talcone and Marcus." Kelly paused when she felt Nora's hand brush her back. She glanced over her shoulder at her. Nora had tears in her eyes.

"He was killed over some archived records? I can't believe it."

Kelly slipped her hand around Nora's waist and hugged her. "I'm sorry. I wanted to tell you last night, but . . ."

"I'm glad you didn't." Nora leaned her head on Kelly's shoulder. "Did Marcus ask for money to erase Talcone's name from this list?"

"I don't know if he was asking for money or not. But I doubt he ever realized he would be killed over this."

"What is Rick waiting for? Let's end this thing." Nora let go of Kelly and rubbed her face. She glanced around the room. The sheets were in disarray and clothes were strewn about from the night's foreplay. She stared at Kelly. "You won't come back once the case is finished, will you?"

Kelly shook her head. "I won't need to be here. There's no reason to worry about Rausche once Talcone is caught since he was on Talcone's payroll. If he knows what's good for him, he'll be getting out of the state." She stared at the unmade bed, remembering the wonderful weight of Nora's naked body and the smoothness of her skin. "Besides, Terrance will be home soon."

Nora glanced away at the mention of her fiancé. "I don't know if I'm more upset that you're leaving my life now because the case will be finished, or if I'm upset because of how this case is finishing." She sighed and brushed her fingertip over Kelly's lips. "I want another night with you."

Kelly shook her head. "I can barely leave now. I can't spend another night knowing I'll leave all over again and never touch you."

"Why never?"

"You're engaged." Kelly turned from her and went to pick her clothes off the floor. Nora kept her eyes on her as she dressed. She hugged Nora and kissed her, only once more. "I'll be late for work. I'll call later."

Chapter Fifteen

Colin was the first to approach Kelly that morning. She had just unlocked the doors and the camp kids were slowly filtering in to the dojo.

"Ma'am?"

"What is it, Colin?" Kelly asked. She flipped the window sign to read Open and swept her finger over the sill checking for dust. The waiting room needed a thorough cleaning, she decided, staring at her now fuzzy gray fingertips.

"I wanted to remind you that the schedule says it's ice cream day."

"Thanks, Colin. We can't forget about the Thursday ice cream, now can we?" Sam was going to be pissed that she was leaving him with the kids today. They were always rambunctious after ice cream. Monkey came up behind Colin and reached out to Kelly with his belt in hand. "And what'd you want to say, Monkey?" She smiled at him. He'd gained more confidence over the past week but was still a disaster on the mat. Not only was he unable to kick in a straight line to save his life, he didn't seem to care about hitting a target. If left to his own devices, he'd hit everything in the room except the target. Tomorrow was his last day at the camp. His mother had signed him up for only two weeks of karate, despite his begging for more. Kelly had hoped that he'd have learned more karate moves, but she was satisfied that he'd at least learned a little more confidence.

"Can you tie my belt? I have to practice."

She leaned down to tie his belt. "We haven't started class yet. What are you going to practice?"

"Flying side kicks." He grinned at her. "I was practicing at home and my mom got upset."

"Oh really?"

He nodded. "She said I couldn't kick the sofa anymore and I couldn't have another week of karate camp."

"Well, then we'll have to make the most out of our last couple days of camp, won't we?" She picked him up so his feet dangled in the air and he laughed as he towered above the other children in the waiting room. "I bet if I threw you from here, right into that bag over there, you could do a perfect flying side kick." She swung him through the doorway, pretending to let go of him and then catching his belt before he fell.

He shrieked in delight. Then he cried out, "Wait, put me down, I forgot to bow!"

She dropped him and watched as he made a perfect bow at the doorway. One other thing he'd almost learned, she noted. Respect.

Monkey turned around and held up his arms. "Okay, do over!"

Kelly shook her head. "Go practice your front kicks on that bag." She pointed to one of the heavy bags hanging three feet away from the back wall. "By the end of today, you are going to show me that you can kick that bag all the way to the wall. That's how you'll pass karate camp."

He opened his mouth to protest but stopped when he saw her stern look. She pointed to the bag and he trotted over obediently.

"Hey, Colin," she called. "You're in charge of Monkey's front kicks. Go make sure he's doing each kick correctly."

Colin nodded.

"And by the way," she said as she pulled a blue certificate out of her pocket. Colin's eyes widened with surprise when she handed it to him. She had never been so happy to give any of her students a test notice as she was with Colin now.

"Really, really?" He jumped up and down, clutching the notice.

"Yes, really." Kelly smiled. "You'll test for blue belt next week. Good luck, Colin."

Colin raced over to his backpack and carefully tucked the test notice in the front pocket. He bowed as he entered the mat area and kneeled to tie his purple belt around his waist, looking officiously in the mirror. After getting the belt set just as he liked it, he ran to help Monkey with his front kicks.

Kelly had to admit she was impressed. Colin had earned his purple belt three years ago. Ordinarily, there was only a five- to six-month period before each intermediate belt test, yet he'd stubbornly refused to learn his material and his test was continually delayed. Then at the beginning of summer, she'd taken the belt away from him because of discipline issues. He had made a dramatic change after losing the belt and earned it back a few weeks ago. Now he was eager to help out the beginners at the camp and rivaling the top students in his abilities. She knew he was ready for a reward and he seemed finally overdue for the next rank. They'd both know by next week if she'd made the right decision. Sam would administer the test for Colin's blue belt.

Sam arrived at ten minutes to noon. He often came in on Thursday afternoons to do office work and he didn't seem upset at taking the camp over for the next few hours. He didn't even seem to mind the idea of chaperoning the group to the ice cream parlor. Kelly thanked him, promising that this wouldn't turn into a daily occurrence. She quickly changed out of her karate gi and into a pair of slacks and a blue blouse. Kelly hadn't worn the blouse before, having picked it up on the clearance rack at a department store the day before. As soon as she saw herself in the mirror, she almost decided to change back to her karate T-shirt. The blouse had a low v-neck cut and revealed too much skin to seem professional. Unfortunately, a T-shirt also wouldn't appear professional. She decided not to worry about it and slipped out the back door of the dojo, hoping none of her students would notice her in this attire.

When Kelly reached the GPAC office building, it was just after twelve-thirty. A tall woman with short black hair and an eyebrow piercing opened the door at her knock. "Is John Rainsfeld in?"

"No, he's at lunch. I'm his secretary, or was, until I gave my notice this morning." She laughed sardonically and extended her hand. "Anyway, I'm Heather."

Kelly introduced herself, saying she was a friend of John's, and then asked if she could wait for him to return. Heather led her inside the office and pointed to a chair near the front desk. The phone rang and Heather hurried over to her desk to answer it.

"No, he's out. Do you want me to leave him a message?" She scribbled something on a pad of paper.

Kelly glanced around the room while Heather was distracted by the phone call. Marcus's fern was still on the top shelf above the computer. His desk didn't seem any less, or more, organized than when she'd last been here.

Heather hung up the phone and eyed Kelly. "So, how do you know John? Have you been friends long?"

Kelly considered the question. For some reason, she hesitated to tell the secretary that she was working on the investigation of Marcus's death. "No. We've only just met."

Heather sighed. She leaned back in her chair and crossed her knees. "Can I give you some advice, hon?"

Kelly nodded.

"He's a real lemon, let me tell you. I broke up with him a month ago when I found out he was seeing another woman on the side. And I should have left him sooner, but I was worried about my job here, you know . . . dating the boss and all. Anyway, I wouldn't wish that bastard on any girl." Heather smiled sympathetically.

Kelly was struck dumb with this piece of information. "I thought he was gay."

"Did he tell you his little secret? Yeah, he pretends to be gay here, but don't worry. I dated him, sweetie, and I know the truth. He uses that line on everyone." Heather stood up and headed over to John's desk. "He'd kill me if I showed anyone this, but . . ." She reached under his desk and pulled out a few *Playboy* magazines. "He's one hundred percent straight. Trust me, there isn't anything gay about John except his act."

"Wow. That's unbelievable. I mean, I really thought he was bi, or something." Really, she had never doubted that John was gay.

"Don't worry, hon. Everyone falls for it. You weren't the first and won't be the last, either, if I know John."

Kelly needed to keep her talking. She sensed that this woman had more to tell. If John wasn't gay, why was he working for GPAC? "So, that's why you're quitting your job? Because you broke up with him?"

"Oh, it's a long story." Heather shook her head. She motioned to Marcus's desk. "We lost an employee here last week. He was a really great guy—died in a car accident. It was tragic, really." She went to Marcus's desk and leaned against his chair. "He was quiet, you know, but sweet. I always kind of hoped he'd ask me out."

"I thought John said he worked for a gay political action group—isn't anyone here gay?"

Heather shook her head. "Crazy, isn't it?"

"Everyone who works here is straight?" Kelly repeated, just to make sure she had this clear.

"Well, the Board of Directors for GPAC are made up of gay and lesbian community members, and everyone thinks that John is gay. Which is exactly what Da' Boss wants. Most people assume that I'm a lesbian, since I work here and I've got short spiky hair. No one ever really knew for sure with Marcus. I think he was straight."

"Who's Da' Boss?" Kelly knew she meant DiBaca. Who else

could it be? Marcus must have picked up on this nickname, but why did Heather know about DiBaca?

"Oh, he's this old guy that John works for. Long story." Heather went back to her desk. She glanced at the time. "Well, I have four more hours of this job. I think I'm going to start cleaning out my desk. You can still wait for John, if you want. I honestly hope I've convinced you to leave though, for your own sake."

Kelly nodded. "The last thing I want to do is date John."

"Well, then I've done one good thing for the day. Chocolate?" She had opened the top drawer of her desk and pulled out a box of chocolates.

Kelly picked one and then asked, "You know, I remember John mentioning Da' Boss. I just assumed it was someone who worked here. But there's only three desks in this office."

"He mentioned him? I'm surprised at that." She sighed. "But then again, John has such a big head he doesn't think anyone will catch him. You see, Da' Boss is kind of a big secret. John reports to him, but the board doesn't have any clue about it. I've never met Da' Boss, but John used to talk about him a lot. Marcus got in a fight with John about Da' Boss once last month. I really thought John was going to fire him over the whole thing. John's got such a fast temper. Anyway, guess that's all water under the bridge now."

"Why does John report to this guy if the board doesn't know about it?"

Heather glanced at Kelly with a suspicious look. Maybe she was starting to suspect that Kelly had more questions than a new girlfriend should about her boyfriend's work. "I'm only telling you this since I've already quit this job . . . He writes John an extra little paycheck each month as long as John keeps the information pipeline flowing. Da' Boss wants to know all the new contributors to GPAC and also keeps tabs on the plans of the board. It's his way to monitor the gay political agenda—and he has his ways to make sure GPAC goals are never achieved."

"That's terrible." What an understatement, Kelly thought. She was having trouble keeping her voice ambivalent about John and Da' Boss. So Marcus knew all along that DiBaca had John

Rainsfeld as his puppet. She should have suspected the connection much sooner. The sketches were in Marcus's journal, and though she'd stared at the pages for hours, she hadn't seen the blatant message. "It must have been hard for you to work here, knowing that John was undermining the whole organization."

"I felt like I've been living a big lie for the past year. I'm so ready to get out."

Kelly shook Heather's hand, thanking her for the advice about John. She asked her to please not mention that she'd stopped by, saying that she preferred to keep the ball in her court until she broke up with him that evening. Heather agreed, seemingly quite pleased at her afternoon's work and showed Kelly out of the building.

Kelly was on the phone as soon as she reached her car. Her mind was racing with the thought that all along she had known. John was in fact DiBaca's puppet. "Well, I've got some more juice to add to the mix."

"What's that?" Rick asked.

"John Rainsfeld's not gay. I just finished a conversation with his disgruntled secretary, otherwise known as his ex-girlfriend. Apparently John gets paid by DiBaca to feed him information on GPAC sponsors and who knows what else. Sounds like the GPAC board has no clue."

Rick was silent and she guessed he was taking a moment to process the new information. He never jumped on anything too quickly. "Who'd you say you talked to?"

"The secretary, Heather."

"Last name?"

"I don't know, Rick. We were talking about annoying boyfriends. I wasn't about to stop her and ask her last name once I had her talking."

Rick sighed. "Okay, meet me at the office. I'll track down this secretary's info. We'll probably need her as a witness. I have something here that will validate her story about John's connection to DiBaca."

As soon as Kelly walked into the office, Rick held out a photocopied picture of Jared DiBaca with a newspaper clipping about the CVA. "Recognize this guy?"

"Da' Boss," Kelly said. "You know, Marcus called him Da' Boss in a sketch. The resemblance is uncanny."

"This is a copy of something that was found in Leo Rausche's place. The FBI investigated Rausche shortly after he tried to kill you for doing the same." Rick paused as if he needed to add emphasis. "Apparently, the guys who searched Rausche's room found a briefcase with Marcus Edwards's name on it. One of my FBI pals gave me a call about it. He just stopped by and took a look at that recording you took from Marcus's place. The briefcase that Rausche is carrying in the recording is identical to the one they found in his room."

"What else was inside?"

"They found all of these newspaper articles about DiBaca and Talcone. Marcus had drawn a map of DiBaca's connections. According to this, DiBaca was the unseen force who spearheaded GPAC. He designed the organization so it would feed information to the military about homosexuals. You wouldn't believe all of the contacts that DiBaca has and the reach of the CVA."

"You're saying that DiBaca made a gay political organization? Why the heck would he do that?" she asked.

Rick shook his head. "Why use a mole in an organization when you can control the whole organization?"

"What about the board of directors? Nora has friends on the board and I know she wouldn't be part of something like this."

"Maybe not. The current board probably has no idea who gave GPAC its first donation. DiBaca wouldn't want the board members to know how he's controlling them. But John Rainsfeld knows." Rick took a cigarette out and started to light it. Kelly shot him an indignant look. "Don't tell me I can't smoke in my own office."

"Well, you shouldn't."

Rick lit the cigarette anyway. "Most of the board members are just gay figureheads who are too busy with their own lives to pay much attention to GPAC. They've had a few good leaders filter in and out, and it sounds like DiBaca does his best to make sure the good ones filter out sooner rather than later. Long story short, GPAC exists only to feed information to the CVA and the military. They have files on everyone who has ever given money to GPAC, and the military has access to all of this through CVA."

Kelly interrupted. "Wait a minute, you said that you got this all from things that Marcus had figured out and then stored in a brief-case? I wonder why Rausche kept that briefcase."

"He was probably going to blackmail DiBaca."

"I'm surprised Marcus didn't try that."

Rick shook his head. "Maybe he considered it. After he figured out that the Gay Political Action Coalition was in fact the off-spring of the Conservative Veterans Association and DiBaca's brainchild, sounds like Marcus wanted out of the whole thing. CVA had let him in on their little secret, assuming he was an ally, what with a shiny military background and no homosexual past, you know."

"Marcus didn't know GPAC was run by the CVA when he started there?"

"It was highly classified information. DiBaca was in charge of everything and John only reported to him."

Kelly nodded. Given Heather's story, that made sense. "And what about the GPAC board?"

"Like I said, they're just figureheads. The GPAC board is a bunch of gays and lesbians who were handpicked by John Rainsfeld or DiBaca. They have the wool wrapped over the eyes of the board members so tightly that their contacts must itch." He smiled grimly. "The thing is, in order for GPAC to be successful at drawing in information about the gay community, it needs to have gay leaders and it needs to actually do something. So John sets up lawsuits that GPAC has no hope of winning and runs legislative crusades that look good on paper but have no political backbone."

"What about Talcone? Is the FBI still going to investigate him?"

"They're sending an agent to his office tomorrow morning."

Rick stretched his arms. "And I'm going to call Nora to tell her about the developments with John Rainsfeld and DiBaca. And good work with Heather Brown. Brown's her last name, by the way. I'm sure the FBI will be happy to have a statement from her and I've given the agent on the case her information. It's always nice to have a live witness."

Kelly left Rick's office and headed back to the dojo. She still had a few hours left of the karate camp and Sam would be happy to be relieved from the sugar-high kids. She knew that the FBI agent would find everything Kevin had described to her. She knew he hadn't misled her. Of all people, she had to trust her sparring partner.

After sending home the last camp student, Kelly went to her locker to change. She checked her phone messages and noticed that Gina had called twice. She didn't listen to the messages and had no desire to return the calls. By the time she had reached Alex's place, guilt set in. She showered and ate a peanut butter and jelly sandwich, staring at her cell phone. By seven o'clock, she decided to drive over to Gina's house. They needed to talk in person and there was no sense in delaying things. She phoned ahead to make sure Gina was home, hanging up just as she answered.

Gina was sitting on her porch when Kelly pulled up to the curb. She came out to Kelly's car. "I thought that was you. Why'd you hang up?"

"I wanted to talk to you in person." Kelly guessed Gina had been crying. Her eyes were red and the lids puffy. Gina's dark curls weren't pulled back in her usual ponytail but fell over her shoulders in a tousled array to frame her face.

"When you didn't pick up your phone, I thought you were avoiding me. You always used to pick up."

"I was at work. And I was avoiding you." She avoided Gina's eyes and focused on the dashboard. The odometer read 053999 and she thought the oil was overdue for a change. Of course, the actual mileage was a hundred thousand miles more than the odometer claimed. The one digit never appeared in the first space after the car had driven a hundred thousand miles.

Gina shook her head. Her eyes were moist. "I fucked up with Vicky, I know that. But fuck you for avoiding me. Did you even listen to my messages? You're not worth it if you're still acting like this after hearing the messages. I wasn't lying, you know."

"I couldn't listen to them. I was too mad at you," Kelly admitted. The overflow of emotions showed the tenderness that she usually concealed. "I'm sorry for not returning your calls." And she was sorry now. Before, she'd only been pissed.

Gina nodded. "I want to believe you." She swore softly. "I hate when people avoid me. And you have the audacity to tell me that?"

"Is Vicky inside?"

"No. We had an argument—right after we bumped into you at the restaurant. I hadn't told her that I'd been seeing you." Gina sighed. She pointed down the street. "Walk with me?"

Kelly reluctantly agreed. Gina led the way down the street and Kelly followed a few steps behind. She kept her eyes on the pavement or on the houses that they passed. The evening was a perfect temperature now that the sun had set. They reached the end of the cul-de-sac and took the bike path that cut between two houses. The path led behind the housing tract to Ashton High School and Kelly felt a wave of nostalgia as they reached the campus.

"It's strange to be back here," she said. She hadn't set foot on the campus since graduation three years ago.

"I forgot that you grew up in this town—an Ashton High alum." She interlaced her fingers with Kelly's. "So, tell me, did you have a crush on your gym teacher? Or was it the homecoming queen?"

"Neither." She let go of Gina's hand and slipped her arm around her waist. "Although there was this cute girl in my tenth-grade drama class, but I never even talked to her."

"Why didn't you make a move?"

"Her boyfriend. He was this popular guy and she was into him, you know. But he was a real asshole. She would have been better off with me." She laughed at the memory. "I was too shy then."

"And what's your excuse now?" Gina cocked her head and gazed at Kelly. "Are you still feeling shy? 'Cause I don't have a boyfriend."

"No, but you have Vicky." Kelly stepped around her and kept walking. What did Gina want? she wondered. Seeing her now, Kelly felt more attracted to her than ever. But she didn't want to play second fiddle to Vicky.

Gina caught up to her at the basketball courts and grabbed her arm. "I don't know why I keep stopping myself from telling you this . . . Look, I told Vicky more than just that I'd been dating you." Gina kept hold of her arm. She seemed nervous. "I said I was falling for you. I don't want to let you go. I've tried, all week, to not think about you. Do you know you're driving me crazy?" Gina's voice cracked. "And fuck you for avoiding me. I needed to talk to you."

"I was giving you space," Kelly said in her own defense. "It was your choice to sleep with Vicky so don't blame me for driving you crazy. While she's in town I just don't want to be involved."

"Vicky spent one night at my house—that was it." Gina lowered her voice. "I've already broken up once with her and I'm not about to start anything again."

"You were with her last night. Remember, I saw you holding hands." Kelly stared at her. "I thought you were the one that hated lying."

"She held my hand. I wanted to kiss you as soon as I saw you there, but she had my hand."

"That's not the point. We agreed that we wouldn't sleep with anyone else while we were together." Kelly knew she was walking a thin line. But Gina would never know about Nora. They'd made an agreement not to sleep with other people and they had both cheated. She wondered if their relationship would last another round.

"I made a mistake," Gina said. She held on to Kelly as though she couldn't let her go. "You're the one I want in my bed."

"I don't want to think about who's in your bed when I'm not around." Kelly wanted to kiss Gina but stopped herself. She didn't trust her emotions. Only last night she had been in bed with Nora and had loved every moment. Every moment until daybreak, when reality had set in, she reminded herself.

"Then sleep in my bed every night."

Kelly kissed her. She couldn't think of what was right or wrong. She just wanted to be with Gina tonight. Her cell phone rang and Gina scowled.

"Don't answer it."

Kelly shook her head. "You know I have to."

Gina took the phone from Kelly's hand. "Actually, you've gotten a lot of experience at ignoring calls lately. Let's see who this could be. Oh, look, it's your other girlfriend, Nora."

Kelly took the phone from Gina and answered the line.

"Hi. We need to talk. Can you meet me in an hour?" Nora asked.

"I have plans." Kelly glanced at her watch. It was half past eight already. "I can meet you tomorrow."

"No. It has to be tonight, as soon as you can get here. Cancel your plans," Nora said.

The phone line clicked and Kelly shook her head. She glanced at Gina and tried to think of a lie that she could use, but she knew she had to be honest now. "I have to go."

"To bed with me?" Gina asked, teasing.

"Not exactly." Kelly shook her head. Although she was frustrated that Nora would expect her to drop everything to meet her tonight, she had to admit she was looking forward to seeing Nora.

Gina wouldn't look at her. "When are you going to be done with this investigation? I want you back."

"Soon. Very soon."

"Give me a call then, okay?" Gina turned and walked away.

"Thanks for coming," Nora said as she opened the door. "I'm sorry about asking you to cancel your plans, but we have a deadline tonight."

"Deadline?"

Nora headed upstairs to the den and Kelly followed a few steps behind. She remembered climbing the stairs only last night to make love to her. Kelly shook her head to erase the thought.

They entered the den and Nora went directly to the computer. She sat down in the oversized leather chair and typed something on the keyboard. "Come over here. I want you to see this," she said, beckoning Kelly to her side of the desk. "These are the files that Rick sent to me. I guess the FBI agent found these computer disks in Marcus's briefcase. Rick said he didn't have the computer disks when you two met this afternoon. I think you might want to take a look."

Kelly waited as Nora selected the file and moved the cursor to the document labeled "Contacts." A list of names appeared on the screen and Jared DiBaca was near the top. Nora scrolled down, pointing out the information that Marcus had stored on his computer about CVA and GPAC.

"I'm trying to decide if Marcus's info on DiBaca and GPAC should be in tomorrow's press—if we make the deadline. I have a friend who's a journalist for the *Tribune*. I called her and mentioned that I had a story for her politics column. She was excited to get it, but I'm not sure if I should give her this information before I've had a chance to go through everything—there's almost too much information here. I feel like I'll miss something if I hand this over too soon."

Kelly scanned the file. Marcus had made a timeline of the past five years of GPAC's activities, noting every contact DiBaca had with GPAC. John Rainsfeld's name was mentioned several times. He also had information on DiBaca's links to military discharge cases involving a suspected gay or lesbian charge. Kelly read through the first two pages and then stopped. "Looks like DiBaca was at the center of a witch hunt."

Nora nodded. "And he was getting the information from GPAC records, straight from John Rainsfeld. My journalist friend really wants to break the story, then do an exposé on GPAC and DiBaca."

"And what about Talcone?"

"The FBI already has his number. They'll take care of him tomorrow. I want to focus on DiBaca and John Rainsfeld now."

"Leo Rausche's name is on this list. Did you check out Marcus's info on him?" Kelly asked. She had seen his name on the list of people connected to DiBaca. "And why is DiBaca linked to Rausche? I thought he worked for Talcone."

Nora scrolled down to Rausche's name and then highlighted that section. "And this isn't all. Rick said that Rausche has an FBI file as well as a police file. It makes my skin crawl just to read everything that he's linked to. This sounds like he's been on DiBaca's payroll and 'helped' him out several times before."

"I'd sleep better if that guy was in jail," Kelly admitted. She read over Nora's shoulder. Marcus had described the projects that Rausche had helped DiBaca with as if he was writing a recommendation letter. His own name wasn't included. "Do you find anything else on Rausche in the files?"

"Not really. There's a link to some newspaper article that—"

Kelly held up her hand to interrupt Nora. "Did you hear that?" The sound of breaking glass was unmistakable. It sounded like it had come from the front of the house, but it was hard to pinpoint. There were too many windows.

Nora stared at her. "Hear what?"

Kelly immediately headed for the door. She pointed toward the balcony window. "Check the backyard. Can you see anyone?"

Nora looked at her in disbelief. "We can't leave through the window. There's no ladder."

"We don't have a choice."

"Are you kidding?"

"No."

She went to the window and looked down at the yard. "I don't see anyone."

"Good. Then this is our exit. Call the police." Just then Kelly heard the creaking sound of the floorboards. Kelly knew that the wood floor at the entryway creaked if you stepped off the red carpet runner. She closed the door of the den and shoved a chair against it, wedging the handle.

"What's going on? Is someone inside?" Nora asked.

"I think so," Kelly whispered. There were windows on both sides of the front door and if someone smashed a window, they could easily reach the bolt and chain that secured the door.

Nora picked up the phone and started to dial, then glanced at Kelly. "There's no dial tone. Do you think someone cut the phone lines?"

Kelly tossed her cell phone to Nora. "Make sure you tell the operator your address. They can't trace cell phones easily."

Immobilized, Nora stared at the cell phone. "Maybe you should make the call. I don't—"

"Do it. Now," Kelly ordered. She still couldn't hear any sound, yet the breaking glass and the creak of the floorboards had been unmistakable. Whoever was inside would find them soon enough. They were sitting ducks in this room. She went to the balcony window and glanced outside at the backyard. Everything seemed to be in place. She headed back to the door and listened again. There was no sound.

Nora was giving the operator her address in a shaky voice. "Yes, I have an emergency—" There was a loud crashing sound from somewhere in the front of the house and she glanced at Kelly anxiously. "Sounds like a bookcase fell over." She continued, "Yes, this is an emergency. Can you send someone right away?" She paused. "What? Why will it take that long?"

Kelly already had the window open. There was a ledge under the window and an oak tree whose thick branches brushed against the eaves. She grabbed the phone from Nora. "We have to leave now."

Nora gazed at the window. "There's no ladder. We can't go out the window."

The chair wobbled as someone tried the handle. They stared at each other silently, waiting for the door to burst open, but nothing happened. Maybe he was trying another door down the hall, Kelly thought.

She grabbed Nora's hand. "We have no choice," she whispered.

Nora shook her head. A loud thud sounded against the door, and this time Nora headed for the window on her own. She climbed halfway out and then glanced at Kelly. "What now?"

"Put your feet on that ledge, under the window. Then you'll have to reach out for that branch there and climb down the tree. If you can make it down, go directly to your neighbor's house. Wait there. Don't leave for anything."

Nora placed her feet on the ledge. Kelly held on to her waist as she reached out to grab the tree branch. She swung her foot up and over the branch and then started shimmying down the tree. Kelly smiled with amazement. Nora made the trick look easy. Kelly climbed out of the window just as another thud sounded at the door. They scrambled down the tree, barely pausing at each branch intersection.

Once Nora hit the ground, she screamed to Kelly and pointed up at the den window. Leo Rausche was hanging half out of the window, aiming a gun at Kelly.

"Run!" Kelly shouted down to Nora. She fully expected Rausche to shoot, but he held his fire. She glanced up at the window. Rausche had disappeared. Either he was waiting for them to run so he'd have a clear shot, or he was on his way down the stairs to get Nora.

Nora took off through the backyard. By the time Kelly reached the ground, Nora was already gone. She saw the back gate was open and sprinted toward the side of the house, knowing Rausche was on his way. She slipped behind the back porch and found a broom leaning against the side of the house.

If she waited here, Rausche could ambush her, and a little broom would be no match for a gun. She peered around the back porch. The yard was strangely quiet. The crickets and birds were silently waiting for the intruders to leave.

Kelly ran her hands along the broom handle. It was shorter than her Bo staff and made of a lighter wood, but it would have to do for now. There was no choice but to run. Run, or be found by Rausche and shot before she had a chance to fight. The only way to win this, she thought, would be to get the first strike in. Her heart was pounding and the blood rushing in her ears distracted her. She couldn't wait for Rausche to come. She glanced to both sides and then up at the window one last time before dodging around the back porch steps and racing down the other side of the house toward the street. She saw Rausche and froze. His back was to her and the revolver was in his hand, hanging at his side, as he gazed down the street in the other direction. She edged up to him, keeping alongside the house. He started to look her way and with less than ten yards between them, she charged. His gun came up just as she decided to jump him. There was no turning back now, she knew.

She yelled and jabbed the butt of the broom handle into the cement and lunged into the air. Her foot struck his throat in a side kick and then skidded down his chest. The full weight of her body hit Rausche's throat and he immediately stumbled back, clutching his throat and coughing for air. Kelly had landed five paces from him. His gun had gone off, then fallen out of his hands, and lay in the gutter a few feet away. As soon as she went for it, Rausche looked up and lurched toward her. She kicked the gun away before he could reach it. The gun ricocheted off her foot and clattered down the street.

Rausche eyed the gun for a moment and then turned toward Kelly. She raised the broom handle and started to swing it when he lunged forward. With a quick shuffle she moved out of his path, but he stepped to the side and threw a jab followed by a hook punch at her head. She dodged the first jab and caught the cuff of his wrist on her cheekbone. The hit stunned her momentarily. She recovered just as Rausche came at her with another punch. She blocked the strike with her forearm and retaliated with a swing of her broom handle at his leg. The wood smashed his knee before he could throw the next punch. Rausche swore loudly, clutching his wounded leg and balancing on the other leg.

Kelly swung the broom handle again, this time at his good knee, striking the leg again and again until he crumpled to the ground, screaming in pain. Without thinking, she swung the broom handle once more, all of her strength focused on Rausche's knee. He rolled to the side and the wood struck his fingers. Kelly stopped then, seeing the horrible look of agony on his face. He cried out again, swearing to kill her.

Suddenly the sound of sirens overrode Rausche's voice. He tried to stand and collapsed on the sidewalk before he'd placed any weight on his knees. He eyed the gun and started crawling toward it. Kelly ran past him, dropped the broom and grabbed the gun. Rausche's hand caught hold of her leg. He clutched at her jeans and she kicked at his face to shake him off. He let go just as her toe clipped his nose. She jumped back and pointed the gun at his face, trying not to look at the blood dripping from his nose. "Don't move, you bastard!"

He started crawling toward her again and she backed up, placing her finger on the trigger.

"Don't move, Rausche." *Please, don't make me shoot*, she thought. "Not another move!"

"You're not going to shoot me. You can't do it." Grimacing, Rausche stood up slowly. He placed his weight gingerly on the leg that Kelly had battered with the broom handle and took one faltering step forward, challenging her.

Her finger was shaking against the trigger. "You don't know me that well, Rausche. Don't make me prove that I can pull this little trigger."

"I don't know you that well?" He took another step closer. "Kelly Haldon, one of sensei Sam Lee's students. You've been working with Nora Kinley, and more importantly, Rick Lehrman. And your lover is a cop with the SFPD. I also know you visited my house and stole a photo that I'd like returned. And another thing—"

She stopped him. "I don't have any photos. I don't know any of those people you mentioned." Her heart was racing. Rausche took another step toward her and she backed away. "But there's something I'd really like to know too. Were you told to run Marcus Edwards off the road or was that a mistake? I was thinking that maybe you're just a bad driver." She couldn't stop her hand from shaking. *Maybe he's right*, she thought. *Maybe I am weak.*

"Some things we'll never know. Like, if you would've pulled that trigger." Suddenly he lunged forward. Kelly threw a hook punch at his temple with the barrel of the gun. He stumbled to the side and crumpled to the ground.

Just then the first police car arrived. An officer, an older black guy with a no-nonsense look, jumped out and pulled his gun, focusing it on Kelly. His partner, a younger white guy, came from the other side of the car and also aimed his gun at her.

"Okay, you're going to set that gun down, nice and easy. Then I want to see everyone's hands in the air," the first cop commanded.

Kelly held the gun still pointed at Rausche. She didn't trust that Rausche wouldn't try to grab for the gun if she set it on the ground.

"Did you hear that? Put your hands in the air."

Rausche didn't move. Kelly wondered if he was unconscious or playing possum. A direct hit to the temple could have knocked him out. She locked the safety and tossed the gun toward the patrol car. She held her hands up in the air.

The younger cop ordered Rausche to put his hands in the air but he still didn't move. Watching his chest, Kelly could see movement and knew that he was breathing.

"I think he's unconscious," she said.

The older cop nodded. "Okay, I want you to back away from him. Slowly."

Another patrol car pulled up and two more cops climbed out, pointing their guns at Kelly and Rausche. Kelly followed the order to back away from Rausche, and she edged toward the patrol car, keeping her eyes on Rausche. His eyes fluttered and he opened his mouth as though he were going to speak. No sound came from him.

The other officers approached Rausche. As soon as they were on top of him, he seemed to come to. He rolled on the ground, trying to resist the handcuffs they fitted on his wrists. He finally submitted and when they ordered him to stand, he stood up slowly, pulled mostly by a muscle-bound officer with a deep booming voice. Once Rausche was in the second patrol car, another officer handcuffed Kelly and helped her into the backseat.

Kelly shook her head and closed her eyes. She leaned back in the hard vinyl-covered seat, wondering what exactly she should say when the police questioning began. Suddenly she remembered Nora. She must have made it to her neighbor's house. Had she watched this whole scene, safe inside someone's living room?

Chapter Sixteen

By Friday morning, Kelly was ready to never see Leo Rausche or hear his name again. She had relived her fight with him over a dozen times just in the ride from Nora's house to the police station, and when a police investigator at the station started asking questions about Rausche, she knew her memory would not fade soon enough. The investigator had big ears that stuck out of his balding head with lobes that hung low on his neck, threatening to touch the collar of his uniform. With those ears, he seemed to be always attentive and she decided to drop Rick's name just to see how the investigator might respond. She mentioned she was working with him on a case and asked if she could call him. The investigator jumped to let her make the one call, and miraculously, Rick had picked up the line. A half an hour later, the police chief informed her that he had just gotten off the phone with someone from the FBI and that she would be released without charges following a brief questioning. Amazed at the strings Rick could pull,

Kelly quickly agreed. She spent the next hour answering questions and was finally released from the station at 4 a.m.

She arrived home before dawn and collapsed on her bed. Her alarm was set for 7 a.m. and she needed to close her eyes just for a moment, she thought. The cell phone rang before she'd fallen asleep and she stared at the phone, wishing that the ringing would simply stop on its own.

It was Nora. "Can I come in?"

"What? Where are you?" Kelly asked. She heard a knock on the front door and sat up. "Okay, give me a minute." She hung up and glanced around the room, wondering if she had any clean clothes to wear. The only thing that she could find was her karate uniform. Alex had done a load of darks and left a pair of her black karate pants neatly folded on the dresser opposite the bed. Kelly pulled on the pants and a tank top. She headed for the front door and then stopped in the middle of the hallway. Nora was sitting on the couch in the family room.

"The door was unlocked," Nora observed. "I didn't think you'd mind if I let myself in, but don't you know how dangerous it is to leave doors unlocked?"

"This is Ashton. There's no crime here. At least, not like the city. How'd you know where I live?"

"Oh, I have my ways," Nora said smugly.

"Rick?"

She nodded. "He also said you spent the night at the police station."

Kelly sat down on the chair opposite the sofa. "Yeah, it was a real party at the station. Cops everywhere. And how are you? I guess you got to your neighbor's house all right?"

"I don't know what happened exactly." Nora sighed. "I've never frozen up like that. I heard Rausche and knew that I should come help, but I couldn't move. Then I was at my neighbor's house and he heard the gunshot and just pulled me inside and slammed the door shut." She picked up one of the pillows on the couch and hugged it against her chest. "But I guess it's over now. Rausche is not getting out on bail. Talcone will be joining him soon enough if the FBI does their job."

"And the exposé?"

"It won't make it in the papers tomorrow. We missed the deadline, obviously. But my friend will get the information and she'll probably put it in the Sunday edition."

Kelly didn't know what else to say. She wondered if Nora had come just to say good-bye. They wouldn't have any excuse to see each other again. Maybe that was for the best. Every time she looked at Nora her heart raced and she could almost feel the sensation of Nora's hands on her when they'd danced together. "Nora, why'd you come here?"

"To apologize," Nora replied.

Kelly shook her head. "There's nothing to apologize for—"

"Yes, there is. You don't even know why I'm apologizing yet." Nora smiled. "By the way, I like what you're wearing."

Kelly glanced down at the loose black cotton pants. "Karate pants. They're comfortable." A thin string tied under her belly button held them on her hips. She felt uncomfortable under Nora's gaze and stood up. "Can I get you a drink?"

Nora followed her into the kitchen. "You look sexy in them."

Kelly shook her head. Why was Nora complimenting her now? "We have beer, orange juice or milk."

"Juice, thank you."

Kelly sensed Nora's gaze on her as she filled two juice glasses. She replaced the pitcher in the refrigerator and felt Nora's hand on her back.

"I wish things could be different. If I'd met you a few years ago, it would have been . . ." Nora stalled. "I love Terrance. But I fell for you even though I knew it wouldn't work. I liked you the moment we met." She took a sip of the juice and set the glass on the counter. "You know, I don't fall for women."

"Why are you telling me this now?" Kelly didn't want to hear it again.

"Because I'm sorry for flirting, sorry that I really didn't have any intentions beyond . . ."

"Sex?" Kelly asked. She was trying to quiet her feelings of anger. "I don't want to hear an apology."

"Then I won't apologize. And I'd give anything for another night." She sighed. "By the way, you're really something in bed. I'm jealous of your girlfriend."

Kelly shook her head. She was jealous of Terrance.

"It wasn't that I wanted to see how it would be, just once, you know." Nora added, "My attraction, or desire, was to be with you, specifically, not just with a woman."

Kelly took a sip of the juice and let the sweet acidity fill her mouth. Unable to listen anymore, she turned and walked out of the kitchen. Nora caught her arm before she'd gotten far.

"What did you feel when we danced?"

They stared at each other silently. Kelly stepped forward and kissed her. Her tongue slipped between Nora's lips as she caressed her neck. She pulled away suddenly and gazed at Nora. "That's what I felt."

Nora pulled her close for another kiss, this one more aggressive yet still soft. After a moment, Nora whispered, "And I've never felt that before. When I look at you I'm excited in a way I've never felt before." She stopped and rubbed Kelly's palm. "Do you understand?"

"I understand that it doesn't really matter," Kelly said. She had to guard her emotions. Nora was already pushing her limits. What would she do if Nora agreed to keep up a relationship with her when Terrance returned? He would be home from his business trip tonight and Nora would probably forget about her then.

"I loved dancing with you. Terrance would die if I tried to lead him on the dance floor." Nora laughed and slipped her hand around Kelly's waist. "I'd take you as my partner for every dance."

Kelly turned away. She couldn't let Nora confuse her. "I think it's too late for dancing. Terrance will be home tonight, won't he?"

"Yes, but that doesn't mean we have to say good-bye. We could meet again, you know, for . . . dancing. I'm sure there's a club in the city where women go to dance with other women, right?" Nora brushed against her, moving in a circle and spinning as if she were a dancer onstage. She smiled at Kelly. "It could be fun."

"Nora, don't." Kelly wanted her to stop talking. "You need to let go." She took Nora's hand off her waist. She could feel her eyes water. Nora saw the tears and brushed her hand gently over Kelly's lashes.

"You're beautiful. I'm jealous of your girlfriend."

Kelly shook her head. "But you still have to choose Terrance."

"We could go dancing sometime."

"No." Kelly knew that she wanted to be with Gina, now more than ever. Nora was choosing Terrance, despite everything she said or felt for her. They were better off not seeing each other at all.

At eight that morning, Rick met Kelly at the dojo just as she was working her wire pick into the lock. He smiled and handed her a ring of keys. "You know, this might make it easier."

Surprised to finally have her keys back, she had to stop herself from thanking him. He had taken them away and didn't need to be thanked for returning them, she decided stubbornly. She quickly found the key to unlock the dojo and smiled happily as the lock turned almost too easily. "Amazing work with the right tools!"

He popped open the lid of his gas station coffee and took a sip. "Yeah, I've heard you're not bad with a broom either."

"So, Rick, how is it that you know all these things about me anyway? For instance, how'd you know I was dating Gina?"

He shrugged. "Intuition."

"No. I'm not buying that." She shook her head.

"I've been following you. I wasn't ready to let you take this case on your own." He paused. "It was a training exercise and I've been watching your back every step of the way."

Kelly shook her head. How many times had she seen a black sedan trailing her? She wondered now if it had been Rausche or Rick. How many times had she missed him following her? "I screwed up last night."

"No. We got Marcus's killer in jail, which half of the SFPD couldn't do. Leo Rausche ain't going nowhere. Talcone is a few hours away from handcuffs, while DiBaca and John Rainsfeld are the next ones up to be investigated by my friends at the agency."

She wondered what other information they would find in the exposé of DiBaca and Rainsfeld.

"But we do have a few things to work on. First, don't try to take on a crazy guy with a gun when you're only armed with a broom." He gave her a sly smile.

"Point taken." She nodded. "Don't worry, I won't forget that."

"Second, you need to look in your rearview mirror more. You are so easy to follow, it's almost sad. We've really got to work on that."

"And third?" she asked, frustrated at herself.

Rick pointed at the key ring. "Don't lose your keys."

Kelly shook her head indignantly. "Oh, hell, no. I didn't lose them. They were stolen. You can't pin that one on me."

"Lost or stolen—it's the same thing, in the end," Rick countered. "You need the right tools for every job." He took another sip of his coffee, clearly pleased with himself.

It wasn't worth it to argue with him, she decided. What mattered was that she had her keys back. She stared at the key ring and counted her keys, which looked so strange now. Then she noticed a silver key that hadn't been there before. All of her other keys were bronze. "This isn't mine." She held up the fifth key on the ring. Although it had been a few weeks since she'd seen the ring, she knew she had only four keys and they were all bronze.

"It is now," Rick said.

"What do you mean?" Kelly asked.

He handed her a piece of paper with an address scribbled in his cryptic handwriting. "I've got a cabin in Tahoe that I never use. I thought you might want to get away for a few days. Take the weekend off."

She stared at the key. "Are you sure?"

He nodded. "You can stay at the place this weekend and whenever else you need a break. Just let me know when you want to get away." He picked up his coffee and started to leave, then said, "One more thing. You nearly shot Rausche in the knee. Would you really have pulled that trigger?"

"Maybe." She was at a loss. How did he know that if he wasn't

239

there? "I'm sure I would have missed. Fortunately, he didn't make me pull the trigger."

"Have you talked to your cop girlfriend yet?" he asked. "I bet they have a lot of rumors flying around the station about you now. They've been trying to catch Rausche for the past few months and then look who finally brings him in . . ." He laughed. "Not bad."

She shook her head, wishing she could talk to Gina before she heard the rumors at the station and feeling more than ready for a vacation in Tahoe. The Feds could handle Rausche and Talcone. Nora and her journalist friend could work on the exposé of DiBaca and John Rainsfeld. It was a relief to finally be done.

Rick turned to leave and then stopped in the doorway. "I'll let you know when your next job comes. Make sure you answer your phone."

By that evening, Monkey's mom was the last parent to arrive for the evening pickup. She was thirty minutes late. Kelly glanced out the window. After parking her SUV in a tow-away zone in front of the dojo, Monkey's mom honked once and then tapped her hand on the steering wheel impatiently. Monkey jumped off the chair where he'd been waiting. He ran to the doorway and then stopped. "Ma'am?"

His mom honked again. She must have seen him pause in the doorway. Kelly ignored the pile of Sam's paperwork that she'd been sorting. She'd taken on the task of organizing his desk and had found a drawer of karate gear supply orders, bank statements and utility bills jumbled together from the past five years. "Ready to leave, Monkey?"

He eyed his mom and then glanced back at Kelly. "Can we do the flying kick through the door? I want to show my mom."

Kelly smiled. She'd had Monkey practicing front kicks everywhere. He had done so many front kicks that she almost felt sorry for him, yet he never seemed to tire. Still, he wasn't kicking straight. So she'd changed the lesson plan to flying front door kicks and he caught on almost immediately.

240

"Sure, we can do one more front door kick." She glanced outside and said, "Remember not to kick until I say *kiai*, okay?"

He nodded. "Then I say aah-saah!" he whispered to himself.

"And kick straight through the door like a fireman." She stood behind him. "Ready?" She picked him up by his belt and shouted, "*Kiai!*"

As soon as he was airborne, he kicked both feet forward simultaneously and yelled, "Aah-saah!"

He cleared the doorway and Kelly caught him just before he landed on the cement.

Brimming with kid-sized adrenaline, he looked up at her and grinned. "One more time?"

She shook her head. "Nope. That was it for now. Next summer, okay?"

He nodded and turned to run to the SUV where his panic-stricken mother was waiting. Kelly stifled a laugh as she heard her scream at him, "What were you thinking? Don't you know how dangerous that was? What if you'd fallen!"

Monkey gazed back at Kelly and waved. He climbed up into the backseat and waited for his mom to buckle his belt. Kelly knew he was trying to explain that it wasn't dangerous. She also knew that his mother would probably never let him come back to karate camp. Maybe he'd come on his own when he got older. At least she hoped so.

Gina called just after Monkey left to ask if she was still coming to the bar that evening. Kelly promised she'd be there. She left the dojo and, after a quick shower, headed over to the Main Street Saloon. Beth and Tasha waved at her just as she was pulling into the parking lot. They waited by the entrance of the bar for her to park.

Tasha gave her a bear hug as soon as she approached. "By the way, Vicky's a tramp. We'll watch out for you, hon."

"Is she here tonight?" Kelly asked, hoping the answer would be no.

Beth nodded. "Vicky came to cheer for our team at the game

tonight. Gina didn't want her to come to the bar, but we couldn't tell her to stay home."

Kelly glanced back at her car. She wanted to leave now, before any scene occurred. But maybe it would be just fine. "Do you think she'll be okay if I'm here?"

"No," Beth answered. "As long as no one brings up your name, she's really quite pleasant. But as soon as anyone mentions you . . . stand back." She laughed.

Tasha rolled her eyes. "Don't listen to her. She exaggerates everything."

They entered the bar and Kelly spotted Gina by the pool table. Vicky was hanging on her side with a bottle of beer in hand. They were both wearing jeans and black shirts. "Looks like they belong together," Kelly said quietly. "I think maybe I'm at the wrong place tonight." The loud rock music and chatter of voices made her long for the tranquil mood they'd just left in the parking lot.

"No." Tasha caught Kelly's arm as she turned to leave. "You're going to hang out with Beth and me. I'm telling you, Vicky is a tramp. If Gina doesn't stand up to her and tell her to get lost, I will."

Kelly tried to smile. Tasha had an uncanny ability to win her over. Reluctantly, she agreed to stay and followed Beth and Tasha to the bar to order drinks. After a few minutes of waiting for the slow bartender, Kelly tapped Tasha on the shoulder. "I feel weird for not saying hi to Gina yet."

"We'll get drinks and meet you at the pool table," Tasha said. She mouthed a "good luck" before turning to whisper something to Beth.

Gina was just finishing her turn at the table. She gave Kelly a hug, no kiss, and then reintroduced her police friends, Aaron and Brenda and, of course, Vicky. Aaron gave her a warm smile. Brenda and Vicky looked like they'd practiced their sneers in the mirror together. The foursome was in the middle of a heated partners' game, with Vicky and Gina ahead by one ball.

Brenda shot next and sank the cue ball. She complained about a distracting overhead fan and handed the pool stick to Aaron. He caught Kelly's eye and winked at her. Vicky was up next. She spent the first few minutes walking around the table and squinting at the angle between each striped ball and the nearest pocket.

Aaron approached Kelly and held out a piece of paper. "I thought you might be here tonight. Well, actually, Gina told me she was going to invite you," he admitted.

Kelly unfolded the paper and laughed. "You've got to be kidding."

Brenda hissed something that didn't sound complimentary. Kelly realized she'd laughed too loud but really didn't care. Aaron had given her the original copy of the ticket he'd started to write for the stop sign that she'd missed. On the side of the ticket he'd scribbled, "Too cute."

Gina glanced over Kelly's shoulder to see the paper. "Aaron, something tells me that excuse wouldn't fly with the captain," she said. Under her breath she added, "But I can't blame him."

Kelly folded the ticket and slipped it into her pocket. Brenda was anxious to know what Aaron had given her but was too haughty to ask. Sensing an impending domestic dispute, Kelly said, "It's a good thing you got called to a more important assignment. I'd hate to see how much that ticket would have cost."

Brenda perked up at this. "What assignment did you get called out for?"

Aaron shrugged. "Just some crazy guy who was running around with a gun and waking up his neighbors. Leo Rausche. The kids in his neighborhood called him the mean pigeon man."

"Did you catch him?" Brenda asked.

Aaron shook his head. "They had a guy staked out at his place every night for a week. Turns out he was wanted on a few counts—besides illegal possession of firearms and killing a dog. Someone said the guy had a murder on his record and had served time for it a while back. And he was in the military—go figure. Makes me sleep well at night knowing who the government wants to protect us."

Kelly didn't tell Aaron the new development in the case of Leo Rausche. She wanted to explain the whole story to him but decided that he would learn all about it soon enough. Leo Rausche would be facing a trial before long.

Tasha handed Kelly a drink. "Uh-oh. Did I just hear you ripping on the military, Aaron?" she asked. "You know, Vicky and I may have to gang up on you if you keep that up."

Vicky shrugged. "He can bash the military all he wants. Everyone else does." She finally made her shot. Two striped balls sank into the same hole, one after the other. "But I'll still jump sand rockets to protect his happy ass back home."

It was obvious that Tasha wished she hadn't been held in San Francisco while the rest of the unit was in Iraq. Kelly couldn't imagine that anyone would willingly sign up for the mission, but here were two women who had—one held back because of an unsubstantiated, but true, charge about her sexual orientation, and the other here only to see her father in case he died while she was away serving her country.

Aaron was subdued by Vicky's comments. He was also the next in line to shoot if Vicky missed her next ball. The pool game continued with some palpable tension. Finally, Vicky sank the eight ball in the desired corner and took the five-dollar bill that Aaron and she had agreed upon as the table bet. The group mingled with the other players and the pool players' tension diffused with a little more alcohol and music. Kelly did everything possible to avoid Vicky. She wasn't able to talk to Gina alone until she mentioned she was leaving. It was just after midnight.

Gina walked her out of the bar. "I'm sorry about Vicky's attitude," she said.

"She's pissed. I guess I don't blame her." They reached Kelly's Volkswagen and stood by the car. Kelly was aware that anyone inside the bar could be watching them. She had parked under the only light in the parking lot—a habit she'd learned from self-defense training that she knew she'd have to break for her work with Rick. "Can you come over later?"

"You're actually asking me over to your place?" Gina asked in disbelief. "Are you sure you're feeling okay? You never invite me over."

Kelly smiled. "Yeah, I'm fine." Gina had come over once or twice of her own volition, but Kelly had never invited her. She never thought this was a problem, until now. "But I'd be happier with you in my bed."

Gina pulled on Kelly's belt until the buckle slipped loose. They kissed as Gina unbuttoned her jeans. Kelly felt a rush of excitement as Gina's hand rubbed her. Her finger slipped down to press against Kelly's clit. She murmured with pleasure. Gina pulled back her hand and kissed her again.

"Wait up for me, chica." Gina turned to head back to the bar. "I'm going to give Vicky a ride home. She's gotten herself drunk because of you."

"Actually, I think it was because of you," Kelly countered. "Just remember whose bed you're sleeping in."

"How could I forget? We're both wet with anticipation." Gina grinned. She blew a dramatic kiss and disappeared inside the bar.

Chapter Seventeen

When Kelly arrived home from the bar, the kitchen smelled of chocolate. She found a plate of chocolate chip cookies that Alex had left for her. Her name was scribbled on a Post-it note attached to the plastic wrap cover. A can of paint was sketched next to the words, "Yes, I'm bribing you with cookies to finish the painting. Only one more coat and then you're done!" Great, she thought, now he's resorted to bribes. She had almost finished painting but the back of the house faced the afternoon sun and she wasn't looking forward to staring at the bright yellow paint in the searing heat. She'd have to do it soon. Summer vacation was almost over and she'd be heading back to San Francisco in two weeks for her senior year of college.

She turned on the television and tried to stay awake watching sitcom reruns. A soft knock came at the front door just as she was nodding off. She carried the plate of cookies out to the front room and greeted Gina. "Chocolate chip cookies?"

Gina rubbed her belly. "I'm starving." She took a bite of a cookie and closed her eyes. "Did you bake these?"

"No, Alex did."

"Can I marry him?" Gina asked.

Kelly laughed. "No. I'd be wrecked with the sin of coveting my brother's wife. And I wouldn't want to try and explain that to the priest at the confessional."

Gina finished her cookie and took another. "Do you have milk?"

After filling two mugs with milk, they stood at the kitchen counter, feasting on milk-dunked cookies and rehashing the night's events at the bar. The plate was empty before long.

Gina swallowed her last cookie morsel. "How many were on that plate?"

"Only six, I think." Kelly caught Gina's hand and licked a smudge of chocolate off her finger.

"Mmm." She closed her eyes as Kelly sucked on her fingertip. Gina stepped closer and grabbed the countertop. She pressed her hips against Kelly's. "I think I want to work off those cookies."

"What do you suggest?" Kelly asked. She kissed Gina as soon as she opened her mouth to answer.

Gina undid Kelly's belt and pulled it through the loops. "Didn't I already unbutton your jeans? Who told you it was okay to button them?"

"Who told you it was okay to unbutton them in the middle of a parking lot?" Kelly shot back. She pulled off Gina's shirt and unfastened her bra, letting Gina's full breasts fall into her hands. Gina murmured approval as Kelly massaged each breast.

Gina had unbuttoned Kelly's jeans and was struggling to pull them off, apparently distracted by Kelly's fingers on her nipples. She finally got them down to Kelly's ankles and then waited as Kelly finished pulling them off.

"And the shirt can come off as well," Gina noted.

"Oh, can it?" Kelly asked sarcastically.

Gina arched one eyebrow and pressed her hips forward. Kelly

was pinned against the kitchen counter now. She pulled off her shirt, as requested, then waited for Gina to work the hooks on her bra. When she'd finished, Gina hung the bra over a kitchen chair. She pointed to the countertop.

Kelly turned around and looked at it. "What?" she asked.

"I want you up there."

Kelly glanced over her shoulder at Gina. She pushed up to sit on the counter's edge and watched Gina approach. The tiles were cool against her skin. Gina placed one hand on each side of her and kissed her.

Kelly loosened Gina's ponytail, letting the curls fall to her shoulders. She slipped her hand to the back of Gina's neck and pulled her close to kiss her again. Gina's tongue slipped inside her mouth. She felt a rush of pleasure as Gina moved lower to kiss her nipples, gently biting and sucking them.

"How'd we end up in the kitchen again?" Kelly murmured.

Gina shrugged. She moved lower on Kelly's body, kissing her belly and just above the line of hair. Kelly watched Gina part her folds and lick her clit. She gripped the edge of the counter as Gina's tongue slipped inside her. She was wet and begging for more. She tried to slow it down but the wave inside her threatened to break as soon as Gina started to suck on her clit. She pulled Gina toward her, feeling every thrust of the finger that was now inside her, pushing deeper while she continued to suck. Kelly cried out as she felt the rush of the orgasm. Gina kept her tongue on Kelly's clit, riding out the tremors of her body's pleasure. Finally, she relaxed. Gina pulled her off the counter and hugged her tightly. Kelly's legs felt weak and she tugged Gina toward her bedroom. She needed to lie down.

As soon as she had Gina in her room, she pushed her onto the bed, not bothering to pull down the sheets. She lit a candle on her nightstand and watched Gina take off her pants. Gina smiled at her when she realized she was being watched.

"Want to try something?" Kelly asked.

Gina shrugged. "Maybe. What do you have in mind?"

Kelly opened the top drawer of her nightstand and pulled out a purple dildo. She slipped a condom on it, sensing Gina's eyes on her. "Is this okay?" Uncapping a bottle of lube, she squirted some in her palm.

Gina smiled and sat back, watching as Kelly slathered lube over the dildo. "Go easy on me, okay?"

Kelly nodded. She kissed Gina and didn't ask for an explanation. "No problem." She climbed on top of her, rubbing over her with a deep burning pleasure. Gina gripped her shoulders as Kelly pressed against her. She pushed Gina's legs apart and spread lube over the wet folds.

The tip of the dildo rested against Gina's clit, and she waited for the moment to push it inside. Gina's hips pushed up from the bed and Kelly slipped it down and inside her then. Gina moaned as Kelly guided it deeper. She lifted her hips when Kelly rocked it out of her, begging to have it again. Sensing Gina's building excitement, Kelly moved the dildo back in and flicked her thumb against the swollen clit. Slowly she pulled out the dildo.

Gina grabbed Kelly's wrist as soon as it slipped out. "Where are you going?"

Kelly smiled. "You like it?"

Sweat shone on Gina's forehead and the sheets were tossed around her. "But you're not finished." She spread her legs farther apart and guided Kelly's hand toward her.

Kelly slipped the dildo inside again. She massaged Gina's breasts and pressed her hips down each time Gina tried to rise up. She kissed her nipples, sucking gently, as she rocked the dildo in and out faster. Gina climaxed suddenly, digging her fingernails into Kelly's shoulders, her hips held up so the dildo could grind deep inside her. She cried out and squeezed her knees together, then fell back against the bed.

Kelly kept the dildo inside her until her body relaxed. She slipped it out and rubbed her hand over Gina.

"Damn." Gina sighed. She caressed Kelly's face and combed her fingers through her hair. "You can do that again anytime you'd like."

Kelly smiled. She rolled off Gina and lay beside her. She traced the curve of Gina's body. "You're beautiful."

Gina shook her head. "Right now, I'm . . . a puddle."

"A beautiful puddle then." Kelly started to pull down the blankets. The sound of breaking glass startled her. She paused, listening. Another glass shattered. "Gina, did you hear that?"

Gina opened her eyes. "What?"

Kelly jumped out of bed and slipped quickly into a pair of shorts and a sweatshirt. "I just heard glass break. I have to check it out."

Gina grabbed her arm. "No, don't go. If you heard something, we should call first. Where's your phone?"

Kelly pushed her feet into a pair of sneakers and handed Gina her cell phone. "I'll yell if everything's okay. If you don't hear me, call the cops in two minutes." She closed the bedroom door behind her. Maybe she had imagined the sound. At least this time it couldn't be Rausche. She flicked on the hall lights and then checked Alex's room. He was sound asleep. She quickly went room to room searching for any broken windows, then ran back to the bedroom. Gina, already dressed, was still holding the cell phone.

"No one's inside. All the doors are locked. I must have been hearing things." Kelly shook her head. She'd never imagined a sound before but maybe the experience with Rausche last night had disturbed her mind.

Suddenly an unmistakable crash of breaking glass shattered the quiet. Gina and Kelly both headed to the front door. The sound was coming from outside.

Kelly grabbed Gina's hand. "Wait, I have a scope. Let me get it." She ran back to her room and grabbed the night vision scope. She pulled back the drapes from the front window and scanned the street. She saw a movement by Alex's mailbox and focused the scope on that spot. Gina's car was parked there and someone was perched on the hood of her car. "Shit, it's Vicky."

"What?" Gina asked incredulously. Kelly handed her the scope and held the drapes back for her to see for herself. Shattered glass littered the street.

"I think she's just smashed a few beer bottles on your car."

"A few?" Gina was seething. "I can't believe she's even here. How'd she find your place?"

"She must've followed you," Kelly suggested.

"How? She was too damn drunk!"

"Maybe she took a cab." And had him stop to pick up a six-pack? Now, that was unlikely, she thought.

"Who took a cab?" Alex asked. Kelly and Gina both spun around, surprised to hear another voice. He looked at them with a sleepy expression and rubbed his face as he came over to the window. "What's going on?"

Gina handed Kelly the scope and went to the front door. "I'm going to yell at my crazy ex-girlfriend. Sorry about waking you up, Alex. By the way, nice boxers."

Alex looked down at his shorts. His boxers looked like a Valentine's present—bright pink with little red hearts all over. He smiled sheepishly. "All right, if it's just girl-drama, I'm going back to bed. Yell if you need me."

Kelly started out the door, but Gina barred the way. "If you come out here it will only make things worse."

She was probably right, Kelly realized. Gina could handle Vicky without her help. "Fine, but if she tries throwing any more bottles, I'm coming out to save you." Kelly caressed Gina's cheek. "Not that you need to be saved."

Gina grinned and kissed her. "I don't mind getting saved by you. But I think I can talk her out of this mess. It looks like she's already broken all of her beer bottles anyway."

Kelly positioned the scope in the front window and watched Gina head toward her car. Vicky jumped off the hood and raised her hands. Kelly couldn't make out what she was saying. They argued for another five minutes before Gina came back to the house.

"I'm going to drive her home," Gina announced. "She's too drunk to be on the road. I can't believe she followed me here." She shook her head. "Then I'll be back here, so don't you dare fall asleep."

Kelly knew she couldn't argue. She crossed her arms and watched silently as Gina gathered her keys and her wallet.

Gina opened the door and then closed it. "I don't want to leave. Not with everything that's happened. The only place I want to be tonight is in your bed."

Kelly kissed her. "I believe you. Pack a few things and come back here. I want you all weekend."

Kelly packed a backpack with some hiking shoes, clean clothes and a bag of cookies. She tossed her cell phone into the backpack as an afterthought, knowing Rick would be pissed if she left it behind.

An hour after she'd left, Gina knocked on the front door. "Do you know how mad I am at her?" Her duffel bag hung off her shoulder and a sweatshirt was tied around her waist.

Kelly shook her head. "I can take a guess."

"You'd probably underestimate." Gina smiled and hugged her. "Anyway, it's great to see you, again." She glanced at Kelly expectantly. "Are you letting me in?"

"No." Kelly grabbed her backpack. "We're going for a drive."

"Where to?" Gina's tone was suspicious.

"Tahoe."

"What? It's the middle of the night. Hell, it's three o'clock."

"And it'll be daybreak soon. We'll have a good sunrise." Kelly smiled and kissed her. "Just come with me."

"You're crazy, chica."

Kelly headed out to her car and Gina followed behind her, reiterating that she thought it was crazy to start a road trip in the middle of the night. She paused halfway down the walkway. "Wait, I have to work Sunday. We can't drive all the way up to Tahoe just to turn around and come home the next day."

Kelly held open the passenger door. "I'll call Rick. He'll get in touch with your police chief and get you the day off. Rick told me that your chief owes him a few favors."

"Are you kidding?" Gina set her backpack on the ground.

"Kelly, I can't miss work. What am I going to tell everyone at the station?"

"No one will ask." Kelly waited with the door still held open. "Rick has a cabin that's ours for the weekend. It's right on the lake with a perfect view of the mountains . . . even a hot tub in the back-yard. Please, I want you to come."

Gina seemed torn. She shook her head. "This is crazy."

"Please?"

"You're the only person I know who'd decide to go to Tahoe at three in the morning." Gina brushed by her and tossed her duffel bag in the backseat. She turned to face Kelly. "And I'm the only person I know who'd actually agree to the plan."

Kelly felt a rush of excitement as she kissed her on the lips. It seemed like forever since they'd kissed.

Gina sat down in the passenger seat and waited for her to let go of the door. "Well, are we going or not?"

She smiled and closed Gina's door, then climbed into the driver's seat and started the car. "I can't wait to get out of Ashton. And don't worry about your work. Rick will have a good story to tell your boss. He'll come up with some excuse—some high-level intelligence training with the FBI, or something." She winked at Gina. "No one will question your absence."

Gina smiled. "He knows how to pull all the strings, doesn't he?"

"You have no idea."

"You're done with the case, aren't you?" Gina asked.

Kelly nodded, hoping Gina wouldn't ask too many questions. She was tired of lying to her. As they pulled out of the driveway, Gina tried to adjust her seat.

"The seat is stuck," she complained. "It won't slide back."

"There's a lever under the seat that you have to pull." Kelly felt a wave of nausea hit when Gina reached under the seat. She tried to say something to stop her, but it was too late. Gina's hands were already under the seat.

"What the hell is this?" Gina pulled the sawed-off shotgun out and turned to Kelly, waiting for an explanation.

"It's a shotgun."

"I know what it is. The question is, why do you have this under your passenger seat?"

"Well, for safety, you know," Kelly said quickly. She glanced at Gina and knew she couldn't lie about this. "Actually, it's a funny story."

Gina nodded. "Good. I'd love to hear it. How about starting at the very beginning? Where have you been for the past two weeks? And don't feel like you need to leave anything out. We have the next four hours to just talk." She set the shotgun in the backseat, carefully concealing it under her duffel bag, then slid her seat back a few notches. "Kelly, what the hell are you doing with a sawed-off shotgun? Did you forget that I'm a cop?"

"No, I didn't forget. And I love the fact that you'll listen to my explanation before handcuffing me."

Publications from
BELLA BOOKS, INC.
The best in contemporary lesbian fiction

P.O. Box 10543, Tallahassee, FL 32302
Phone: 800-729-4992
www.bellabooks.com

SEASONS OF THE HEART by Jackie Calhoun. 240 pp. Overwhelmed, Sara saw only one way out—leaving . . . ISBN 1-59493-030-9 $12.95

TURNING THE TABLES by Jessica Thomas. 240 pp. The 2nd Alex Peres Mystery. *From ghosties and ghoulies and long leggity beasties* . . . ISBN 1-59493-009-0 $12.95

FOR EVERY SEASON by Frankie Jones. 240 pp. Andi, who is investigating a 65-year-old murder, meets Janice, a charming district attorney . . . ISBN 1-59493-010-4 $12.95

LOVE ON THE LINE by Laura DeHart Young. 240 pp. Kay leaves a younger woman behind to go on a mission to Alaska . . . will she regret it? ISBN 1-59493-008-2 $12.95

UNDER THE SOUTHERN CROSS by Claire McNab. 200 pp. Lee, an American travel agent, goes down under and meets Australian Alex, and the sparks fly under the Southern Cross. ISBN 1-59493-029-5 $12.95

SUGAR by Karin Kallmaker. 240 pp. Three women want sugar from Sugar, who can't make up her mind. ISBN 1-59493-001-5 $12.95

FALL GUY by Claire McNab. 200 pp. 16th Detective Inspector Carol Ashton Mystery. ISBN 1-59493-000-7 $12.95

ONE SUMMER NIGHT by Gerri Hill. 232 pp. Johanna swore to never fall in love again—but then she met the charming Kelly . . . ISBN 1-59493-007-4 $12.95

TALK OF THE TOWN TOO by Saxon Bennett. 181 pp. Second in the series about wild and fun loving friends. ISBN 1-931513-77-5 $12.95

LOVE SPEAKS HER NAME by Laura DeHart Young. 170 pp. Love and friendship, desire and intrigue, spark this exciting sequel to *Forever and the Night*. ISBN 1-59493-002-3 $12.95

TO HAVE AND TO HOLD by Peggy J. Herring. 184 pp. By finally letting down her defenses, will Dorian be opening herself to a devastating betrayal? ISBN 1-59493-005-8 $12.95

WILD THINGS by Karin Kallmaker. 228 pp. Dutiful daughter Faith has met the perfect man. There's just one problem: she's in love with his sister. ISBN 1-931513-64-3 $12.95

SHARED WINDS by Kenna White. 216 pp. Can Emma rebuild more than just Lanny's marina? ISBN 1-59493-006-6 $12.95

THE UNKNOWN MILE by Jaime Clevenger. 253 pp. Kelly's world is getting more and more complicated every moment. ISBN 1-931513-57-0 $12.95

TREASURED PAST by Linda Hill. 189 pp. A shared passion for antiques leads to love. ISBN 1-59493-003-1 $12.95

SIERRA CITY by Gerri Hill. 284 pp. Chris and Jesse cannot deny their growing attraction . . . ISBN 1-931513-98-8 $12.95

ALL THE WRONG PLACES by Karin Kallmaker. 174 pp. Sex and the single girl—Brandy is looking for love and usually she finds it. Karin Kallmaker's first *After Dark* erotic novel. ISBN 1-931513-76-7 $12.95

WHEN THE CORPSE LIES A Motor City Thriller by Therese Szymanski. 328 pp. Butch bad-girl Brett Higgins is used to waking up next to beautiful women she hardly knows. Problem is, this one's dead. ISBN 1-931513-74-0 $12.95

GUARDED HEARTS by Hannah Rickard. 240 pp. Someone's reminding Alyssa about her secret past, and then she becomes the suspect in a series of burglaries. ISBN 1-931513-99-6 $12.95

ONCE MORE WITH FEELING by Peggy J. Herring. 184 pp. Lighthearted, loving, romantic adventure.   ISBN 1-931513-60-0 $12.95

TANGLED AND DARK A Brenda Strange Mystery by Patty G. Henderson. 240 pp. When investigating a local death, Brenda finds two possible killers—one diagnosed with Multiple Personality Disorder.   ISBN 1-931513-75-9 $12.95

WHITE LACE AND PROMISES by Peggy J. Herring. 240 pp. Maxine and Betina realize sex may not be the most important thing in their lives.   ISBN 1-931513-73-2 $12.95

UNFORGETTABLE by Karin Kallmaker. 288 pp. Can Rett find love with the cheerleader who broke her heart so many years ago?   ISBN 1-931513-63-5 $12.95

HIGHER GROUND by Saxon Bennett. 280 pp. A delightfully complex reflection of the successful, high society lives of a small group of women.   ISBN 1-931513-69-4 $12.95

LAST CALL A Detective Franco Mystery by Baxter Clare. 240 pp. Frank overlooks all else to try to solve a cold case of two murdered children . . .   ISBN 1-931513-70-8 $12.95

ONCE UPON A DYKE: NEW EXPLOITS OF FAIRY-TALE LESBIANS by Karin Kallmaker, Julia Watts, Barbara Johnson & Therese Szymanski. 320 pp. You've never read fairy tales like these before! From Bella After Dark.   ISBN 1-931513-71-6 $14.95

FINEST KIND OF LOVE by Diana Tremain Braund. 224 pp. Can Molly and Carolyn stop clashing long enough to see beyond their differences?   ISBN 1-931513-68-6 $12.95

DREAM LOVER by Lyn Denison. 188 pp. A soft, sensuous, romantic fantasy.
ISBN 1-931513-96-1 $12.95

NEVER SAY NEVER by Linda Hill. 224 pp. A classic love story . . . where rules aren't the only things broken.   ISBN 1-931513-67-8 $12.95

PAINTED MOON by Karin Kallmaker. 214 pp. Stranded together in a snowbound cabin, Jackie and Leah's lives will never be the same.   ISBN 1-931513-53-8 $12.95

WIZARD OF ISIS by Jean Stewart. 240 pp. Fifth in the exciting Isis series.
ISBN 1-931513-71-4 $12.95

WOMAN IN THE MIRROR by Jackie Calhoun. 216 pp. Josey learns to love again, while her niece is learning to love women for the first time.   ISBN 1-931513-78-3 $12.95

SUBSTITUTE FOR LOVE by Karin Kallmaker. 200 pp. When Holly and Reyna meet the combination adds up to pure passion. But what about tomorrow?   ISBN 1-931513-62-7 $12.95

GULF BREEZE by Gerri Hill. 288 pp. Could Carly really be the woman Pat has always been searching for?   ISBN 1-931513-97-X $12.95

THE TOMSTOWN INCIDENT by Penny Hayes. 184 pp. Caught between two worlds, Eloise must make a decision that will change her life forever.   ISBN 1-931513-56-2 $12.95

MAKING UP FOR LOST TIME by Karin Kallmaker. 240 pp. Discover delicious recipes for romance by the undisputed mistress.   ISBN 1-931513-61-9 $12.95

THE WAY LIFE SHOULD BE by Diana Tremain Braund. 173 pp. With which woman will Jennifer find the true meaning of love?   ISBN 1-931513-66-X $12.95

BACK TO BASICS: A BUTCH/FEMME ANTHOLOGY edited by Therese Szymanski—from Bella After Dark. 324 pp.   ISBN 1-931513-35-X $14.95

SURVIVAL OF LOVE by Frankie J. Jones. 236 pp. What will Jody do when she falls in love with her best friend's daughter?   ISBN 1-931513-55-4 $12.95

LESSONS IN MURDER by Claire McNab. 184 pp. 1st Detective Inspector Carol Ashton Mystery.   ISBN 1-931513-65-1 $12.95

DEATH BY DEATH by Claire McNab. 167 pp. 5th Denise Cleever Thriller.
                                                                ISBN 1-931513-34-1 $12.95

CAUGHT IN THE NET by Jessica Thomas. 188 pp. A wickedly observant story of mystery, danger, and love in Provincetown.   ISBN 1-931513-54-6 $12.95

DREAMS FOUND by Lyn Denison. Australian Riley embarks on a journey to meet her birth mother . . . and gains not just a family, but the love of her life.   ISBN 1-931513-58-9 $12.95

A MOMENT'S INDISCRETION by Peggy J. Herring. 154 pp. Jackie is torn between her better judgment and the overwhelming attraction she feels for Valerie.
                                                                ISBN 1-931513-59-7 $12.95

IN EVERY PORT by Karin Kallmaker. 224 pp. Jessica has a woman in every port. Will meeting Cat change all that?   ISBN 1-931513-36-8 $12.95

TOUCHWOOD by Karin Kallmaker. 240 pp. Rayann loves Louisa. Louisa loves Rayann. Can the decades between their ages keep them apart?   ISBN 1-931513-37-6 $12.95

WATERMARK by Karin Kallmaker. 248 pp. Teresa wants a future with a woman whose heart has been frozen by loss. Sequel to *Touchwood*.   ISBN 1-931513-38-4 $12.95

EMBRACE IN MOTION by Karin Kallmaker. 240 pp. Has Sarah found lust or love?
                                                                ISBN 1-931513-39-2 $12.95

ONE DEGREE OF SEPARATION by Karin Kallmaker. 232 pp. Sizzling small town romance between Marian, the town librarian, and the new girl from the big city.
                                                                ISBN 1-931513-30-9 $12.95

CRY HAVOC A Detective Franco Mystery by Baxter Clare. 240 pp. A dead hustler with a headless rooster in his lap sends Lt. L.A. Franco headfirst against Mother Love.
                                                                ISBN 1-931513931-7 $12.95

DISTANT THUNDER by Peggy J. Herring. 294 pp. Bankrobbing drifter Cordy awakens strange new feelings in Leo in this romantic tale set in the Old West.
                                                                ISBN 1-931513-28-7 $12.95

COP OUT by Claire McNab. 216 pp. 4th Detective Inspector Carol Ashton Mystery.
                                                                ISBN 1-931513-29-5 $12.95

BLOOD LINK by Claire McNab. 159 pp. 15th Detective Inspector Carol Ashton Mystery. Is Carol unwittingly playing into a deadly plan?   ISBN 1-931513-27-9 $12.95

TALK OF THE TOWN by Saxon Bennett. 239 pp. With enough beer, barbecue and B.S., anything is possible!   ISBN 1-931513-18-X $12.95

MAYBE NEXT TIME by Karin Kallmaker. 256 pp. Sabrina has everything she ever wanted—except Jorie.   ISBN 1-931513-26-0 $12.95

WHEN GOOD GIRLS GO BAD: A Motor City Thriller by Therese Szymanski. 230 pp. Brett, Randi, and Allie join forces to stop a serial killer.   ISBN 1-931513-11-2 $12.95

A DAY TOO LONG: A Helen Black Mystery by Pat Welch. 328 pp. This time Helen's fate is in her own hands.   ISBN 1-931513-22-8 $12.95

THE RED LINE OF YARMALD by Diana Rivers. 256 pp. The Hadra's only hope lies in a magical red line . . . climactic sequel to *Clouds of War*.   ISBN 1-931513-23-6 $12.95